LITTLE GIRL LOST

VOLUME 1 OF THE
LITTLE GIRL LOST TRILOGY

by
Cindy Hanna

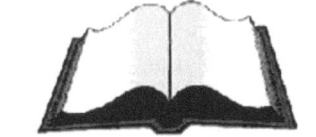

CCB Publishing
British Columbia, Canada

Little Girl Lost: Volume 1 of the Little Girl Lost Trilogy

Copyright ©2010 by Cindy Hanna
ISBN-13   978-1-926585-73-4
First Edition

Library and Archives Canada Cataloguing in Publication

Hanna, Cindy, 1965-
Little girl lost / written by Cindy Hanna.
(Little girl lost trilogy ; v. 1)
ISBN 978-1-926585-73-4
Also available in electronic format.
I. Title. II. Series: Hanna, Cindy, 1965- . Little girl lost trilogy ; v. 1.
PS3608.A558L58 2010   813'.6   C2010-900408-6

Cover design: Arthur Dix – Photographer; Michael Davis – Hair/Make-up Artist

Publisher: CCB Publishing
British Columbia, Canada
www.ccbpublishing.com

I dedicate this novel to my compassionate friend, Arthur. Had it not been for your insight to the creative that lay dormant within me, this book would still be a partially written manuscript tucked away in a drawer. Your artistic promptings and profound wisdom awaken, enlighten and inspire me.

From the bottom of my heart, I thank you.

CHAPTER 1

Sally swings to and fro in the hammock. The sound of rustling leaves, blowing in the wind, causes her to look up. The crisp air caresses her naked breasts, making her nipples stand erect. She begins—slowly—gradually building momentum, backing off at just the right moments. She has chosen the perfect "toy" for this sexual journey and brings herself repeatedly to the edge of climax. She increases the vibration, escalates its rhythmic use and continues, almost in frenzy. Tomorrow she will be raw and sore, but that does not stop her. Faster and faster she pumps until she is dizzy with delight.

The inevitable orgasm approaches and she tenses with anticipation. Her heart rate increases. Her breathing becomes heavier. Her stroking more frantic. She is like a wild animal driven by primitive instinct, unable to stop herself. Her need to climax supersedes all else. The sensation is both excruciating and extreme. Never wanting it to cease, she propels herself further into oblivion.

"Oh, God! Oh, God! Oh, my fucking God!" she repeats through guttural moans and sighs in a near sacred chant. Unable to pull herself back from the edge this time, she allows herself to climax. The sensation explodes throughout her body, causing her to reverberate uncontrollably. Still she cannot stop. When she becomes so sensitive that it hurts, she gently continues on. As she attempts to cry out to her God, Sally begins stuttering just before she reaches her second body-wrenching orgasm.

Exhausted, spent, she leans back, as though a troublesome weight has been placed upon her, and feels herself slipping into that threatening pit known as her past. She offers no resistance, knowing that fighting is futile. She has to surrender herself to the memories, observe them, relive them, mourn them and release them. In blind allegiance, she closes her eyes and allows the images to pass freely through her mind. They flood her consciousness and cause her body to shake from their reality.

* * * * *

Sally, age seven, boldly advances to secretly view them. They are fighting again, but then, they always fight.

Why can't they get along? Can't even go three days without a blow-up.

Recently, however, the disagreements have been escalating in frequency and intensity. Sally is uncomfortable with the things her parents now commonly say to one another.

Don't they know? The name-calling and fights—they scare me. Don't they care?

Sally is aware that her home life is far from normal and longs to have the life of other kids. In an attempt to experience this normalcy, she craves a sleepover with her best friend, Julie Anders, and approaches her mother. "Ma, can Julie spend the night?"

Her mother begins to stammer, "Oh, gee…honey…I don't know if that's…such a good idea. You know how your father can get…."

"I know. You won't even know she's here," Sally continues. "Pleeease! We'll stay in my room and be as quiet as mice."

Her mother sighs. "Oh, all right, but only if you promise to stay out of your father's way. We don't want him getting agitated."

Sally rushes to her mother and gives her a hug. "Thank you, Ma! We'll be perfect angels, you'll see."

Sally hopes that her parents will behave. She even times the sleepover for the day after an argument, thinking her parents might be too weary from battling the night before to begin another episode.

True to her word, Sally and Julie are well behaved. Her parents try to make the sleepover a success. The girls are in Sally's room when they hear her father call, "Does anyone want some of my special popcorn?"

Sally's eyes light up as she scrambles out of her room, calling over her shoulder, "Come on, Julie. My daddy makes the best popcorn in the world! You're gonna love it."

The girls run to the kitchen, where they watch Sally's father work his magic. They marvel at how he patiently waits until the oil heats to just the right temperature before gently pouring in the corn kernels. They begin to pop as he skillfully shakes the pan back and forth over the burner. Giggling, Sally exclaims, "Oh, look, Julie. They're bursting into fluffy white clouds."

Julie closes her eyes and inhales. "Mmm.... It smells wonderful!"

Sally's dad really works his magic. No one can add melted butter to popcorn like he can. Others either make the popcorn soggy or the butter is not heated enough and leaves salty lumps of un-melted butter on the kernels.

"Watch this," Sally says. "It's the best part, Julie. My daddy does this perfect—every time."

They marvel as he drizzles hot melted butter over the popcorn, and then gently tosses it in the bowl. Smiling, he hands the freshly popped treat to his daughter. "There you go. Now see if that isn't the best–tasting popcorn you've ever had."

Sally's heart soars. Her father loves her. He is not a bad guy—just has a nasty temper. Happily, she accepts the bowl, pops one of the fluffy buttery morsels into her mouth and comments, "Mmm, it's delicious, Daddy!"

Sally gives her dad a hug and then skips off to her room with Julie, where they nibble their treat. They enjoy their sleepover, listen to music and munch on their snack for quite awhile before Sally hears the definitive elevated voices of her parents, indicating the onset of an argument. She gets up and, in an effort to drown out the inevitable sounds, nonchalantly increases the volume of her stereo, stating, "I love this song!"

An argument breaks out—a bad one. The raised voices of both her parents can be heard despite the music. Julie becomes upset. "Sally, I want to go home!"

"Don't leave. They're just fighting. They'll stop soon."

Sally manages to convince Julie to stay a bit longer, but soon her father's raised voice and the anxiety in her mother's prove too much. Julie, seeking the safety of her own house, goes home before the hitting begins. That is the last time Sally invites a friend to spend the night.

That's it! I'm sticking to spending the night at my friends' houses. Their parents know how to behave.

Sally is angry and harbors many hateful thoughts towards her parents.

Why don't they just grow up? Other kids' parents get along, why can't mine?

At times, Sally seriously questions who is more mature, her and her younger brother, Eric, or them.

Not all of her childhood is bad. In between their parents' fights, she and her brother live a relatively happy life. Running with the "pack" of kids from their neighborhood, they hurdle over split-rail fences, climb mature trees and scale chain-link barriers, as a shortcut to the street behind them. They live in Covina, California in one of the post-war houses that are evenly spaced up and down the tree-lined streets—a perfect Mayberry town. One can almost imagine Sheriff Taylor and Barney Fife waltzing out of the police station at any given moment while Aunt Bee calls them in for a slice of homemade pie. People leave their doors unlocked and attend church faithfully. Conformity is each community member's number one priority. It is the mid 1970s, when neighborhood kids play outside in large groups until the streetlights come on.

Sally and Eric love being physical. They run and play hard every day. Excelling at physical activity, they dominate their peers whether playing a game of freeze tag, roller-skating, riding bikes, skateboarding or swimming. The siblings are first to be chosen when kids select and break into teams.

Their sidewalk-lined street is on a hill. A patchwork quilt of two-foot squares forms the pathways. The trees flanking the walkways are huge with many of their roots having lifted up sections of the concrete pads. The neighborhood kids love these uneven portions, for they create a rollercoaster track perfect for biking, skating or driving wagons over.

The latter is Sally and Eric's favorite. They drag their red Radio Flyer wagon to the top of the hill. Turning it around, Sally gets in the rear, straddling it so her feet can hang over the sides like brakes. Eric climbs in front and sits cross-legged. His job is to steer with the handle. Once he is settled, Sally raises her feet and off they go, gaining speed, as they hurtle down the hill at a blinding pace. They race over the root-raised sections of concrete, squealing with delight, as their tummies drop, and Eric swerves from one edge of the sidewalk to the other. Sometimes they crash—tumbling out of their wagon, belly-laughing uncontrollably.

The best part of their neighborhood has to be the ice-cream truck. Every afternoon it heralds its approach with its twangy music broadcast over a blown speaker. Hearing it from the next block over, the children scramble to gather their pocket change. Sally and Eric always get the same items: she a Big Stick and he a root beer Popsicle. Those who purchase treats share with the ones who have no money. There are never any hurt feelings or selfishness. No one is ever left wanting. The neighborhood kids all look after and take care of each other like an extended family.

Sally ventures out of her room and down the hallway, where she peeks around the corner to spy on her parents. She notices the crimson coloring entering her father's face. It begins at his neckline and creeps its way up his face, blending almost seamlessly with his hair color. The veins in his neck begin to stand out. Next, the pulsing vein on his forehead will appear.

Oh, God! Time to get away. Don't want to be near him. Danger!

Sally's churning stomach begins to reject what she ate earlier for dinner. She swallows back vomit as she notices her father's arms swinging violently in the empty air called space. His gesticulating intensifies along with his Irish temper. She knows his arms have much power behind them. Each family member has taken his or her turn being her father's punching bag. He does not care whom he turns his wrath upon when he gets in one of his moods—whoever is within striking distance suffices.

Grimacing, Sally knows that his mighty hands long to come in contact with something that they can slug until there is nothing left to pound.

Get away! Leave! Save yourself!

The beatings are bad enough, but the thrashings…they are terrifying! Consumed by one of these furies, Sally's father has no self-control and beats his victim until they escape or are too physically broken to respond. Sally senses this level of fury and her father's need to batter someone.

How long will it take before he kills one of us with his rage?

Guiltily, she is thankful that she will be spared this time.

Thank God, I'm outside his reach.

It will be her mother's turn. Based on her father's ire, the attack promises to be far worse than any Sally has endured—of this she is certain. She feels inadequate, knowing that she cannot help.

Why isn't there someone to save me and make this nightmare end?

This person doesn't exist, though.

How can I make this monster go away before he destroys us? How?

Feeling helpless, she turns and walks silently down the hallway towards her room. Catching sight of her image in a mirror on the wall, she stops, transfixed by the gruesomeness reflected back at her. The entire left side of her face is distorted. Her left eye is nearly swollen shut, encircled by a blended palette of black, purple, red and yellow splotches where the worst of the bruising is. Absentmindedly, her hand raises to caress the area. The minute it makes contact, her image transforms back to normal.

Another memory.

Sally grimaces.

That's what he did to me last time.

Turning from her reflection, she continues down the hallway, passing her brother Eric's room. He is preoccupied, playing with G. I. Joes.

Look how he's gone to great lengths to arrange his soldiers just so. He's trying to block out what's happening around him.

She pauses for a moment in his doorway, marveling at his innocence, envying his naiveté. Eric, her junior by two years, is still too young to fully comprehend what is wrong with their family.

I know he's aware that something is wrong, but am grateful that he doesn't know just how dangerous the situation is. I'm sure he's affected more than he lets on. Wish I knew how to explain things to him without hurting him.

She does not though, so she remains silent.

Every day I feel like a soldier just trying to survive on the battlefield.

Sally feels like a soldier. Eric plays with toy soldiers. Their situation is always on their minds, and yet their father's anger is the elephant never discussed. It sits plainly in the middle of the room, taunting and mocking them, yet they cannot acknowledge it, for if they do, they will have to face just how dire their situation is.

Better to ignore it and stay out of the line of fire as much as possible.

Sally cringes, remembering the family members' endless array of broken bones, bruises and casts. Apparently they all sucked at staying out of her father's way.

Her father's anger has taught Sally well. She has learned to keep a low profile and keep her head down on the battlefield, lest she get it shot off. It has educated her to walk the line and do exactly what is expected and demanded of her—always—without question or having to be told twice.

In school this serves her well. She is an overachieving student who goes above and beyond what is asked of her. Her teachers often openly praise her efforts and use her work as an example to the other students. She loves getting their approval and seeing her work posted on the bulletin boards with A+'s written across the top. Sally lives to please. Her exuberance also serves to keep up the appearance that all is well on her home front. People think she has a normal family—straight out of a Norman Rockwell painting.

Sally shakes her head.

Normal is just a state of mind.

She leaves her brother's doorway and continues down the hallway. Entering her room, she closes the door behind her. Seeking refuge, she climbs in bed and pulls the covers over her head in an attempt to block the sounds coming from the other room. The disagreements always follow the same pattern: the raising of voices, amplified shouting and accusations followed by the unmistakable sound of the first blow.

Sally hears the terrible yelling escalate in volume. She cannot bear to listen to the ear-piercing cries, knowing what will come next. The pitch becomes higher and shriller until she can no longer hear herself think. This is far more intense than other battles.

Somehow I must stop this. I have to do something!

Summoning courage she does not know she possesses, she leaves the safety of her bed, opens her bedroom door and yells, "Stop! Stop fighting!"

Her outcry is met with momentary silence. The awful, dreaded pause in the storm makes her want to disappear.

What have I done?

Her father rounds the corner in an instant, his face a blotchy crimson red. He rushes down the hallway towards her with alarming speed. "What?! What did you say?!"

Terrified, Sally slams and locks her bedroom door. Backing away, she hopes it will hold, but knows it will not. The explosion comes—as expected. Shards of splintered wood erupt into her room as her father crashes through the door and races towards her.

Blessedly, her memory stops there.

* * * * *

Sally opens her eyes and begins picking up her masturbatory toys. That's what her husband James calls them—toys. She swings her legs over the side of the hammock, puts on her robe and, toys in hand, walks back to the house, shivering a bit at the cool breeze.

Crossing the lawn, Sally realizes that although it haunts her, she feels at ease with her past. There she knows what will transpire, where, when and how it will occur. Like a frequently viewed movie, she watches the reels play out repeatedly, gaining a certain amount of comfort in knowing how they will end.

CHAPTER 2

Sally cannot help but question.

How did my marriage manage to survive?

While pondering, she realizes that getting through the tough challenges together is what made James' and her relationship stronger.

"Divorce," Sally mutters aloud. The word leaves a vile taste in her mouth.

What a nasty word. Why do so many people get divorced?

She remembers back to when she was first familiarized with the concept, recalling her "sleepover" friend, Julie Anders, from her youth.

* * * * *

Julie's parents, like Sally's, do not get along—their disagreements end one day when Mrs. Anders announces, "I want a divorce!"

There is no more shouting or name-calling, just that awful word—divorce. Sally, unaware at the time, soon witnesses the life-altering effects it has on individuals. The changes come rapidly. Mr. Anders moves. Next, their house sells. A month later, Julie and her mother move to Texas to live with her maternal grandparents. Sally never sees her friend again. It is all so sudden—so permanent.

Three years pass since the argument where Sally screamed at her parents to stop fighting. She is ten and Eric eight.

It's not fair. Eric and I shouldn't have to grow up this much. We've seen and experienced way too much.

Sally finds that the less she is acquainted with the word divorce, the happier she is. Soon, however, she discovers that she is not immune. Divorce descends upon her own family like a dark cloud, eclipsing the sun's rays.

One day, her mother finally has enough: enough beatings, enough verbal abuse and enough feeling helpless as she watches her husband beat their children. While their father is at work, her mom packs a few belongings for each of them. Completing her task, she calls, "Come on, kids, we're going to stay with your grandparents."

Eric questions, "But what about Daddy? Is he coming?"

"No!" She takes both children and seeks sanctuary with her parents who live in Pasadena. Her father helps her file for divorce. He also protects her and the children, like a ferocious pit bull, when his son-in-law arrives, demanding that his family return home with him.

Time passes quickly after her parents' divorce. Sally and Eric stay with their mother, per the court order. In an act of kindness her father doesn't often show, he moves out so his wife and children can return home.

Sally and her brother grow inseparable. Their community, centered on conformity, places a negative stigma upon them. Sally is protective of her younger brother, often commenting, "It's just the two of us. Gotta look out for each other."

"Promise you won't ever leave me," Eric says.

Sally hugs her little brother tight. "I promise. I'll always be there to protect you."

Eric smiles and hugs her back.

The siblings take solace in being the other's best friend and confidant. They have each other. Alone, their mother shoulders the burden of being a divorcee. Sally watches how her mother is shunned from social circles and repeatedly turned down when she volunteers to help with school and team activities.

She observes her mother's frustration.

I'm never going to put myself through the hell of divorce.

Sally feels the sharp sting of rejection from the same neighborhood kids she has always run with.

I haven't changed or done anything wrong. My parents just got divorced. I don't understand why the other kids avoid me.

Sally is jealous as she watches other kids play together with their complete families.

Look at them with their cocky smiles, the one that shows how happy and safe they feel.

She wants to run up to them and shout, "Wipe that smug grin off your face! Don't you know? Nothing ever stays the same. People change and families crumble right before your eyes." Instead, she chokes back tears and turns to her brother as an ally.

The McFees feel freest at the beach, where they blend in with the masses and have a sense of anonymity. Whenever they can, they drive to their sandy sanctuary for several hours of therapeutic fun and relaxation.

Years pass. Sally becomes a pre-teen and then a teenager. Her mother never remarries. Sally and Eric become more inseparable. The day Sally gets her driver's license, Eric is there to congratulate her, "Way to go! Weren't you nervous?"

"Yeah. I was scared I'd screw up."

Upon arriving home, their mother looks at Sally and suggests, "Why don't you two take the car and drive around a bit?"

"Really?!"

"Sure. Just be back before dark. Okay?"

Sally smiles broadly. "We'll be back before it's dark. I promise."

Grabbing her brother's arm, she makes a dash for the door before her mother can change her mind. "Come on, buddy, let's go."

Eric high-fives his sister. "Partners in crime?"

"Always!" Sally responds, high-fiving him back.

They feel invincible—she sixteen, he fourteen. The world is their oyster. They cruise around a bit to experience Sally's new freedom before ending up at the local pizza joint. After spending the afternoon munching on pizza, sipping ice-cold sodas and playing video games, Sally and Eric head home.

The next day is a spectacular Saturday—perfect beach weather.

Sally and Eric ask, "Please, Ma, can we go to the beach today?"

Their mother shakes her head. "I wish I could, guys, but I'm swamped." She brightens. "But Sally can drive. No reason you two can't go."

"Really?" Sally asks. "You trust me to drive all the way down there and back—alone?"

"Sure, honey. Just as long as the two of you stay together."

"Thanks, Ma," Sally says.

Excited by their new independence, the siblings load their stuff into the car and head down to Redondo Beach. It is a glorious day, complete with blue skies, waves calling to them and the smell of sunshine on their hair and skin. Sally grabs her boogie board and says, "Last one in is a rotten egg."

They race out into the waves. Due to the riptide that day, they keep repositioning themselves back near the lifeguard tower and stay out in the waves for hours, catching one good run after another, having the time of their lives. Eric looks at Sally as the day begins to wane. "One more ride? Then we can leave."

Unable to resist his puppy dog face, Sally says, "Okay, one more, then we've got to head home."

They paddle out on their boards and wait for the perfect wave. It arrives, and they align themselves to ride it in. Positioning themselves side by side at its crest, the two smile broadly at one another. Sally says, "See you on the other side."

They both paddle in earnest and begin to ride the top of the wave. By the time they realize their mistake, it is too late. They have over paddled and drop out over the crest of the eight-foot, monstrously powerful wave. Unable to stop what is happening, Sally desperately looks at her younger brother and yells, "Hold on, Eric, this is gonna get rough!"

"I'm scared!" he says, his eyes opened wide.

Sally offers him a reassuring smile. "I won't leave you."

Over the top they both pitch and are immediately sucked headfirst, straight down into the foaming churn of the whitewater. Sally cannot distinguish which way is up or down. Unable to hold her breath any longer, she gasps for air, her lungs filling with burning salt water. She begins swimming as hard as she can, clawing her way to the surface, choking and gagging. Breaking free, she fills her lungs with air, spews

12

out the saltwater she has taken in and then swims for land. She pulls herself out of the water and staggers onto the shore, dropping to all fours still gagging and coughing up saltwater.

Turning around, she expects to see Eric alongside her. All she finds is his boogie board. Gooseflesh blankets her skin. Standing up, Sally scans the water to locate him. He is nowhere to be seen. She runs up and down the shore calling his name. She sees him, limp and broken at the water's edge. Lifeguards encircle him.

Running to her little brother, she hears someone call his name in guttural tones—it is herself. "Oh, my God! Eric. No! Eric!" She drops to her knees by his side.

One of the lifeguards tries to pull her away but she fights him, crying, "Get off me! This is my brother."

A second lifeguard steps in to help pull her away. "Miss, you've got to let them do their job."

Sally relents. "What's wrong with him? Why isn't he moving?"

One of the lifeguards answers, "Looks like he's broken his neck, probably when he hit bottom."

Horrified, Sally looks at her brother's lifeless form.

He's so...pale.

"He took in a lot of water," the lifeguard continues. "They're trying to breathe life back into him...."

The lifeguard cannot bring himself to finish. Sally helplessly watches as they work on Eric for what seems like forever. She hears the shrill wailing of approaching sirens in the distance and mumbles, "What am I going to tell her? How will I— She trusted me— I was— I was supposed—"

She rides with her brother in the ambulance as the EMTs furiously attempt to revive Eric's still, small body.

He's so grey. Come on, buddy, fight. I'm right here. Don't leave me.

Every mile they drive draws Sally into a deeper state of shock. Her heart pounds, her skin grows cold, and her mind thrashes against the horrific scenario playing out before her.

Upon arriving at the hospital, they pronounce her baby brother— her buddy—her soul mate—her confidant—dead.

Sally falls into a zombie-like state, going through the motions of life, yet gaining no enjoyment from them. All she wants is to smile—really smile again. She simpers on the outside while crying on the inside.

I just want to laugh with him again. I loved belly laughing with him until we couldn't breathe. I feel so cold—frozen—like an isolated iceberg.

Sally hates to be cold. She is alone and feels alone. Nothing she does has any real meaning. She awakes, sobbing, every night reliving that dreaded moment on the beach.

Why did we take one more ride? If I'd insisted on leaving, Eric would still be alive. Why did I let him talk me into catching that wave? Why?

Sally avoids going to bed until the wee hours of the morning, fearful of nightmares. Her stomach muscles hurt from constantly crying. She hugs herself in an attempt to halt the impending ache. A sickening artificial smile appears on her face and her eyes burn as tears flood them, endlessly streaming down her cheeks. Silently, they come like Ninja soldiers making a stealthy attack. Without warning, they overwhelm her.

Just once I want to win this emotional war. But I can't. This is what I deserve—this hell I'm living. This is my punishment for failing my little brother.

And so her torment continues. Sally falls asleep sobbing and awakes crying out to Eric. Every night and morning, there is a fresh puddle of salty tears soaked into her pillow. She hates the mornings most, for with them comes the gut-wrenching reminder that she has to face yet another day without her beloved brother. There seems to be no end to her purgatory.

Sally's mother has her own demons to contend with. Wracked with the grief and guilt only a parent can feel, she questions her every decision of that fateful day and seeks clarity by journaling.

Why did I let Sally and Eric to go the beach alone? Why didn't I go with them? Surely I could have saved Eric from that horrible accident-if only I'd been there. Why was he taken from me? What did I do to deserve this? What did he do wrong? Why wasn't I allowed to say, "goodbye"?

I can't stop scorning myself for not giving him a hug before they left for the beach. It's stupid. I was washing dishes at the time and my hands were wet. I was too worried about dripping water on the kitchen floor to give my son his final hug goodbye...and now I'll never be able to hold him again. Why didn't I just take the time to embrace my child?

When will these incessant daunting questions stop plaguing my every thought? At times, I think I'm going mad. Might be easier if I did. At least then I wouldn't be aware of the immeasurable pain I'm in.

I'm a horrible mother! A good mother would have kept her son safe. A good mother would have saved him. A good mother would have been there with him as he lay dying: to hold him, to hug him and to comfort him. Why wasn't I a good mother? How can I do right by Sally, *after so completely failing her brother? I can't. She's better off if I just stay out of her way.*

I know Eric's death isn't Sally's fault, but... Why did Sally let them ride an eight-foot wave? She should have known better. As the older sister, she should have seen it coming and protected him. I am a horrible mother. I just realized that deep down I do blame Sally for the loss of my son.

At a time when they should be drawing on one another for strength and comfort, Sally and her mother fall into the pit so often visited by those overwhelmed with grief. They grow further and further apart. They speak to one another only when necessary and spend little time together, avoiding the house that reminds them of their terrible loss.

Just as Mr. McFee's violent temper had never been discussed, Eric's death is their elephant to ignore. It takes its toll on Sally and her mother. Since the day of the accident, neither has been able to bring herself to face Eric's bedroom. Instead, they close the door. This allows them to fool themselves into thinking that perhaps Eric will come bounding out of his room in his goofy manner at any moment. But they both know better. His contagious laughter will never again liven their house.

We'll never see his twinkling green eyes or feel the warmth of his embrace.

These are the realities that neither can bear to accept, so Eric's room remains sealed—unaltered—as if a shrine. Their loss and shame is never faced.

Collectively, mother and daughter come to realize that it is better to keep his room shut and ignore it, than to face their shattered emotions.

CHAPTER 3

Sally's mom cannot bring herself to go home after work, following Eric's death, and finds herself volunteering to work longer hours. She runs meaningless errands to avoid the inevitability of returning home.

Sally cannot stand how *everything*—school, house and neighborhood—reminds her of Eric. She begins hanging with the druggie kids from school in an attempt to block out her pain and loneliness.

I hate being alone. These druggies have reached out to me. They accept me and it feels good to be wanted. And their drugs numb my pain.

Their leader, Grease, presents a proposal to her. "We'll let you in our group. But you have to prove your allegiance."

Sally asks, "What do you want me to do?"

Grease looks her straight in the eye and responds, "Shoplift."

It is almost the end of the school year. Sally is seventeen years old and lured by the numbness the drugs will offer. Feeling confident that she can pull this off without getting caught, she does not back down from Grease's penetrating gaze and replies, "All right."

During lunch, Angel and the other druggies drive Sally to the market. They wait in the parking lot by their car as she goes inside. Sally nervously walks up and down a few aisles, summoning courage to go through with her initiation.

I can't believe I'm doing this. It's not too late. Just turn and walk out the door. But then I'll lose my new friends. Come on. Stop being such a coward. Suck it up! You can do this.

Sally approaches the bins of nuts and dried fruits.

Ah, hell, if I'm gonna do this, I might as well stick to being healthy. She fills two bags and then walks towards the back of the store.

17

Placing one of the bags in her oversized purse, she heads towards the front of the store and drops the remaining bag on a shelf.

If anyone saw me, they'll think I just changed my mind about buying the stuff.

Sally walks out of the store to the percussion of her heart pounding in her ears. "I did it," she mumbles under her breath.

Not twenty feet outside, she hears rapidly approaching footsteps and knows, without looking back, that they are headed for her. She hears a male voice call, "Hey, hey, you, miss. Stop, I need to talk with you."

Oh, my God! What have I done?

Back inside the store, Sally's terrified eyes fall upon the shoplifting forms neatly attached to the steel clipboard. Threateningly placed atop is a shiny pair of adjustable handcuffs. The steel badge nearly jumps out at her, screaming Los Angeles County Sheriff's Department, Officer O'Reily, 61610.

That's gonna be me—nothing but a number. Just a number— entered into some steel-shelled computer, lost amongst millions of other faceless, nameless numbers.

Her gaze drops from his badge to his ominous gun.

I hate guns.

Sally shivers. Clipped to the left rear of the officer's holster belt is a second set of handcuffs. Seeing them causes another shudder to roll through her.

"Stand up, turn around and put your hands behind your back," Officer O'Reily commands.

Silently, Sally does what she has been told. He places the cuffs on her wrists: first, one on the left and then the other on her right. The cold steel edges bite into her flesh. She marches obediently down the stairs from the staff lounge with her hands securely clasped behind her and is then paraded past onlookers.

This is so humiliating. I know these people...and they know me.

She is escorted down the frozen foods aisle, through an unattended register and out the door to the awaiting squad car where she meets another steel enemy, the protective grate between the front and back seats of the vehicle. Sally feels trapped by all the steel.

Stupid! Why did I agree to this? I'm not a thief.

She sees her new friends acknowledge her when the squad car begins to roll out of the parking lot. Their simple gesture warms her heart and eases some of the humiliation she is feeling. Sally stares at the steel grate before her on the drive down to the police station, trying to avoid eye contact with people along the way.

Everyone's staring at me, wondering what horrible crime I committed to be riding in the back of a police car.

She slides further down in her seat. Officer O'Reily turns the unit into the station's lot. They pass down a two-lane drive, past the department's gas pumps, make a right turn and pull up in front of the steel door that leads into the booking area. Sally is directed from the car to the door—a frightful steel door.

Sally is questioned, once inside the booking area, and has the handcuffs removed. Her belongings, all of them, are taken from her and accounted for. Her possessions are spread out on a steel countertop in front of an iron holding cell, and she is asked to account for each. Having her things seized and sorted through leaves her feeling degraded. To her left is a pay phone on the wall. She desperately wants to make a call—to connect with the outside world.

A female officer leads Sally down a hallway and into a room around the corner, which houses a jail cell. Sally assumes that it will soon become her new home. The policewoman escorts her to the center of the room and says, "Take all of your clothes off."

Sally does as she is told.

"Bend over and spread your cheeks."

Sally obeys, allowing the officer to confirm that she has no drugs, lethal weapons or any other foreign objects inside of her.

This is so demoralizing.

She is told to remain there, nude, while the officer goes to question whether or not she can put her bra back on. Before leaving, the officer sees Sally's puzzled expression and answers her unasked question. "Your bra has a steel underwire. Normally we don't allow prisoners to enter a cell with any metal objects in their possession. I'm not sure about the bra. I'll have to ask."

While she is gone, Sally remains frozen.

Don't move a muscle. Don't break any other laws.

Sally stands, as rigid as a tree, fearing to even breathe. The policewoman returns. "It's okay for you to put your bra back on. Get dressed."

Once clothed, Sally is escorted out of the room, back up the hallway, to the steel counter where her things had been laid out earlier. Officer O'Reily, the sheriff who had arrested her, stands waiting to receive her. He slides a piece of paper towards her. "Please read this document listing your possessions and then sign it."

Sally complies and is guided to a row of wooden chairs lining a wall. A single handcuff hangs to the left of each seat with one end bolted to the wall.

"Sit down," Officer O'Reily says, pointing to one of the chairs.

Sally does and he leans across her to grab one of the handcuffs, clamping the bracelet to her left wrist, before walking away. Chained like a dog with a collar that is too tight, Sally cannot escape. She looks through an open door into a small room across the hallway where two custodians are on break.

They're staring at me.

The men turn their backs towards her.

They're talking about me. I wanna run and hide.

She sits there until Officer O'Reily returns and removes the handcuff from her wrist. He leads her to a table attached to the wall. There, he holds the fingers of her right hand over a rotating inked pad and has her make several fingerprints on her new criminal record. Sally washes her hand, but is unable to get all the ink off her blackened fingers. She looks at them.

I wonder if this will ever come off.

She is re-handcuffed to the wall where she waits until another officer comes and fetches her. This policeman leads her back down the hallway to the stripping room. They round the corner and stand before the formidable cell door. "Enter," he says.

Reluctantly, Sally walks into the cell. Once inside, she hears the awful slam of the heavy door, followed by his words. "You're doing time now," he says before walking away.

She stands just inside the cell door and observes her new housing layout. There are three beds: two on one wall, a third located on another. There are a steel sink, drinking fountain and toilet in the opposite corner.

She takes her place on one of the bunks and huddles in its farthest corner. She begins to shudder, shake, sing, cry and think. Desperate for something to do, she commences counting the number of bars on the cell door—ninety-one in all. She hears another girl enter the stripping room. The same female officer tells *her* to disrobe.

The girl begs the policewoman, "Please, just one light. That's all I want—just one smoke."

God, please don't have them put her in my cell. I've heard stories of what happens in jail.

The strip-search is completed, and the other girl leaves, her request for a smoke having been denied. Alone, Sally resumes thinking. Isolation creeps in. She hates to be alone.

How long have I been here? I can't keep track of time.

She gives up. Looking for something to occupy her mind, she finds herself down on her hands and knees reading the messages that have been carved into the cell's floor. Disturbing questions pass through Sally's mind.

How did the previous cellmates carve sayings into the concrete floor?

Wasn't I told that no metal objects were allowed? These carvings were made with something sharp, but what?

A detective comes to talk with her after what seems like years. The lighting is poor and there is an iron mesh welded to the cell's bars, making it difficult for Sally to clearly distinguish what he looks like. She longs to see the outline of a human face.

I'm so desperate to talk to someone—anyone—that even talking to this officer feels good. It makes me feel less alone.

The detective addresses her. "I've spoken with your mother and think it would be a good idea for you to start seeing a counselor on a regular basis. The charges against you will be dropped, as long as you agree to apologize, in person, to the store manager. Do you agree?"

"Yes."

"Good. Your mother is waiting outside for you. Someone will come and get you when we're ready to let you go." Having said his piece, he gets up and leaves.

After a time, an officer comes to get Sally. She is escorted out of her cell, hopefully never to return, through the stripping room and back to the steel counter where her belongings are returned to her in a manila envelope. The officer firmly places his massive hand beneath Sally's elbow as he directs her through the door and out to the waiting area. Seeing her mother's face, Sally feels as though she has been released from one prison to another.

Mother and daughter leave and drive in silence to the Ralph's store so Sally can apologize to the manager before heading home. Once en route, her mother asks, "Why did you do it? What were you thinking?"

Her queries are met with silence. Both have become accustomed to the deafening silence that lies between them like an impenetrable fog.

Sally uses the drive to process what has happened to her.

I was dared to steal, stole and have spent the majority of my day surrounded by steel. Now, as a common thief with inked fingers, I'm returning to the scene of my crime to apologize. I never want to go through this again.

At the store, she faces the manager, sincerely apologizes and promises that it will never happen again. He says he hopes not and he forgives her.

The drive from the store to their house is filled with more deafening silence.

CHAPTER 4

Sally's only salvation is to stay away from home and be anesthetized with drugs that her new friends provide. Her favorites are marijuana, which she smokes and cocaine, which she snorts. Both afford the opportunity to escape her painful reality.

Rather be with my friends than home where everything reminds me of Eric. Can't stand the memories that slice through me like a knife.

Sally's mother and she barely speak anymore.

This is more unbearable than the memories of Eric.

Mrs. McFee beats herself up mentally. Sally, once a top student who prided herself on being amongst the best, no longer cares about being the poster child for her teachers.

Nothing matters. What's the point? My own mother doesn't care. Why should I?

On the school's recommendation, Sally begins seeing the district's psychologist. Dr. Dave Glenstein is small in stature, with a hunched back, pasty skin tone and a severely pocked face from a lost battle with acne as a youth. He speaks with a whiney voice and reminds her of a mouse, always wiggling his nose to readjust his thick horn-rimmed glasses. His beady eyes unnerve her as they peer out over the top of his lenses.

She easily manipulates Dr. Glenstein by telling him what he wants to hear and going through the motions of being helped. He accepts her act.

He's an idiot! I'm stoned half the time, and he doesn't even notice/care. Maybe if I go through the motions, he'll stop asking me how I feel about Eric's death. Shit! Can't he see? I don't want to know how I feel!

Her act is convincing—for a while. Then Sally starts to spin out of control, her mind warped from the drugs she is taking. Her mother wants to help but is too engulfed in her own grief. Sally spends more time with her new friends.

It feels good to be accepted again. The best part? Nothing about these friends reminds me of Eric.

She is paid special attention to by the boys and enjoys their interest. She begins to click with one in particular—Grease, the leader. He is a dead-ringer for John Travolta from the movie *Grease*. He has the same bad-boy charisma, chiseled good looks, piercing blue eyes and slicked-back black hair—hence his name. He is used to getting what he wants and has Sally in his sights. Sally begins having sex with him.

This sex thing is awesome! Can't get enough. Can't stop thinking about it or Grease!

Sally engages in casual intercourse with the other boys in the group through the holiday season, the ringing in of the New Year and well into spring. She does Tiny, Spike, Blade and Taz and likes all their nicknames. Each offers anonymity.

Sally runs with the group as the warmer days and evenings hint towards the coming of summer. She stays out all night and disappears for days on end while on drug binges.

In the group, she finds a new best friend—Angel. Like her, Angel has had a rough upbringing. The group gave her the name Angel, claiming that she must have a guardian angel watching over her to have survived being continually raped and beaten by her father.

Angel is five-feet nothing, weighs a hundred nothing sopping wet, is Hispanic and has a mane of gorgeous raven-black straight hair that cascades down to her rear. Her eyes are the color of milk chocolate, with flecks of caramel sprinkled through them, and have a way of looking right into a person's soul when she is talking to them. Despite her size, she is a fierce fighter. Those who cross her do not end up walking away from the battle.

Sally manages to graduate. "Yeah! We're done with school, Angel! Now what?" She lets out a sigh. "You going to college?"

Angel laughs. "Yeah, right, like my dad is gonna spring for me to go to college."

"Me either. Ma can't afford it...besides, I've had enough of this school shit."

Angel high-fives Sally.

"Guess we're gonna have to get jobs."

"I suppose."

Angel fills the hole that Eric's death created in Sally and tells her of a friend she wants to introduce her to. "Sally girl, you're gonna love Ax! He's awesome!"

Sally agrees to be introduced. The girls take a bus to Pasadena where Sally meets Ax, and they learn all about his setup at a motel on Colorado Boulevard where rooms can be rented by the hour, day, week or month. He tells them that he always keeps three rooms paid up—parading an endless stream of his prostitutes through them.

Sally is shocked that Angel would think to introduce her to a pimp.

A pimp? Why a pimp? Well, then again, why not a pimp? It's not like I don't like this whole having sex thing. It's fun. Why should I just give it away to a bunch of horny boys? Why not charge for it?

Ax is an impressively large black man with skin the color of dark chocolate. A towering six-foot, five-inches tall, he is a formidable opponent with a slight waist that is exaggerated by his monstrously large upper torso. He looks like a Mr. Universe with a waist that appears almost corseted through his tight clothing. His sizable physique is enough of a deterrent to stop most from engaging in trouble with him. He is a living specimen of a shorter, black Paul Bunyan.

He tells the girls that he carries a concealed gun tucked into the back of his waistband that is always loaded, ready to fire, can be accessed at a moment's notice and that he has never missed a moving target.

They also learn that he carries an ax behind his driver's seat. Honed razor-sharp, he claims that it is used as a "reminder" to forgetful customers. If a john forgets to pay one of his bitches, he gives them a reminder by chopping off whichever hand the offending customer jacks off with.

Hmmm, chops their hands off with an ax?   Maybe he has....
Don't know...but then, this is a whole new world to me.

Ax tells them how he takes care of his girls. Keeps them fed.
Gives them a roof over their heads. And primes them with drugs to
help them relax.

Ax sounds like a good guy who would take care of me and keep me
safe. That would be nice. And he sure couldn't keep his eyes off of
me. I think he likes me.

The girls ride the bus home.

"What do you think?" Angel asks.

"Ax seems too good to be true."

The next day the girls decide to run away and begin a new life with
Ax. They pack a few meager belongings in knapsacks and catch a bus
to Pasadena, arriving at Ax's door. He takes them in and works his
magic, telling them they are beautiful, desirable and full of potential.
He takes them under his wing, protecting, housing, loving, training
and manipulating them.   He feeds them and provides them with
cocaine, which they gladly snort. Sally and Angel become his top
bitches.

After a few weeks, he drops the bomb, citing, "I took you in when
you had nowhere else to go. Fed, clothed and looked out for you.
Now it's time to give back and earn your keep."

With their judgment dulled by the drugs, the girls are enticed by
the thrill of sex-for-pay and willingly become his new whores. Sally's
first time is in the carport of the motel. Ax, parked in the adjacent
Colton Organ and Piano parking lot, has full view of her business
dealing.

Sally struts her stuff in the alley behind the motel. Dressed as a
prep school girl, her appearance soon attracts the attention of a
customer who circles several times before pulling up alongside her in a
newer Mercedes Benz. He is in his mid sixties, well groomed, with
silver hair and flawless clothing.

"Hey, little girl. Haven't seen you around. Want to share your
candy?"

Sally, standing on the passenger side of the vehicle, leans
provocatively in the window, giving him a teasing view of her breasts.

"What did you have in mind?"

"A B.J. What would that set me back?"

Sally names her price. He parks his car in the carport and has her climb in the passenger side. He pays her fee and they begin.

Smiling, Sally leans over and works her magic as the john runs his fingers through her long hair. "What's your name, beautiful?"

"Anything you want."

"Think I'll call you Brandy. That's the color of your hair."

"Mmm, I like that," Sally mumbles, her mouth full.

The john seems to enjoy the vibration of her speaking. "Oh, yeah, baby, work it. That's right. Stroke it. Suck it. Take it all."

Sally mixes in gentle nibbles, which enthrall her client. She goes down deep, his penis pushing deep into her throat. She does not gag, having been taught well by the druggie boys. Excited herself, she brings him to an explosive climax, eagerly swallowing all his body has to offer.

Finished, she exits the car, walks to where Ax is parked and hands him the money. He tells her she has just served one of their better customers, and that he is pleased with her performance. He then sends her back to work while grinning to himself.

Sally likes doing exactly what she is told by the johns and following their instructions to the letter. She enjoys bringing them to orgasm. Sometimes she screws up, and Ax beats her.

It's only 'cause he loves me. If I do what I'm told, I won't need to be beaten.

The thrill and excitement of their new life continue to intoxicate them through summer. But as time wears on, Ax gives Sally and Angel fewer drugs, choosing to control them instead through fear and intimidation. The girls are easily dominated and controlled—a role each learned from their fathers.

Sally, by the end of summer, falls into a state of deep depression from her depleted coke supply and at last realizes how screwed up her life is.

I want to stop using. Go home. Be a kid again. Can't go back, though. Look what I've become. Ma would be so ashamed of me.

Hell, <u>I'm</u> ashamed of me.

Sally remains with Ax.

Ax owns me. Screws me whenever he wants and sends me out to be screwed by the johns. He's like a pit bull watching my every move. How did I ever feel protected by him? Now I feel used—owned.

At the end of her first year of hooking, Sally tells Angel, "I'm pregnant!"

"What?! Are you shitting me? That's nothing to joke about."

Sally begins crying. "No joke, I'm really pregnant."

"Are you sure?"

"Of course, I'm sure. Haven't had a flow in two months, so I took one of those home pregnancy tests—it was positive. What am I gonna do? Oh, God! What about Ax?"

"Calm down. Let's think this through. Been throwing up?"

"Yes. But only a little." Sally's eyes brighten. "Maybe the test was wrong."

Angel nods. "Let's have you take another. We can decide what to do if that one's positive."

That test conforms the last.

Sally is beside herself. "Angel, Ax's gonna kill me! I swear to God."

"Not if he doesn't know. Turn sideways."

"What?"

"Just do it."

Sally strikes a profile pose, while Angel examines her. "Excellent! We can keep this from Ax. You don't even show. Girls hide pregnancies all the time. We'll just—"

"Hide mine?"

"Exactly!"

Ax finds out about Sally's pregnancy, just after the start of the New Year. She is six months along and unable to hide her expanding figure. He beats her savagely. Ax's anger is terrifying. "You stupid bitch!" he roars. "How the hell could you forget to take 'em damn pills? It's a simple thing. What the hell are you gonna do now? It's too late for an abortion." He slaps Sally hard across her face. "Stupid cunt! You're gonna work that pussy till that kid drops. Some johns really dig that shit." He throws his hands up in the air. "So much for the innocent schoolgirl image. Consider your coke dried up. I ain't gonna have no crack-addicted motha fucka under my care."

Angel helps Sally clean up after the beating.

"He isn't going to throw me out," Sally says. "He's gonna take care of me and the baby."

Ax feels empowered. Some pimps really frown upon one of their bitches getting pregnant. Not him, he knows some johns really enjoy exploring and going down on a pregnant hooker. He's a crafty businessman who never misses an opportunity to make more money.

Oh, yeah, I'll take care of Sally and her baby. I'll take real good care of her brat and never let it out of my sight. She'll earn back every dime she's cost me and then some.

An evil grin spreads across his face.

Damn naive pussy. Don't know what the hell she's just handed me. She's gonna find out—soon enough.

CHAPTER 5

The remaining three months of Sally's pregnancy pass by quickly. She suffers through withdrawals, but feels healthy and has a radiant glow by the end of winter. She continues to sell her body, attracting a whole new clientele who are only too eager to have sex with a pregnant whore.

On Sally's twentieth birthday, one month prior to her baby's due date, she poses a question to Angel, "How about we become family-of-choice."

"What's that?"

"Well, there's family, which you can't get rid of and then there's family-of-choice—the ones you aren't related to, but you adopt into your heart, as if they are."

"Hmm, family-of-choice. I like the way it sounds. So, we'd be like, related?"

"Exactly!" Sally grows serious. "Of course, we have to say the sacred vow."

Angel rolls her eyes and laughs, "I knew there was gonna be a catch."

Sally shoots her a glare. "Oh, shut up! Listen, and if you agree at the end, say, 'Yes.'"

Angel snickers, "Do we have to seal this with spit or blood or anything like that?"

Sally stares at her with subdued fury. "Do you want to do this or not?"

"Yeah, yeah."

Sally continues. "All right, here goes. We promise to stand beside one another—always—as if the same blood ran through our veins. We'll be connected, as one, and fight for each other until the bitter

end. We're family now and will allow no one to stand between us."
She looks expectantly at Angel.

"That was real pretty."

"Well...?"

"Well, what?"

"Do you agree?"

"Yeah!"

The girls clasp hands and spin in a circle while laughing.

On St. Patrick's Day, Sally's labor pains begin with her friend by her
side. Sally cries out, while seized by an intense contraction, "Jesus
Christ, no one told me it was gong to hurt *this* much."

Angel holds her hand in an attempt to comfort her. "It'll be okay.
Try to picture this. You're on a gorgeous beach in a beautiful bikini
instead of lying here in labor."

Sally, momentarily taken aback, looks at her friend as if she has
lost her mind. "What?! Fuck the beautiful bikini! This really hurts.
Besides, why the hell would I be wearing a bikini? Girl, have you
seen me lately, I look like a damn whale. And last I checked, whales
don't wear bikinis!"

Angel tries another approach. "Okay, forget the beach—bad idea.
Try to concentrate on your breathing."

Sally loses her patience. "My breathing? Why the fuck would I
want to do that? I don't have to concentrate on it. Just happens.
Honestly, where do you come up with this shit?"

"I don't know." Angel replies, near tears. "On TV, they always
tell the pregnant woman to concentrate on her breathing. I don't know
what I'm doing. Just trying to help."

Sally softens as her contraction subsides. "I know." She takes
hold of her friend's hand. "I'm glad you're here." Sally squeezes
Angel's hand as another powerful pain overtakes her body.

Nature runs its course. Sally's contractions wrack her body and
her instincts tell her what to do. She delivers her son, with Angel by
her side, on one of the same beds where she has laid hundreds of
johns. No doctors, nurses, or midwives. Just two sister prostitutes,
alone in a grungy motel room, welcoming a new life into the world.

31

Angel hands the new mother her son. The minute she sees him, there is no question in Sally's mind as to what his name will be. "Oh, look, Angel, he has his brilliant green eyes."

"Whose eyes?"

Sally answers almost in a whisper, "My brother's. He has Eric's eyes." She continues, her voice denoting her wonderment, "He looks *just like him*."

Tears begin rolling down Sally's cheeks as she clutches her son to her chest. She begins sobbing uncontrollably for all she has lost, all she has given up and how screwed up she has allowed her life to become. "Angel, why have I been given such a precious gift? I'm not worthy."

Angel sits on the edge of the bed beside her friend and wraps an arm around her shoulders. "Maybe you're being given a second chance. Don't question it, just accept it."

Sally looks up, her eyes moist with tears. "A second chance?"

Angel nods.

Sally honors her brother and her best friend by naming her child, Eric Angel McFee. Her eyes solemnly fall upon her son as she promises, "Little man, as God is my witness, I promise to do right by you and always protect you. No harm will come to you while there's a breath left in me."

She looks at Angel and asks, "Will you be his godmother and swear to look after him should anything happen to me?"

"I'll kill anyone who tries to hurt him."

Within weeks of Eric's birth, Sally realizes the leverage she has handed her pimp. She begs to be allowed to stay with her son but Ax says, "Let me tell you how it's gonna be. I'm gonna keep that motha fucka with me each and every day until you work off your debt to me. You cost me plenty of dough, not working for the past six weeks. Now it's time to pay up or I'll chop that fuck'n brat up and make you watch!"

Horrified and desperate to protect her son, Sally does as she is told. Ax comes and goes daily from his favorite parking lot with Eric Angel in the backseat of his car. Sally often hears her son's cries, which tear at her soul, as he is ignored by Ax.

She is only allowed to fulfill her son's needs (food, change of diaper, bonding, etc.) after she has serviced several johns and hands over her payments to Ax. She is then allowed to take Eric Angel into one of the pre-paid motel rooms for a short time. Sally treasures this time. She snuggles him close as she feeds him and looks lovingly into his twinkling eyes. "Hey, there, precious, do you know how much mama loves you?"

Responding to his mother's soft voice, Eric Angel locks eyes with Sally and coos.

Sally makes faces at and tickles her son, causing his face to erupt into a beaming grin. She revels in watching him track her every movement with his inquisitive eyes and often lays on her back holding him above her, gently rocking him from side to side. Occasionally he drools down onto her, causing her to laugh. She justifies, in her mind, how she works extra hard to bring in and service the johns.

It's just a job...a means to an end...a way to be with my son.

Eric Angel learns to crawl, to say his first words and then begins running—everywhere. Sally continues to sell herself for Ax while her son is held hostage. The time she does get to spend with him is a precious gift they both embrace. She begins to teach him his numbers and the alphabet as he grows. They play, giggle and have in-depth conversations only a mother and small child can share. She teaches him about his world and he, like a sponge, soaks up all his mother has to offer.

Sally loves to watch her son sleep. She spends long hours, late into the night, watching the rhythmic rise and fall of his tiny chest as he peacefully snuggles against her side. His laugh is as contagious as his uncle's had been, and Sally cannot help but belly laugh along with him. *These* are the times that make her heart soar. *These* are the instances that make her mess-of-a-life worth living. She treasures every moment of Eric Angel's existence.

At the end of each workday, Ax rounds up his girls and brings them to his home. There, he locks all five in a room, where they exist, as college girls might, in an overcrowded space with only two beds.

The prostitutes share everything, including their love of Eric

Angel. He is their ray of sunshine, their glimmer of hope and a way for each of them to forget just how dire their existence is. Sally falls asleep every night with her son clutched tightly to her chest, just as a small child might cling to its teddy bear.

One prostitute, Misty, shares stories of her former life in Las Vegas. She tells them of the gentleman's club where she worked as a stripper and of its house mom, Mama Pearl, who took care of the dancers. The three girls vow that if they ever get out of this mess with Ax, they will head straight to Las Vegas and Mama Pearl. Sadly, they never get the chance. Misty overdoses on cocaine while with a john, and dies. Her death serves as a chilling reminder of just how fleeting life is.

* * * * *

Sally awakes in a pool of sweat, attempting to breathe. Her hair, T-shirt and bedding are soaked through. Disoriented, she sits up and tries to remember where she is. She feels Eric Angel nuzzle closer to her as the fog begins to lift, his small body fitting neatly against her own. With a start, Sally remembers the dream—another one of her dreams.

Damn it! I have try to remember. What did I see? A bug? A bee? A bumblebee coming straight at the windshield.

She recalls the disjointed, nonsensical fragments.

It hit the windshield, but it didn't splat. Why didn't it splat? Bugs always splat. Yet this one broke through the glass, leaving a neat little hole as an entry point.

A veil of blackness drapes itself across her dream memory as her vision flees. Sally lies back down. Shutting her eyes, she feels the inevitable onset of a headache.

What the hell does it mean? Why am I dreaming about bumblebees and little black holes in windshields?

She knows that her dream is trying to tell her something and senses that a terrible event is going to transpire, but what, when, where—she cannot say. Instinctually, she wraps her arms around her sleeping child and pulls him closer.

* * * * *

Sally is cursed with her dreams. Most people dismiss their night visions as fantasy—not meant to become reality. Not Sally, she knows better. For her, dreams are warnings, premonitions. Although they often lack important details such as where and when certain events will occur, she has come to realize that they *always* become reality. Her dreams, like a good mystery, keep her guessing and searching for more clues. Sometimes the puzzle pieces come quickly. Sometimes they take weeks, months and even years to reveal themselves to her.

Sally lies, hugging Eric Angel close, remembering her very first premonition dream. It had been several months prior to her brother's fatal accident. She recalls how she had awoken in a pool of sweat, feeling disoriented and trying to make sense of her bizarre nightmare. The pieces of that dream had been so fractured: wetness—darkness— sun—eternal bonding—a smile—her brother's face. She had no concept, at the time, of what the dream foretold. Its only lasting impression was how unsettled it made her feel.

Not until after the fateful day at the beach did the full meaning of her vision become clear. The dream snapped into crystal-clear focus as she sat alone in the emergency room, beside her brother's dead body, waiting for her mother to arrive. A cold chill had worked its way down her spine as the realization of the dream's powerful message had sunk in, causing her to shiver. It was then and there that she had vowed to *never* ignore another one of her visions.

* * * * *

Sally lies there, pulling Eric Angel closer to her, as a chill creeps its way down her spine—her body convulsing and shivering. A long time passes before she finally drifts into a restless sleep.

Along with the dawn comes another day for Sally to sell herself in order to spend time with her son. The johns, seeming to be more abundant this day, allow the girls to bring in extra money for Ax. Pleased, and in a rare act of kindness, he allows his bitches to call it an early day.

Sally is delighted. This means extra time she can spend with Eric Angel. They giggle, bond and play one of their favorite games. Angel even gets in on the fun. They turn on the radio to a rock-and-roll station and begin to silly dance.

* * * * *

One day, when they were quite young, Sally and Eric had been dancing to some music in her room when their father appeared in the doorway, watching them. Afraid that they had somehow angered him, the children immediately stopped. He had smiled, not unkindly, but encouragingly. "No. No. Keep going. You look like you were having fun."

Seeing his reassuring grin, the siblings resumed their dancing. In a rare and cherished moment, their father joined in. A few minutes later, their mother, drawn by their laughter, came into the room. She stood and watched for a moment, a wide grin upon her face, as she looked from her children to her husband. She, too, joined them.

Both parents winked at one another as they mimicked their children. Seeing their parents dance so silly made Sally and Eric dissolve into uncontrolled belly guffaws. Soon they were all trying to catch their breath. Thus the game of silly dance was created. This memory always brought a smile to Sally's face and warmed her heart, for, to her, it represented the best of spending quality time together as a family.

* * * * *

Angel, Sally and Eric Angel silly dance until they fall to the ground with belly laughter. The three play late into the night, until Eric Angel falls asleep. Sally bears a content look.

Wish time would freeze. Those whom I love most surround me. Can't ever remember feeling happier.

Most five-year-olds are not content to sit silently in the backseat of a

36

car day after day for long hours, yet this was normal for Eric Angel. Oh, sure, he had protested once or twice and received vicious beatings from Ax. Even at this tender age, he had learned—just as his mother had—to do exactly as instructed, without having to be told twice. He had discerned that it was better to be bored than to meet the wrath of Ax.

On a cold afternoon, not long after Eric Angel's fifth birthday, mayhem breaks out at the motel. Another pimp tries to move his girls into Ax's territory. Ax rises to the occasion to defend his turf. "Ain't no motha fucka gonna mess with my turf!"

Needing someplace to secure Eric Angel, Ax locks the boy in his car, located in the parking lot, before bolting across the street to the rear of the motel to confront the would-be squatter pimp. An angry argument erupts. Their voices rise and they begin to throw blows. Ax dominates the other man in size and strength.

The other man manages to break free of Ax's vise-like grip and runs towards Ax's car across the street. Ax nonchalantly follows suit, an evil grin curling the edges of his mouth. "Not so fast, motha fucka."

The other pimp has a good fifty-foot lead. Ax pursues him into the street, fetches his revolver from his waistband, aims and repeatedly fires at the man, emptying his gun. There is no large bang like in the movies, just a series of little pops. The man pauses for a moment, then slumps and falls to the ground.

Ax slows his pace, knowing the police will soon arrive, and continues towards the downed man. Stepping over him as one might step over a piece of garbage, Ax walks to his car, gets in and calmly drives away. He does not bother to check the man's pulse, certain that his prey is dead.

Ax notices an eerie silence from the rear seat after driving a few blocks. Looking back, he sees Eric Angel's tiny, limp body, with a bullet hole neatly in the middle of his forehead. The boy, who had been peeking over the front seat of the car to view the fight, had been struck in the head by one of Ax's bullets and killed instantly. His small form lies crumpled, in a pool of his own blood, on the floor. His head is upturned, as if questioning, "Why." His once-brilliant green eyes remain open, the light having gone out of them.

"Ah, fuck!" Ax growls aloud. "Now how the hell I gonna control that bitch?"

The cops descend upon the murder scene like locusts on a Kansas farmland. They scour every inch of the place, interviewing everyone, not surprised that no one seems to have seen anything. They spend long hours gathering their hollow details.

The police have their suspicions of what went down—one pimp crowding another's turf. Blah. Blah. Blah. They know the dead man to be a scum-ball pimp, yet they must treat the investigation into his death with the same respect and thoroughness as any other. Of course, nowhere is it written that they have to *solve* the case. What was one more dead pimp to them, but a service to society? As the detectives know, street vigilantism does serve a purpose.

The police run their investigation while Ax disposes of Eric Angel's body, cleaning every speck of blood out of his vehicle. The deed done, Ax cruises by the motel several times, careful not to draw attention to himself, to see if the officers have left.

After the officers leave, Ax pulls into the motel's carport and summons his bitches to come with him. Sally sits in the rear seat, where just hours before, her son had been shot. She finds it odd that Eric Angel is not in the car. Sensing Ax's ire, however, she decides not to question where her son is, choosing instead to look straight ahead and keep her mouth shut. That is when she sees it—the neat little black hole in the windshield directly in front of her.

Suddenly, the meaning of her dream becomes clear and she begins screaming, "No! It can't be. No. Not my baby!"

Ax roars, "Somebody shut that fucking bitch up before I do!"

Sally realizes that the bumblebee she had seen in her dream had been the bullet as it approached her son. She had witnessed it in her vision the same as her son watched it approach him. Sally hears the mournful wailings of a wounded animal—herself—moments before she blacks out.

With no mention of a murdered little boy or a body, Eric Angel's death goes undetected by the authorities, affording Sally the opportunity to avoid getting caught up in the investigation surrounding the pimp's death. Ax, on the other hand, is not as fortunate. In his efforts to stay just outside the questioning reach of the investigating officers, Ax becomes a scarce sighting at the motel, which lessens the scrutiny with which his whores are accustomed to living under.

Sally goes on a massive three-day cocaine binge following the death of her son with a cleverly "squirreled away" emergency supply of coke Ax's other prostitutes have stolen from Ax's supply. Wanting to provide her with instant relief, they opt to have her smoke crack instead of snorting cocaine. One of the girls offers her some, coaxing, "Here, Sally, this will help ease your pain."

Sally smokes the crack and is instantly rewarded with a euphoric feeling, shorter-lived than with coke, but releasing. She does not eat or sleep while on her binge, is talkative about everything, feels energetic and self-confident and is able to continue performing her sexual services with the johns.

Following her binge, Sally slips into a state of deep depression and tries to come to terms with her son's death. When that proves too overwhelming, she tries to block it just as she does with what johns routinely do to her body. She continues to smoke crack as a means of escape, but does not binge again. She knows she has to break free of Ax, that this may be her only opportunity to escape, and that she will need to be thinking clearly in order to make a getaway. She minimizes her drug use and manages to compartmentalize her grief over Eric Angel's death while she waits patiently for her opening.

A window of opportunity presents itself, and she flees, taking Angel with her, while Ax is preoccupied with avoiding the police. The girls realize that they cannot stay in California without Ax finding them. They had heard of it happening before. One of Ax's prostitutes would run, he would track her down, drag her back and execute her— right in front of the others—by chopping her up with his ax.

While talking with Angel, Sally's voice drips with foreboding.

"Ax won't ever stop looking for us. You know he doesn't like losing his possessions—especially the ones who can rat him out."

"Yeah."

Both girls shiver.

CHAPTER 6

Needing distance from Ax, having nowhere else to go and intrigued by the glittery opportunities Vegas might hold for them, Sally and Angel decide to hitch rides-for-favors towards the strip club Misty had told them about and Mama Pearl. They arrive in Sin City a couple of days later and rent a motel room off the main strip a block down from the gentlemen's club. Exhausted, they decide to wait until the following day to meet Mama Pearl and talk to the club's owner about getting jobs. They shower and climb into their own beds. Sleeping separately seems strange after having shared a bed for so many years. Sally stretches out in an attempt to touch all four corners simultaneously. "Look, Angel, I can almost reach."

The vision of her friend splayed like a human cross makes Angel laugh. "You're strange."

Sally grins broadly. "That may be, but I've got my own bed, and I'm loving it. Did I ever tell you that you hog the sheets?"

"Yeah, right, little miss elbow-me-in-the-ribs-all-night-long."

Both girls giggle. Angel grows serious, props herself up and looks at her friend and says, "Sally, there's no one I'd rather go on this adventure with. Love you."

A contented look lightens Sally's face. "Love you, too. Good night."

Sally's eyes fall on a wall picture of Dorothy, Toto, the Tin Man, the Scarecrow and the Cowardly Lion just before Angel clicks off the light. The room falls silent as both girls close their eyes. The only sound is their deep rhythmic breathing.

Sally has a final thought before drifting off to sleep.

There's no place like home. There's no place like home. There's no place li....

* * * * *

Sally sees the shards of wood splinter from around the doorjamb as it explodes inward. There is no sound…just visuals. An intimidating hulk fills the doorway—Ax.

A thousand images strobe through Sally's mind: Ax's sardonic grin, a scrap of paper with writing upon it, Angel screaming, Sally desperate to help, unimaginable pain. Then silence. Deafening silence….

* * * * *

Sally awakes in a pool of sweat with her heart racing. She cannot catch her breath—her chest rapidly rises and falls. Panicking, she breaks out in a cold sweat.

Ax…oh, my God…Ax. Where is he?

She opens her eyes and looks around, fearing the worst. There on the wall is the picture of Dorothy, Toto, the Tin Man, the Scarecrow and the Cowardly Lion from her motel room. She looks to the bed beside her and sees Angel sleeping peacefully. She tries to push the sleepiness from her head in order to think. Sitting up in bed, she rubs her eyes. Gradually, her breathing resumes its normal pace, her heart rate slows and her mind begins to clear, as she realizes where she is and what has happened.

Another dream. Another one of my fucking dreams. Quickly! Quickly! I must pull together the facts. I've got to try to remember what the dream told me. A…a…room. A dark room…at night. There was something else. What was it?

"Damn!" Sally says aloud. "I'm missing something...something *very* important.

Concentrate. Concentrate! I have to try to remember. My dreams are never wrong. There's no room for mistakes. That's it!" She states this somewhat loudly, startling herself. "That's got to be it! It has something to do with mistakes. No. Not mistakes, but *a* mistake...a very important one!"

Sally lies down, exhausted. The dream is gone. She knows it is useless to try to rack her brain. Detecting the beginnings of a headache, the jackhammer pounding at her temple, she closes her eyes in an attempt to dull the pain and seeks comfort from her crack pipe. Inhaling deeply, she feels its euphoric sensation wash over her. Sally scratches without mercy at her skin.

Goddamn bugs! Why can't I get them off of me?

She looks down at her arm, where she has been scratching. There are no bugs. She scratches harder in hopes of release from the sensation and takes another drag from her pipe. She is rewarded with a blissful bug-free feeling for a few minutes. When it subsides, the insect-ridden-skin feeling returns. Unaware that she has drawn blood, Sally resumes scratching.

Can't believe I left that damn piece of paper behind with Mama Pearl's name and the club's address on it. Ax is gonna find it.

Sally gets out of bed and walks over to where her friend slumbers and shakes her. "Angel. Angel! You've got to wake up. We're not safe here." Sally takes another drag from her crack pipe.

Angel awakes, rubbing the sleep from her eyes. She takes note of Sally and the pipe. "Hey. It's okay. No one's gonna hurt us here."

Sally says, "But I saw him!"

"Who?"

"Ax. He was here. He found us."

Angel gets up and puts her arm around her friend. "Look at us. We're fine. It's just the crack playing tricks with your mind."

Sally pulls away. "No! I had one of my dreams."

Angel freezes, and the color drains from her face. "One of your dreams? Oh, my God! Ax *is* gonna find us!"

"That's what I've been trying to tell you. We're not safe here."

Angel sits on the bed, pulling Sally down with her. Placing her hands on her friend's shoulders, she turns so each of them is facing one another. "What exactly did you see in your dream?"

"We've got until Ax finds that note."

"What note?"

"The one we left behind with Mama Pearl's name and the club's address on it. The one Misty wrote."

"There's no note," Angel says. "Misty didn't write down the

information. She told it to us so there wouldn't be any record for Ax to find." A look of dawning understanding crosses Angel's face and she continues, "Come on, let's get you something to eat."

Stamping her foot, Sally's voice rings with the defiance of a small child. "I'm not hungry!"

"Then why don't you put down the pipe and take a break."

"Okay."

Putting the pipe away, Angel states, "I think that's enough for tonight."

Sally scratches mercilessly at her skin. "I can't get these damn bugs off me."

"I know. Let's get you a shower. That'll wash 'em off."

"Promise?"

"Yeah."

Angel showers Sally and tucks her into bed.

"I'm so tired. I can barely keep my eyes open."

"Me too." Angel looks at the clock on the nightstand. "It's the middle of the night. Let's go back to bed. We'll wake up feeling better in the morning."

"Sounds nice. Stay with me? I don't want to be alone."

Angel lies down beside her friend and hugs her close. "I'll be right here. I won't leave your side."

Sally relaxes in the safety of Angel's embrace and repeats her words while drifting off to sleep, "Won't leave your...." She smiles and lets out a heavy sigh. "Hmm. That was the last thing I told my brother before we crashed over the wave." She falls into a deep sleep.

Tears stream down Angel's face.

Oh, Sally girl. Wish you could see what this shit's doing to you. Wish I could save you. I'd give anything if I could, but I can't. All I can do is stay by your side.

CHAPTER 7

The following morning, Sally goes to Angel and puts a hand on her friend's shoulder. "Thanks for last night. Never been that bad before. Don't know what happened."

"It's okay. Stay away from that shit when you're scared or upset. That's when you binge and not even I can reach you."

"Sorry."

"Promise that you'll reach out to me before your crack pipe."

"Deal."

The girls pack bags with outfits they can strip in (tight mini skirts that leave nothing to the imagination, clingy low-cut tops that expose their chests, five-inch stiletto come-fuck-me heels, lacy bras and g-strings) and leave them on their beds. They dress in jeans, T-shirts, comfortable shoes and then head out to explore Las Vegas.

They are twenty-five, the year is 1994 and Las Vegas is undergoing a major facelift with amazing themed hotel/casinos replacing the old Mafia-owned ones. Never having been to Vegas, the girls stroll the strip awestruck. Sally is dazzled, even in the daylight, by all the neon lights. "Look, Angel. There's the Flamingo with its fanned-out neon tail feathers over the entrance."

They cross the street and continue up the other side where they come upon the sprawling Caesar's property. Having heard about the Forum Shops below and what treasures they contain, the girls choke their way through the smog-like cloud of smoke, which hangs from the ceiling of the hotel's main casino like a cancer cloud. The girls are hypnotized by the noise and chaos created by the *ding, ding, dinging* and flashing lights of the slot machines. Stopping in front of the nearest one-arm bandit, Angel comments, "Look, it's just like the ones in the movies."

Angel reaches into her purse and draws out a couple of quarters. Placing them in the coin slot, she looks at Sally and winks before pulling the handle. Both girls watch with mounting anticipation, as first one BAR, then another and finally a third fall into a horizontal line in the center of the display. A light on top of the machine begins to flash. Alarms blare. And the unmistakable *tink, tink, plunk, plunk, tink, tink, tink* sounds as the machine belches out its coins. Sally looks for something to place the coins in and locates a large plastic coin cup. She hands it to Angel, who begins scooping up her winnings as the slot machine continues to spew out an endless cache of quarters. Both girls beam.

"This is awesome!" Angel announces with childlike abandon. "Las Vegas is fun. I like it here!" She looks at Sally. "Go ahead, you try."

Sally fetches a couple quarters from her purse and places them in the machine next to the one Angel has just emptied. She pulls the handle and waits—BAR, double cherries and an orange. She laughs, "Well, at least I got healthy fruits."

"You and your damn healthy eating," Angel says. "I've never seen anyone so into fruits and vegetables before."

Sally shrugs. "What can I say? You are what you eat."

"Yeah, yeah, heard the pitch before. Save it. I like chemicals I can't pronounce in everything I eat. If we are what we eat, then I'm damned smart cause I'm chock full of big words."

"Ah, Jesus, Angel! Where do you come up with this crap?"

Angel shrugs. "Don't know. Gift, I guess."

Both girls laugh and follow the signs to the Forum Shops. Once there, they pass a giant fountain that features animated figures and a laser light show. Sally and Angel silently watch the presentation. Next, they pass by high-end stores, many of whose names neither girl recognizes. Sally lets out a whistle. "Someday I'm gonna walk in these shops and buy whatever I want."

They leave Caesar's and continue up the main boulevard to the Treasure Island hotel/casino. Sally exclaims, "Oh, my God! Giant pirate ships? In the middle of the desert? Who would have thought?"

As the girls approach the hotel, they cross a long, wide, wood-planked boardwalk flanked by several enormous pirate schooners. The girls join the gathered crowd and wait for the show to begin. About fifteen minutes later, the rumblings of loud music can be heard as the ships come to life. Hordes of "pirates" enact their roles in a mock fight. They battle, climb rope ladders and fall—presumably to their deaths—into the water below. The show is intoxicating. The performance ends with one of the ships sinking. Stunned, both girls turn and silently walk back towards their motel. Sally breaks the silence. "This place is unbelievable! And of all the people, the Elvises seem the most normal."

After freshening up in their room, the girls grab their bags and head to the strip joint. The parking lot at Luigi's Gentleman's Club is filled with expensive cars and a valet service. As Sally and Angel approach the entrance, a gorilla-like bouncer visually undresses and sizes them up. "Come to have a good time tonight, ladies?"

"Hope to."

He eye-fucks them one final time before granting them passage.

Inside, there are three stages: a large one in the center of the room, with two smaller platforms flanking the main one. Each has brass poles mounted vertically from the ceiling to the floor—the kind one would expect to see in a firehouse. The room is dimly lit with the stages surrounded by a bar. Individual booths line the room, each large enough to hold four to six people.

Two girls are performing on the center stage, with each of the smaller platforms supporting a single-girl strip act. Each of the performers looks as if she has just walked off the pages of a Playboy magazine. Angel lets out a sigh and remarks, "Jeeezus, Sally girl! How we supposed to compete with them?"

"Let's grab a table in the back and watch for a bit. See what we're in for."

The girls on stage, having stripped to their sexy g-strings, are doing their damnedest to screw the brass poles. The spectators are going wild, hooting, hollering and tossing money at their feet. Angel and Sally navigate their way to a corner booth. A few minutes later, a waitress decked out in a rather revealing micro mini skirt and bikini top that leaves nothing to the imagination, arrives to take their drink order.

The girls watch with fascination as one girl after another gets up on stage to perform her act. Each is unique and lasts the length of a song. The center stage always features two girls rubbing themselves against one another in a seductive manner. Sally and Angel cannot help notice how every guy in the place is reduced to a pile of goo within a matter of seconds.

Following each performance, the dancers walk around the edge of the stage where the audience members, exclusively male, slip one- and five-dollar bills into their g-strings, while others toss their money on stage. It takes several minutes for each girl to gather her earnings.

The waitress returns with their drinks.

"Where's the club owner?" Angel asks.

"Over there," the waitress says, pointing to an Italian godfather Mafioso-type sitting on a stool at the end of the bar.

"Thanks." The girls tip the waitress an extra five dollars.

As they pick up their bags and head towards the club manager, Angel says, "I feel like I'm gonna barf."

"Don't flake on me now," Sally responds.

Drawing in a calming deep breath, Angel manages a smile. The club manager's shirt, undone almost to his navel, exposes his hairy chest and belly. He is short, robust with a stomach that hangs over his trousers. Layers of heavy gold chains hang around his neck, several with pendants large enough to be doorknockers. His hair is black, thinning and slicked back. They catch sight of his gaudy, loose-fitting, gold nugget watch when they arrive in front of him and notice that each of his short, chubby fingers is outfitted with an oversized gold ring. He appears to be making a snack out of the cigar, which bobs up and down with each chomp.

Sally is first to stick her hand out and introduce herself. The man takes her hand, pulls it to his mouth and kisses it, while introducing himself as Luigi, the club's owner/manager. Before either girl has a chance to speak, he pops the question, "Here for a job?"

"That obvious?" Sally asks.

"Honey, *every* female who comes here is looking to become one of *my* dancers. I run a class act and can't seem to beat the girls away with a broom." He stops a moment to size them up before continuing, "Now, you two…. Ever danced before?"

Angel responds, "No, we were sent to you by Misty. You remember her? Worked with her out in LA for a while."

"Let me see," Luigi says, scratching his head with a chubby finger. "Misty, ah, yes, I remember her well. An amazing brunette with a tight little ass and a great rack—really knew how to work the pole. How's she doing?"

Angel answers, "Not so good. She's dead. Overdosed a few weeks ago."

"Ah, sorry to hear that. She was a sweet girl. I liked her. Any friend of Misty's is a friend of mine. Bring something to dance in?"

Angel points to their bags.

"All right then, why don't you get changed? When you're ready, we'll see what you've got."

The girls walk the length of the bar, down the hallway and through an unmarked door into the dressing room grateful to find themselves alone when they enter. Sally looks at Angel and questions, "Are we really going to do this?"

"Come on. This is our chance…a way to a better life. I'll be right there rooting you on and," Angel pauses for impact, "checking out your ass from behind."

Sally laughs. "Thanks, Angel. Let's do this!"

The girls change from their street clothes into the outfits they packed for the audition. After getting dressed, Angel goes over to the long bank of mirrored dressing tables and begins touching up her make-up. Sally, uncomfortable with mirrors, opts to remain by her locker and use a small compact from her purse. When Angel is done, she turns slowly and looks at her reflected image. Satisfied with what she sees, she walks over to Sally. "Okay, let's see."

Sally stands up and pivots for Angel, who responds, "Girl, you look hot!"

They give each other a hug for good luck and walk out of the dressing room to the bar. Luigi is waiting for them along with a group of employees. One of the small stages has been cleared for their audition.

"Ready?"

Sally looks coyly at two enormous hunks standing by the edge of the stage. "Give a lady a hand up, boys?"

They eagerly lift her onto the stage. Once there, she nods at Luigi, who clicks a button on a recorder. Not quite sure what to do, Sally begins gyrating her torso slowly and grinding the air with her hips, all the while imagining that she is having sex with an invisible man. Before long, she forgets where she is and really gets into the song while seductively removing her clothing. The "judges" hoot and holler, urging her on. She barely hears them. When she is stripped down to nothing but her black lace bra and g-string, she positions herself against the pole and begins sliding up and down, rhythmically grinding it with her pelvis. The men go wild. Sensing the song is coming to an end, Sally steps away from the pole and removes her bra, tossing it to one of the judges. She leaves her clothes where they lay when the song ends, and walks confidently (or so it appears) to the edge of the stage to address Luigi who bears a wide grin.

"You're a natural. Don't change a thing." He looks over at Angel. "Let's see what *you've* got."

Sally gathers her strewn clothing and has the men assist her off stage. Angel walks over to the stage and looks at the huge hunks. "Boys?" They lift her onto the stage. Like Sally, she nods at Luigi who begins the music. Her audition goes as smoothly as Sally's. When she is done, she walks over to hear Luigi's verdict. The smile on his face speaks volumes. She, too, has a job.

"Can you start tonight?" he asks. "I'm a couple of dancers short. It would really help me out."

"Sure," Sally says.

He nods towards a black attractive woman now seated at the other end of the bar. "Go see our house mom, Mama Pearl. She'll put you in the rotation. Come see me before you leave tonight for your tip-out."

"Thanks!" Angel says.

While walking over to Mama Pearl, Angel leans over to Sally and whispers, "What the hell's a tip-out?"

"Don't know. Don't worry about it. We'll find out at the end of the night." She squeezes Angel's hand. "We've got jobs!"

Mama Pearl must have been an attractive woman in her day. Her complexion is flawless. It is obvious, although she has gained pounds with the passage of time, that she was once a real looker. She has an ample chest and an hourglass figure. When she smiles, her eyes twinkle, lighting up the room. The girls are immediately smitten with her. Sally says, "Mama Pearl? We've just been hired and need to be put in the dance rotation for tonight. I'm Sally and this is Angel. We were friends with Misty."

Mama Pearl smiles broadly at the mention of their friend's name. "How is that girl? Shame on her for losing contact with me. You'll have to scold her for me the next time you see her."

Angel breaks Mama Pearl's heart with the news of Misty's untimely death. "Tsk, tsk, what a waste.... Such a lovely girl. Ain't no good dwelling on the negative. What's done is done. Let's get you set up in the dressing room."

Both girls dance six hours that night. By the end of the evening, their legs feel as if they might fall off, and they learn from Luigi that a tip-out is a procedure where the dancers each give a percentage of their nightly earnings to be divided up by the bartenders, doormen, DJ and house mom.

Even after paying their percentage, they walk away with just over $300 each in their pockets. Ax never allowed them to have this much money. Both are giddy and head to the dressing room to change into their street clothes. They return to the bar before leaving, and drink to toast their good fortune.

CHAPTER 8

The next day Sally and Angel sleep in, a luxury they could never indulge in while working for Ax. Over coffee Angel asks, "How about we go shopping and treat ourselves to a little TLC? I know we could both use some new outfits and there's *always* the need for more shoes."

"I've been wanting a French manicure and a good foot massage," Sally says. "Let's do it!"

They ask a motel clerk where the nearest discount clothing shop and nail salon are and take a bus there. They get their nails done first. Sally and Angel giggle like two schoolgirls the whole while. Each decides to get a French pedicure with little rhinestone hearts on their big toenails and a set of pink and white square-tip acrylic nails. Neither has ever been pampered this way before. While at the salon, Sally grows silent. Noticing her friend's change in demeanor, Angel reaches over and places a hand on her arm. "Why so quiet?"

"Just thinking. Last week we were Ax's slab-of-meat prisoners. Now we're getting our nails done."

"What's wrong with that?"

"Nothing. It's just so—"

"Different?"

"Yeah."

Angel turns in her chair to face Sally. "I hear ya. Keep thinking I'm gonna wake up and be under Ax's control again."

Sally shifts uncomfortably. "Shit! What if he finds us?"

Angel reassuringly squeezes her friend's arm and musters a convincing smile. "Maybe he will. Maybe he won't. Either way, we should treat ourselves like we're special."

Sally relaxes a little and returns Angel's smile. "You're right. I like pampering myself. It makes me feel like I matter."

The girls finish at the nail salon and walk down to a discount clothing store where they spend several hours. When they leave, each has new outfits, come-fuck-me heels and sexy new lingerie for their job. Angel is positively giddy. "That was fun. Gotta do that again."

They grab a leisurely bite to eat, gather the items they will need for stripping and then head over to the club, hoping to meet some of the other girls. Upon arriving, they are greeted by Desmond, the bouncer who met them at the door the previous evening. He is a huge black man who looks as if he could play nose tackle for a pro-football team.

"Evening, ladies."

The girls greet him. Upon entering the club, Byron, the bartender says, "Evening, dolls. Looking for Mama Pearl? She just stepped out for a minute. Said she'll be right back. If you want, I can let her know you're here."

"No, that's okay. We're a little early. We'll get ready and check back in a bit."

Sally and Angel proceed to the dressing room where they find several performers changing clothes.

Jasper is a beautiful petite Filipino girl with wavy black hair that cascades down her back to her rear. The night Angel and Sally first came into Luigi's, Jasper was one of the two girls on stage who had mesmerized their clientele.

"Hi, I'm Angel. This is Sally."

Jasper looks up, a warm smile on her face. "You must be the new girls."

They talk with Jasper as she finishes getting ready. She looks up at the wall clock. "I'm up. Good luck!" She leaves to go perform.

Sally and Angel get ready. When done, they meet up with Mama Pearl who says, "I've got you girls dancing on the smaller stage. I'll start you out easy tonight. You're on in an hour." Noticing their uneasiness, she offers a reassuring smile and continues, "You'll do fine. Don't worry about nothing. Do what comes natural, and you'll have those fools eating out of your hands in no time. Now make your Mama proud." She gives each an affectionate squeeze and sends them on their way.

Sally and Angel scan the main room for tables to give private dances to. Angel locks onto a table of four twenty-year-olds who seem to be from the nerd patrol and out of their element. The only things missing are their pocket protectors. Angel nods in their direction. "Watch this. I'll have those fools begging for a lap dance in sixty seconds or less. Clock me."

She heads for their table. Zeroing in on the most uncomfortable-looking one, she sits on his lap—to his horror—and addresses his friends. "Hey, there, fellas. Your boy here looks like he might need some loosening up."

She leans up against the young man, giving him clear view of her cleavage and strokes the side of his face. His friends soften while he looks greener than the Wicked Witch of the West. Angel throws on the charm and convinces the others that they could benefit from watching their buddy get a personal lap dance. They agree, and she begins. The three hoot, holler and cheer her on while their pal warms to the idea.

Sally cannot help but be impressed. True to her word, Angel pulled it off in less than a minute.

You go, Angel!

Turning, Sally looks around the room and locates her own table of needy guys—a group of six rowdy businessmen looking to have a good time. Eager to relieve them of their cash, she approaches them. "Hey, there, guys. Anything I can do to make your evening more…memorable? Perhaps a dance or two?"

The men hungrily undress Sally with their eyes and agree to her offer. She dances up a storm. The men invite her to a VIP room after her dance concludes. Sally plays upon the natural competitive nature of men. She takes the smallest by the hand, sidles up next to him and whispers into his ear.

Her ploy works. His fellow horny businessmen follow behind like a group of frustrated sheep. Smiling to herself, she can almost hear their internal thoughts.

Why him? Why is she holding his hand? I'm stronger. I'm bigger. I'm better looking.

Sally and Angel manage to spend a fair amount of time in the VIP rooms in between dances on the side stages. At the end of the evening, they meet up with Jasper, in the dressing room changing. "How did your first night go?" she asks.

Angel beams. "Great! Getting those guys to pay us all they have is a cinch."

Jasper grins and turns to Sally. "How about you?"

Sally responds, "Easiest money I've ever made."

Jasper smiles. "You want to go out?"

Two other dancers, Honey and Cinnamon, enter the dressing room. Jasper invites the girls to join them. Everyone changes into their street clothes, tip out and walk over to Denny's where they grab a booth.

Cinnamon is a stunningly beautiful African-American, with legs a mile long, flawless skin the color of mocha, a small chest and a rear shaped like a perfect peach. Honey looks as though Hugh Hefner himself handpicked her for a centerfold spread. She has an ample chest and shiny honey-colored shoulder-length hair, transparent crystal blue eyes, a cinched-in waist, curvy hips and is absolutely drop-dead gorgeous. Every guy in the restaurant turns and stares at Honey, practically drooling from the corners of their mouths.

The women talk about themselves, their pasts and why they are stripping. Angel addresses Jasper. "Mind if I ask you some questions?"

"Depends.... What about?"

"Why do you dance?"

"Well, that's certainly direct.... I've got three little kids, no man, and I live with my mama. This job pays real well and allows me to be with my children during the day while Mama stays with them at night."

Sally joins in the conversation. "You're a great dancer. Couldn't help but notice how comfortable and natural you looked on stage the other night. How do you make it look so easy?"

Jasper shrugs. "I give the customers what they want. I find one guy in the audience, during each show, and dance for him...or so I make him think. When I'm done, he usually wants to go to one of the

VIP rooms with me—that's where the real money is."

Angel asks, "How much do you charge in the VIP room?"

"It's not tough to get a guy to drop one to two hundred if he's happy with your performance."

Sally and Angel's eyes widen in disbelief. They decide that the VIP room is where they want to spend most of their time. Sally inquires, "Does *anything* go in the VIP room?"

"Oh, no!" Jasper says. "Luigi has a strict policy against full nudity—the customer's *and* ours. We gotta have our bottoms on at all times and contact is to be up close and personal...to a point." Relaxing a bit, she continues, "There are other clubs, mostly skanky, where the girls might turn a trick, but not here."

Angel questions, "If you don't mind my asking, how much do you average per week?"

"I work four days a week and take home around two grand. Like I said, this job pays decent."

Both Sally and Angel are stunned into silence.

Sally mentions how she and Angel had worked with Misty in LA. "Misty told us about Luigi's. We had a pact to break free of our pimp and come out here together."

Cinnamon asks, "So where is that girl? Haven't heard from her for the longest time. Why isn't she here with ya all?"

Sally takes a deep breath before responding, "About a month ago, Misty was with a john. They were smoking crack. She overdosed and died."

There is a collective gasp as the girls try to digest what they have just been told. Jasper shakes her head. "I knew Misty liked crack but thought she had it under control. We all smoked from time to time. It was never a problem."

Angel ventures a quick glance at Sally.

Jasper continues, "It...it's just...."

They all sit silently for a moment before Honey changes the subject. "So what was the deal with your pimp? Was he really that bad?"

Sally answers, "Fucking bastard! He held us hostage, locked us in at night and kept us under guard during the day. He owned us. Misty stopped contacting you because he wouldn't let her."

"That's awful! How'd you get away?"

Sally tells them about her son, his death and the opportunity it afforded for them to break away from Ax. Cinnamon, Jasper and Honey embrace these girls as their new sisters, and assure Sally and Angel that Luigi and Mama Pearl are nothing like Ax—that they will be safe with them.

Angel turns to Honey and inquires why she is working at the club.

"Like, I wanted to go to college, but didn't have the money. One day, I was talking to one of my friends, when she asked if I'd ever considered stripping. I was horrified and said, 'No'. Like, I've always had a real self-confidence problem and couldn't imagine myself getting up on stage, much less taking my clothes off in front of an audience. My friend invited me to come to the club where she worked and watch her perform. I did.... The money's real good and pays for my tuition and books."

Sally and Angel learn that Cinnamon is a mom with two kids and a husband who works days while she works nights, which allows both of them time to spend with their daughters. "My husband doesn't like me stripping," Cinnamon says. "But it pays the bills. He knows this is just a job to me. Outside the club, I'm like any other soccer mom, taking my girls to and from school and practices. This isn't who I am, it's just a way to put food on the table and spend time with my family."

Both Sally and Angel are impressed with the women and how normal they seem. The five-some continue talking long into the evening. Sally and Angel are full of questions concerning the business, and their new sisters are more than willing to share their wisdom.

Honey, Cinnamon and Jasper tell how, in their combined years of stripping, they have never come across a bouncer who has anything remotely intelligent under the hood, but that these Neanderthal men will protect them to the bitter end. "Believe me," Honey states. "These guys are like, your best friends. They take their jobs seriously and treat us like their First Ladies. They'll *always* take your word over that of a customer's—bounce first and ask questions later. If a customer touches you wrong or upsets you, they're gone. These are good dudes. They've got our backs."

"Then there are the bartenders," Cinnamon laughs. "They're all a bunch of mini Donald Trump wannabes, always working on the next great get-rich-quick scheme. When they're not dipping their toes in real estate, they're constantly checking the want ads."

Jasper adds, "They do serve a purpose, though. Don't know how they do it, but bartenders know *everything* that happens inside the club. Don't matter if it's in the club, on the stage, in the bathroom, dressing room or VIP rooms. Those cats are on top of everything! And, if you tip them well, all sorts of opportunities become available to you."

Sally asks, "What's the deal with Luigi? He seems like a stand-up guy."

The three affirm that he is an excellent boss who takes exquisite care of his dancers. He is ex-Mafioso, highly respected in the business and nobody screws with him or his girls. They assure Sally and Angel that Luigi is what he appears to be—a good guy.

CHAPTER 9

After a month at the motel, Sally and Angel rent a condo behind the strip. A year later, they rent a fully furnished luxury condo located in a nice gated community just north of the strip. The day they move in, Angel is dizzy with delight. "Can you believe it? A gated community with a guard tower and everything?"

"I hear you. I love the fountain and the mini lake just inside the entrance complete with ducks…real live ducks. Sure is a long way from when we were with Ax."

"Yeah…. I like living like a person."

The girls' stripping careers blossom. Happy with their freedom, their circle of friends and the money they make, they purchase a red Chevy Silverado. Occasionally, they take a day or two off to celebrate their good fortune.

One sunny afternoon, Angel and Sally head to the Forum Shops. Sally gets a mischievous grin on her face. "Remember when we went there our first day in town?"

"Yeah."

"And I told you that someday I'd come back and buy anything I wanted. Today's the day. You up for some serious shopping?"

"Always! Sounds like fun."

Once inside the Forum Shops, they forget the triple-digit temperature outside and are soothed by the tranquil periwinkle blue sky dotted with fluffy white clouds skillfully painted on the arched ceiling throughout the common areas. Angel spots a beautiful wall mirror in one of the stores. "Look. Isn't it gorgeous?"

Sally barely glances at the piece. "I guess."

"Wanna get it?"

Sally abruptly spins around and faces Angel. "No! How many times do I have to tell you? Fuck! I'd think you'd get it by now. I—don't—like—mirrors!"

Angel flinches from the verbal attack. "Oh…yeah. Sorry." They leave without the mirror.

Sometime later, Sally and Angel get coffee and nibble on chocolate delicacies. By the end of their shopping spree, they have satisfied grins and their arms are weighted down with bags. Angel suggests, "Wanna put this stuff in the truck and walk over to the new Bellagio? Last night, one of my clients told me that they have a cool glass ceiling in the lobby. It's by some famous artist with a weird name."

"Yeah, I heard about that, too," Sally says. "Something like Chubby."

"No."

"Chevy?"

Angel laughs.

Sally snaps her fingers. "I know. Chewy. Wait. I know—Chihuly."

The girls put their bags in their truck and head over to the Bellagio. Inside the main lobby, they look up in awe. The ceiling is a collage of hundreds of multi-colored glass dinner-sized plates with various colored designs marbled throughout. It is spectacular and lit from behind. Sally looks at Angel. "How long do you suppose it took him to make all those? There must be hundreds of them."

"Don't know. I was wondering how he managed to get them all *up there*. He must have been like that Michelangelo dude. It must have taken him forever."

Sally and Angel learn that most of the strippers at Luigi's look out for one another. However, Bunny, a new girl, is only interested in herself. Sally approaches her one night. "Got a minute?"

"Sure."

"I'm gonna be off for the next couple of nights. Would you be willing to cover for me if any of my regulars come in?"

"How so?"

"If one of my customers comes in, would you take care of them and split the earnings with me when I return? I'll do the same for you."

"Sounds fair enough. Sure. I can do that."

"Thanks."

The following night, Sally is off when one of her regulars comes in looking for a VIP room dance from her. Bunny takes the client to a private room, never tells Sally about it or splits the money with her.

Sally finds out the following week and asks Bunny, "When I was out last week, did any of my regulars come in requesting me?"

Bunny looks as if she is trying to remember. "No." Still lying. "If they had, I would have told you about it. Why do you ask?"

Sally conceals her fury and responds, "No reason. Just wondering if you'd covered for me."

"No, didn't have to, but I will."

"Appreciate that."

Bunny leaves the dressing room, and Sally, scheming to teach her overambitious colleague a lesson she will not soon forget, searches through her purse. She pulls out a small bottle. Smiling to herself, she conceals the container in her hand and leaves the dressing room.

While on one of her breaks, Bunny leaves her beverage unattended to use the restroom. Winking at the bartender, Sally squeezes several drops of Visine into Bunny's drink. Bunny returns, finishes her drink and goes to perform. The Visine works its magic quickly.

Before she knows what is happening, Bunny's bowels loosen. Horrified, she looks around and sees Sally and the bartender grinning at her. That's when she knows her deception has been discovered. Making a mad dash for the restroom, she hears Sally comment, "That'll teach you to steal my customer, you back-stabbing bitch!"

Sally and Angel avoid most of the Special Events nights at the club but cannot resist the Baby Oil Event. The house sets up a kiddy wading pool on the main stage, filling it with a few inches of baby oil. The girls enter the pool stripped to nothing but their g-strings and do their best WWF impersonations. Sally and Angel love this event.

On one of these nights, a customer becomes unruly and jumps up on stage into the kiddy pool with Angel and Sally. "Hey, girls, how's about rubbing me down?" he says in his most charming voice. "I'm sure we could get things heated up."

Three is one too many, and the pool splits, spilling its contents like an oil slick across the stage.

Thor, the closest bouncer, leaps up on stage. "No, you don't, bastard! No wading in the kiddy pool with the girls."

Chaos breaks loose. The inebriated overzealous customer latches onto Angel with a boa constrictor grip. Thor slips and slides his way across the stage towards them and yells, "Let go of her, mother-fucker, before I break your arms!" Thor attempts to grab hold of the man, who immediately lets go of Angel and slips away. Furious, Thor tries to catch him. "Get back here! When I get hold of you, I'm gonna enjoy breaking every bone in your scrawny little body. *Nobody* touches my girls!"

The man, like a greased pig in some perverse race at a county fair, slips from Thor's grasp. He slides off the stage where two other bouncers dog-pile him. Thor, enraged at this point, slides off the stage and grabs the man by the back of his shirt and crotch. He carries the squealing man to the back door and launches him into the parking lot, stating, "If I ever see you in here again, you fucking little bastard, I'll kill you!"

Angel and Sally often take road trips to locations where they can hike and explore to their heart's content. A favorite destination is Bryce Canyon, located in Utah. The colorful palette displayed on the canyon walls catches their breath.

Hawks fascinate Sally. They mesmerize her with their grace and power. When she sees one riding the thermals, she looks up and calls out, "Ah, baby, you're gorgeous! Go, baby! Fly. Be free."

She asks Angel, "Ever seen such a grand creature?"

Angel smiles.

When they are not hiking or exploring, Sally and Angel often get together with Jasper, Honey and Cinnamon. They love indulging in pampering dates where they spend the entire day treating themselves, in typical girly-girl fashion, to a day at the spa. They begin with massages, get their nails done and end with their hair. Once presentable, they go to dinner and dance at local clubs, where they often meet guys who invite them on weekend trips to Lake Mead.

On one of these trips, Sally attempts to water ski wearing only her string bikini and ski vest. Each time she tries to stand up, the rushing water pulls down her bottoms. To cover the problem, she lets go of the rope and drops to her side. At sixty miles per hour, she is instantly thrown into a barrel roll. She pulls up her bottoms, laughing at the view Angel and the guys must have from the boat, as well as the irony of her modesty.

The driver circles the boat around to pick her up. "What happened?"

"The rope slipped, and I couldn't hold on," Sally fibs, shooting Angel a knowing look.

On another of these water adventures, two bronzed muscular studs accompany Sally and Angel. There is no water skiing but plenty of tubing. Angel is a die-hard and refuses to give up easily. The guys gun the engine, swerving the boat in an attempt to knock her off the tube. The harder they try, the more she laughs. Being stubborn and strong, she wraps her fingers around the tube's handles and holds on for dear life. She smiles broadly and taunts, "That all you got? Can't that bucket of yours go any faster? I've seen grannies who swerve more on the freeway."

Sally laughs. Defending his honor, the driver floors the engine and whips Angel back and forth behind the boat. One minute she is riding the crest of the boat's far left wake, the next, she jumps the right one while flying across the surface of the water. Angel laughs and calls, "Boys. Boys. I'm so disappointed. Thought you'd know how to show a lady a good time."

The guys, defeated at their own game, slow the wild ride and tow her back to shore where Angel smiles and asks, "When can I go again?"

On a night off, Sally, Angel, Cinnamon, Jasper and Honey gather at Sally and Angel's condo to sip wine and nibble on cheese, crackers and fresh fruit while sharing some of their VIP room stories.

Sally begins with the story of her ice cream sundae client. "One night I went to the VIP room with a client who had a bag with him—a sure indicator that a fetish was about to be played out. When we entered, he asked me if he could transform my feet into ice cream sundaes. Since I'd just had a pedicure, I named a higher price than usual, thinking he wouldn't want to pay. To my surprise, he agreed and had me sit down. He removed a container of baby wipes from his bag and proceeded to thoroughly clean both of my feet. When he finished, he placed them in a large ceramic bowl and scooped three large balls of the ice-cream on top of my feet."

Honey interrupts, "Like, how did you stay still? Wasn't it freezing?"

"As soon as the ice cream landed on my feet, I jumped. When I got back into position, the man sliced a banana into coins around the edges of the bowl. It was hard not to laugh. He then drizzled caramel sauce on top and covered the whole concoction with whipped cream, chopped nuts and a maraschino cherry." Sally notices her friends are drooling.

"What he did next was almost too much. Placing his hands behind his back, he leaned forward and began eating his creation, as one would a pie in a pie-eating contest. Every now and then, he'd look up at me—his face covered in the gooey mess and a wide smile spread across his face. He looked like a little kid and licked my feet clean, even between my toes. Of course, the next day, I treated myself to another pedicure with his money."

Cinnamon laughs. "Don't know about ya all, but now I'm starving for an ice-cream sundae. Sally, Angel, you got any fixin's?"

Everyone agrees that they, too, are craving an ice-cream treat. Giving into their desires, they break to make sundaes.

When they're done eating, Angel shares how one of her regular customers really enjoyed her playing the role of a dominant. "This guy had been encouraged by my stage act with my whip. We went back to one of the VIP rooms where he confided that he wanted me to spank him. He explained that he'd been naughty and needed to be punished. Of course, never one to back down, I agreed."

Cinnamon interrupts, "We know. You just like to beat on the

guys."

The room erupts into laughter.

Angel continues. "I explained that the spanking would have to be done over his underwear and had him bend over and grab his ankles. Since he asked for it, I was going to teach this bad boy a lesson he wouldn't soon forget. I really laid into his upturned ass. Upon hearing the slaps, Desmond, one of the bouncers, came rushing into the room, fearing that it was me who was being struck. As soon as he saw what was going on, Desmond began laughing uncontrollably. It took quite a bit of persuading, but I finally got him to leave so I could complete my client's request."

"Oh, my God!" Sally manages. "Is *that* why Desmond says, 'takes a licking, but keeps on ticking' whenever he passes you?"

Angel grins.

Finally, Honey tells them of her Cupid. "This client stood only four feet tall. He had come into the club a few times before working up the courage to ask me to the VIP room. Enchanted by his littleness, I took him by the hand and led him back to one of the rooms. Once there, I noticed the bag he had with him."

The room falls silent, with all of the girls on the edge of their seats, wanting to hear about Honey's little man and his VIP room fetish.

"He told me he'd always wanted to play Cupid and wondered if I wouldn't mind allowing him to dress as such and shoot suction cup arrows at me while I danced. The idea of having things shot at me, period, was not appealing, much less while I danced, and I told him such. He offered to pay me whatever price I wanted if I would please grant his request. Like, not being one to turn down money, or a little person, I named an unbelievably high price, to which he agreed."

The girls stifle their laughter.

"Just as Cinnamon had with her client, I stepped outside the door while the man changed into his Cupid costume. He hollered when he was done, and I re-entered. I'd agreed to only one dance, not wanting to be shot at for longer than that, no matter what he was paying me. Like, a girl's gotta have principles."

Sally cannot contain her laughter. "Yeah, right! You having principles? You'd do just about *anything* for money."

Honey thinks before replying, "Well, that may be but I can *want* to have principles."

"What? That doesn't make any sense."

Honey says, "Shut up and let me continue my story. I began to dance. When the music started, my Cupid circled, like a gleeful child, and shot random arrows at me. He was a pretty good shot. By the time he was finished, I looked like a damned porcupine."

The girls laugh at the image.

CHAPTER 10

Detective "Doc" Jones' reputation was legendary at the Pasadena Police Station. Others had given him the nickname Doc because of his knack for solving any cold case he put his mind to. Some said Doc was gifted, others said he was driven like a demon, but he knew different. He solved the cases for his daughter.

Years earlier, she had gone missing while walking home from school. They desperately tried to find her and did...two weeks later, in a shallow grave located in an empty field. She had been raped and suffocated. She was all Doc had, her mother having died during childbirth. For eight years, Doc had raised her by himself. She was his heart and soul. He existed for her.

Instead of falling apart after her death, Doc became driven. He vowed to leave no stone unturned until he found the bastard who took his little girl from him. Doc eventually did find Caroline's assailant, and the prosecution put together an excellent case against him. Unfortunately, they screwed up. Some of the evidence the detectives had gathered was collected without a proper search warrant, causing the case to be thrown out. Caroline's killer went free. Doc promised to never allow another child killer/rapist to go free if he was working the case.

Your killer/rapist may have gone free, sweet Caroline, but, baby girl, Daddy swears he won't allow another parent to go through the same anguish I've had to endure.

Doc became obsessed with solving cases and putting scumbags away. One afternoon, a father and mother who had heard about his perfect track record came to the station and approached him about solving their son's cold case.

"Please, Detective Jones, you're our last hope," the mother said while sliding her son's picture across the desk. "Everyone else has given up on our little boy."

Doc picked up the photo and ran his fingers through his thick white hair. "Doc, please. Everyone calls me Doc."

He glanced at the boy's picture and froze. A tingling began at the base of his neck and crept its way down his spine. In the photo, the boy looked to be about the same age as his daughter when she was killed. The boy's eyes haunted him—the same transparent sky-blue eyes as his Caroline's. They almost seemed to cry out, "Hey, mister, please don't give up on me. Find who did this to me." Intrigued, Doc laid the photo down and looked up at the father, his grey-blue eyes shining. "Tell me what you know."

Leaning forward, the father told how his son had been killed six years earlier, and how the killer was still at large. Something deep within Doc clicked into place.

The father continued, "The case was finally reclassified as a cold case."

A passionate fury began to smolder deep within Doc.

Another cold case...another fucking child cold case. How.... How could it be considered cold?

"I'd be happy to look into your son's case."

The mother rushed around the desk to give him a big hug. "Oh, thank you! Thank you, Detective Jones...I...I mean, Doc. I knew you wouldn't let us down." Looking at her husband, she added, "Our boy will finally have justice."

Three months later, Doc solved the case. Someone in the investigation had overlooked an important piece of information, which Doc found, latched onto and allowed to lead him directly to the child's killer.

Cold case files began mysteriously appearing on his desk. Just as curiously, his regular workload eased up. He solved every cold case he was assigned. His track record was unprecedented. Within a year, he switched to handling cold cases exclusively and was given a new title—Investigator Jones.

A few months later, the file involving Ax and the pimp he shot in the back appeared on his desk. He read that early on in the investigation, an anonymous woman had called the police station mentioning that during the motel pimp shootout, a five-year-old boy had been killed.

That got Doc's attention. Poring through the file, he discovered that the anonymous caller had provided accurate information pertaining to the case. It was never followed up on, however, since no evidence of the boy had ever been found.

In the end, the call was written off as a crank caller trying to get their name in the paper. The original investigating officers knew that one scumbag pimp had killed another. Doc could understand how the case may have gone cold if it had just been the death of one pimp by another, but with the possibility of there having been a small child involved, that changed things—at least for him....

* * * * *

"God damn it!" Doc roars as he slams the file down on his desk. Getting up, he feverishly paces the room while his partner, Dan Kowalski, sits across the desk watching him. "How the hell could they have missed a small boy? What the fuck! How do you not follow up on a lead like that? Are they all a bunch of morons?"

Dan, having seen his partner worked up like this before, lets out a deep sigh. "So, we've got our next case?"

"Damn straight! These bumbling baboons can't tell the difference between a crime involving a dead pimp and one that involves an innocent child. Guess I'll have to school them. God damn fucking idiots!"

Dan smiles.

"What are you grinning about, pardner? You look like a damn Cheshire cat."

"Nothing. Just love seeing you like this."

"Oh, yeah, why's that?"

"'Cause this means another cold case is about to be solved."

"Sure thing, 'cause Doc's here to fix it." He sits down at his desk. "All right, pardner, as of this moment, we drop everything else." Doc taps his finger on the file, continuing. "*This* is our number one priority."

Dan nods. "Anything you say, pardner."

"And wipe that damn Cheshire cat grin off your face. I hate cats!"

Dan stops smiling.

Several hours later, having committed each word contained in the file to memory, Doc looks up, leans back and interlaces his fingers. "What do we know so far?"

Dan gets up, begins pacing and responds, "Well, we know the anonymous caller was female. We know that one man, a pimp, was killed by a handgun and that no one was willing to come forward with information."

Deep lines crease Doc's forehead as he leans forward in his chair. "Not a lot to go on." He wags his finger. "But what do we suspect?"

Dan returns to his chair and sits down. "There's a lot more to go on there. Thanks to our six-month investigation of Ax and his prostitution ring, we know that rival pimps were trying to move in on his territory. We suspect that a turf war between Ax and the victim prompted the shooting—Ax being the gunman. I'd be willing to bet that the female caller was one of his prostitutes."

Doc's hair springs back into place as he runs his fingers through it. "We know what a tight leash Ax holds on his girls—how closely he guards them. They can't take a piss without him knowing about it. So, how did one of them manage to call us?"

"Don't know. While Ax was busy trying to avoid us?"

"He's a slippery bastard, all right. Don't know about you, but I'm getting sick of him slipping through our fingers. How many times have we arrested his girls? Feel like I'm getting to know them personally. Just once, I'd like to get something concrete *on him*. Should have turned up something by now. Nobody is that clever." Doc pounds his fist on his desk for emphasis. "I want this bastard!"

"The caller had to be one of Ax's girls. No other females were in the area at the time and the caller provided exact information that was never released to the press."

"And she said she knew the boy—that she lived with him and his mother." Doc is out of his chair, angered again. "How the hell do you ignore the suggestion of a phantom little boy?"

Dan attempts to calm his partner. "Happens all the time. Overworked investigators, sloppy work, you name it."

Doc slumps in his chair. "That's not good enough, damn it! There may be a nameless little boy out there that no one knows about, who's buried in some shallow grave with no justice." He shakes his head. "Too many of those kids. I want this one found. I want to know who he is, where he came from and why no one seems to have a record of him. Phantom children don't exist. Somebody knows something about this one, and I'm gonna find out what. Let's start with that anonymous caller."

"How you going to get to her? Ax won't allow it."

A knowing grin spreads across Doc's face. "Thought about that. I think it's time for you to bring Ax in for some additional questioning, while I talk to his girls."

Dan smiles and then looks serious. "Do me a favor?"

"What?"

"Stay calm this time. You ain't a spring chick. Your fifty-two-year-old heart can't take the stress you put it through."

"Yeah, yeah. What are you? My mother?"

"Just expressing concern."

Letting out a deep sigh, Doc softens and replies, "Okay, I'll *try*. Happy?"

"Downright giddy."

Both men chuckle.

Dan heads to the motel where he finds Ax in clear sight when he pulls up.

Cocky little bastard. Look at him, strutting his stuff like we can't touch him.

Dan pulls his unit up next to Ax, rolls down the passenger window and calls, "Got a minute?"

Ax casually leans down and places his forearms on the lowered window—a taunting grin on his face. "Well, well, if it ain't Officer Kowalski."

Dan corrects him under his breath, "*Investigator* Kowalski."

Ax brushes off the information as meaningless. "What do you

want this time? Don't you have some doughnuts to go eat?

"Ah, how nice, you're concerned about my diet."

"Yeah, hope you choke."

Dan says, "Well, now that we have all the pleasantries out of the way, I was wondering if you'd be willing to answer a few questions?"

"What about?"

"We're still trying to wrap up this whole pimp shooting mess."

"Sucks for you. What's that got to do with me?"

Dan gives Ax a cocky smile of his own. "Seems it might have quite a bit to do with you. We've received new information and would like to have you come to the station and clear a few things up."

Ax, arrogant as ever, returns Dan's smile with one of his own, responding, "Why, sure. I have nothing to hide."

In the interrogation room, Dan circles behind the massive black man seated in the chair before him. He leans in close to Ax's ear and states, "Come on, you scumbag. We both know you killed him."

One side of Ax's mouth draws up to a sneer as he leans back, causing the chair to creak from his impressive size. "Prove it."

Dan completes his circle and stands across the table from Ax. Laying his hands on the table, he leans in for emphasis and states, "That's exactly what I plan to do." He stands and turns, as if to leave. Almost as an afterthought, he looks back at Ax and adds, "Oh, by the way, what's it feel like to be a child-killer?"

Ax coldly returns Dan's stare. "Not saying I killed any little motha-fucka brat, but if I had, I imagine it would feel *real* good."

Hearing Ax's words, a cold chill runs down Dan's spine.

Later that day, Dan and Doc meet up to compare notes. Doc notes his partner's troubled expression. "Okay, spit it out. What's bugging you?"

Dan gets up and begins pacing the room. "Been doing this a long time. I've seen it all. That Ax, though, he's a cold bastard who gives me the creeps."

"What happened?"

"During my interview, I asked him what it felt like to be a child-killer. He never flinched. Instead, he smiled and said that if he had killed the kid, it would have felt *real* good.   Honest to God, he's pure evil. We're gonna want to watch our backs with this one."

CHAPTER 11

Doc questions Ax's prostitutes and comes up with nothing. Then Bambi slips him a note just prior to his leaving. Turns out she is the one who made the anonymous phone call. She wants immediate protection from Ax for sharing what she knows. Doc agrees to her terms.

Bambi tells how Ax knows where Sally and Angel are and that she is concerned for their safety. She recaps how Ax held Eric Angel hostage to force Sally to continue working and how he had killed the boy and then disposed of his body. She mentions how she overheard Ax talking on the phone to someone about where he buried the boy's remains and relays the location.

Doc sets up a team to search the area, overseeing the site excavation personally. Sure enough, they find remains that the lab confirms are those of a five-year-old male.

Armed with information obtained from Bambi, Doc tracks down and calls Sally in Las Vegas. The phone rings at the club. Mama Pearl picks up. "Luigi's Gentlemen's Club."

"Hello, my name is Investigator Jones. I'm calling from Pasadena, California. I'm looking for a Sally McFee. Is she there?"

Mama Pearl's protective nature kicks in. "What you need her for?"

"Well, ma'am, that's confidential."

Mama Pearl sounds like a ruffled hen as she replies, "Unless you give me a good reason, I ain't putting her on the phone."

Doc lets out a sigh. "Tell her it's concerning her son."

"Her son? He's dead."

Doc continues, "Yes, ma'am, I know. Would you please tell her I'm on the line?"

"Oh, all right, just a minute, please."

Mama Pearl looks around the club, locates Sally and discreetly tells her that there is an investigator from California on the phone.

Sally, instantly on guard, questions, "What's he want?"

"Seems he wants to talk with you about your son?"

The color drains from Sally's face, and she begins to sway like she might faint. Mama Pearl reaches out to steady her. "Hey, there, sweetheart, you look like you've seen a ghost. Want me to tell this bozo to take a hike?"

Sally regains her composure and responds, "No. I'll take the call. Okay if I take it in Luigi's office?"

Mama Pearl wraps a protective arm around Sally's shoulders. "Sure, darlin'. Luigi's gone now, so you've the office all to yourself."

Sally walks past Mama Pearl and then reaches out and gently squeezes her arm. "Thank you."

"Be right here if you need me. He's on line three."

In the office, Sally picks up the phone. "Hello?"

Doc's voice sounds relieved. "Ah, Miss McFee, my name's Investigator Jones. I'm calling from Pasadena, California regarding the death of your son."

At the mention of Eric Angel's name, Sally sits down heavily in Luigi's chair and begins shaking. "How...how did you find me?"

Doc tells her about his conversation with Bambi, and how they have discovered the body of a five-year-old male, which they believe to be that of her son.

"Miss McFee, I know this must be difficult for you."

Her emotions having been triggered, Sally almost spits into the phone, "How could you possibly know what I'm feeling?"

Doc's voice is full of compassion. "I lost my child to a violent crime as well. I'd like to help get the bastard who did this to your son."

Sally leans back in her chair, closes her eyes and rubs her temples. "You...you don't know who you're dealing with.... You'll never catch him."

"Miss McFee, I'm quite aware of how evasive Ax can be. I assure you, he won't get away from *me*. Dealt with individuals like him before. Haven't lost one yet."

Sally, seeing a glimmer of hope for her son's justice, opens her eyes. "What can I do to help, Investigator Jones?"

"To begin with, you can call me Doc. Everyone does."

"All right—Doc."

"I'm going to need background information on your son. Anything you can tell me. Also, I'll need a sample of your blood."

"Mine? Why?"

"Our lab can run tests against it to confirm the likelihood that you and our victim are related."

"Do I need to come there?" Panic edges its way into Sally's voice as she continues, "I...I can't go back there!"

"No, that won't be necessary. I'll call a lab there in Vegas and let them know you're coming. They'll take a sample and send it to me."

Sally, relieved, exhales heavily and states, "I don't want to be difficult. I...I just.... If you were able to find me, Ax can't be far behind."

"I understand. Is there another number where you can be reached?"

Sally provides him with her home number. After hanging up, she sits for a long while in Luigi's office, trying to digest the call. When she leaves, Mama Pearl sees her pale face and rushes over to give her a hug. "Hey, darlin', everything okay?"

Sally leans into Mama Pearl's ample bosom. "Yeah. Can I take the rest of the night off?"

"Of course, honey. Take as much time as you need."

"Thanks."

The lab crosschecks Sally's blood sample to that of the boy's. Doc calls Sally with the results.

"Sally?"

"Yeah."

"This is Doc from Pasadena."

"Oh, hey. What's up?"

Doc lets out a deep sigh before proceeding. "We received the sample of your blood. Our lab ran it against the remains we found—they match. Sally, we've found your son."

Nearly dropping the phone, Sally falls to her knees, her eyes well up with tears and her chest tightens. She begins crying and barely manages, "Oh, my God! You found him? You found my baby?"

"Yes. We need you to claim the body."

Sally slumps to a sitting position on the floor and does not respond.

"Sally? Are you still there?"

After a lengthy pause, she responds. "I'm here. Can I call you back?"

"Sure. You know where to find me."

"Thanks, Doc. I'll get back to you."

Sally tells Angel that Investigator Jones has confirmed the discovery of Eric Angel's remains and that they need her to come to claim the body. Next, she goes to Luigi. She looks drained and aged. Luigi, concerned, offers her a chair and asks, "Hey there, darlin', what's troubling you?"

"You know about the ongoing investigation surrounding my son's death."

"Yes. How's that going?"

She attempts to steel her emotions before proceeding with a quivering voice. "They...they've found my son." The minute the words tumble out, tears begin streaming down her soft cheeks. Luigi, out of his chair and by her side in an instant, wraps his arms around her in a protective hug. "They need me to come and claim his body," she adds.

Sally completely breaks down sobbing uncontrollably while Luigi holds her. After awhile, her crying subsides and Luigi asks, "What can I do?"

"I'll need some time off to go to California."

Luigi pulls back. He places a hand on either of her shoulders, looks deep into her eyes and states, "You let me take care of

77

everything. I think of you as family and I always take care of family."

Sally looks at him, her emerald green eyes sparkling with tears. "Thank you, Luigi."

Luigi makes the arrangements to claim Eric Angel's body and has it transported to Las Vegas. He contacts the best mortician and pays to have the most elaborate funeral with the finest casket and a zillion flowers. Aware of Sally's love of the great outdoors, he selects a cemetery with rolling green lawns and mature trees. He secures a plot under a stately oak. Angel and their friends help hold Sally together.

Sally and Angel are driven in a limousine to the cemetery the day of the funeral. Mama Pearl, Cinnamon, Jasper, Honey and Luigi, who doesn't leave Sally's side, meet them. Sally makes it through her son's funeral and gives Luigi a bear hug at the end. Choked with emotion, she manages, "I...I don't know how to thank you." She spies a squirrel and says, "Eric Angel would have loved it here with all the squirrels."

Her mind recalls how her son had belly-laughed watching squirrels scamper across telephone wires while he was alive. Their playful enthusiasm had made Eric Angel illuminate with pure joy. At the memory, Sally's throat tightens and she begins to sob.

Luigi holds her in a tight embrace. "It's okay, little darlin', your son is safe now, nobody can hurt him anymore. Your baby is at peace. He can finally rest."

CHAPTER 12

Although Doc and Dan are ruthless with their investigation, they find plenty of circumstantial but no concrete evidence that Ax killed Eric Angel. Doc, beside himself, vents his frustration to his partner over burgers and beers one night. "God damn mother-fucking bastard! I'm not gonna let Ax slip through my fingers. I made a promise to that boy's mother—a promise I don't intend to break. I'll do whatever it takes to bring that scumbag to justice! Eric Angel didn't deserve to be held prisoner his entire life, only to be killed and then dumped in a shallow grave. I won't sit back and allow Ax to hurt another innocent child. I can't."

Dan lets out a weary sigh and asks, "What can we do? We know he did it but can't prove it. It's like when O.J. was accused of killing Nicole. At least *they* had a glove to go on. We have nothing."

Doc squints his eyes. "You know? You're absolutely right. Only this case is going to turn out different. If *we* can't get him, maybe we should unleash his own kind on him."

Dan leans forward in his chair. "Are you suggesting what I think you are?"

"Absolutely! I think it's time we disclose what Ax has been up to. I'm sure his peers would love to hear about how he killed an innocent child while shooting a pimp in the back."

"Doc, you know what they'll do to him if they find him."

Doc sits taller in his chair and looks Dan in the eye. "I do."

Dan nods his head, signing on to the plan. "Didn't I read in the file that the dead pimp has a brother on the East coast?"

Doc stands up and begins pacing before answering, "Yeah. Can't recall his name." He wrinkles his brow and thinks hard. "Give me a minute." He snaps his fingers. "Leonard! His name is Leonard

White."

"I'll bet it wouldn't bode well with him that the scumbag who killed his brother is also a child-killer."

Doc stops pacing and faces Dan. "Oh, yeah, I think it's time we send a message to Mr. Leonard White."

Dan grins. "I think Leonard is going to enjoy taking care of Ax for us."

Doc holds up his beer bottle. "To Leonard!"

Doc sends word through the underground about Ax and then sits back and waits for vigilantism to do the rest. It doesn't take long.

Leonard discovers that Ax is the one who killed his brother and that he committed the unpardonable sin of killing a child. Leonard sends word that he is coming to California and wants his identity to remain concealed. His request is respected. Eager individuals who have been wronged by Ax offer assistance. Fellow pimps, not fans of how Ax treats his girls for the bad reputation it gives other pimps, step up to help Leonard.

When the information is leaked that he killed an innocent child, Ax, fearing for his life, goes underground. Unaware that his allies have joined forces with his enemies, Ax accepts their help to hide him and puts another pimp in charge of his girls during his absence.

His "allies" drive him to a remote mountain cabin. Using a key, Ax unlocks the door. It swings inward and he steps inside. As his eyes slowly adjust to the dim hazy light within, he sees a familiar face and comments, "What the—"

Before he can finish his sentence, he's knocked unconscious with a blindingly powerful blow. Ax regains consciousness and realizes that he is tied up. He finds himself looking at someone's back as the fog leaves his head. The man purposely turns around to face him. Ax is stunned. "What the fuck? I...I killed you."

The man, who bears a striking resemblance to the pimp Ax shot in the back, walks over and squats down. "You don't know me, but you knew my brother. He's the one you shot in the back and left behind like a piece of garbage."

Ax sniffs the air. "Thought I smelled a familiar stench."

"That was my twin brother, you motha fucka!" To punctuate his comment, the man hooks Ax on the right side of his head with another powerful blow. Ax's head jerks back. He tastes blood and spits it out. Although he knows it is useless, he tries to fight back but the rough-hewn ropes hold tight, cutting into his flesh.

The man, rubbing his knuckles, calmly continues, "His name was Lynol. The day you killed him, you killed half of me."

"Ah, my heart breaks for you."

Through clenched teeth, the man growls at Ax. "Not yet it doesn't—but it will. My name's Leonard...Leonard White. Perhaps you've heard of me?"

Ax's eyes widen with recognition. This man's reputation is well known on the East coast. The story of how he, using his past skills as a butcher, fillets individuals who cross him, is legendary. Ax looks around and for the first time spots the three men, gargantuan in size, standing around him. Realizing he is outnumbered, his mind races.

Leonard steps in close enough for Ax to detect his expensive cologne and calmly states, "Listen here, motha fucka. Let's not make this any more unpleasant than it has to be. My boys here are gonna rough you up a bit. Once they've got your attention, you and I will have a little chat. How's that sound?"

"Go to hell!" Ax says, spitting on him.

Leonard looks down at the splattered saliva on his Italian shirt. "Why'd you have to go and do that? This is just gonna make things worse for you. Makes no difference to me. You're a dead motha fucka either way."

He motions to his goons. "Boys, make him *feel* my unhappiness." Leonard lights a cigarette and walks over to the sofa where he takes a seat while his men move in on their prey. One of them is carrying a lead pipe. He swings, allowing it to connect with Ax's left knee. *"This* is what I think of motha-fucking child killers!"

Ax howls as the pipe shatters his kneecap. "Ah, fuck!" Through clenched teeth, he begs, "Stop! God, please stop!"

The pipe man is unmoved and responds, "God ain't gonna waste his time on a scumbag like you." He swings again and allows his weapon to land on Ax's other knee, while calmly explaining, "And *this* is what I think of motha fuckas who leave innocent children in shallow graves for the coyotes to dig up!" The man inspects his pipe. "You better not have hurt my pipe. It's my favorite."

Stepping back, he motions one of the other goons. "Hey, Vincent, why don't you share with Mr. Ax how you feel."

Vincent bows with an exaggerated wide sweep of his hand and answers, "Gladly." He knocks the chair over with Ax still tied to it and proceeds to kick Ax in his face, ribs and anywhere he can connect. Still restrained, Ax is unable to defend himself or fight back. Every movement is agonizing to his knees. He groans and cries out with each additional blow.

Vincent turns his back on Ax and addresses one of the other men. "Tiny, why don't you share how *you* feel."

Tiny grins. "Why, I thought you'd never ask."

Reaching down, he picks up the chair with Ax in it. "Ah, seems like you fell over. Let's get you upright. Wouldn't want to strain my back or anything."

Laughter can be heard from his buddies.

"Haven't had a good workout with a punching bag for about a week. How about you be my punching bag?"

"Like I have a choice."

Tiny turns to Leonard. "Wow, did you hear that? I think he's catching on."

Tiny punches Ax like a pro boxer. He has a good rhythm going when he speaks again. "So, motha fucka, how's it feel to be helpless? Probably like what that boy felt like when you killed him." He closes with a mighty left cross. "Did I mention? I have a little brother about his age, you fucking scumbag."

Ax never gets a chance to answer. The final blow knocks him out cold. They rouse him by dousing him with a bucket of water. Coming to, he looks up and sees Leonard squatting down at eye level with him. "So, do I have your attention?"

Ax manages to mumble, "Yes," through his swollen mouth with its broken teeth.

Leonard looks satisfied. "Good. We're gonna get to know each other real well." Leonard stands up and paces in front of Ax, who watches him closely through his good eye. He continues, "I'm sure you noticed on the drive up that we're all alone. This party of ours will go completely undetected. In fact, the boys and I have had quite a few parties up here." To his men, "Haven't we boys?" They nod their heads in agreement.

Leonard returns his attention to Ax. "Well, I think that's just about enough fun for today. Wouldn't want to wear ourselves out. Gotta pace ourselves."

He addresses his men. "Put Ax in the bedroom."

Tiny and the pipe man drag Ax, who is still secured to his chair, into the next room. They leave him and close the door behind them. Ax hears their voices as they laugh and play cards through the night. He tries to stay awake, but exhausted, drifts off.

The next morning, Vincent and Tiny come to get him. They untie him, lift him by either arm and carry him, since he can't walk, out of the room.

Leonard, wearing a fresh shirt, motions Ax to join him at the table, where a delicious-smelling breakfast is laid out. "Come. I hate to dine alone."

Vincent and Tiny place Ax in a chair at the table where he watches Leonard eat his entire breakfast—slowly—without acknowledging him. When he is done, Leonard takes his napkin, dabs at the corners of his mouth, folds and places it on his empty plate. Despite his pain, Ax's stomach gnaws on itself. Leonard pushes back from the table and states, "That's better. Always best to conduct business on a full stomach. Where did we leave off yesterday?"

Ax tries not to anger the man while responding, "I'm not sure, this is your party."

"Now, now, don't go getting all testy with me after I was just kind enough to let you watch me eat. Are we going to have any trouble with you today?"

Ax lowers his eyes. "No."

"Excellent! How civilized."

Leonard turns his attention to his men. "Take our friend here and show him our *special* accommodations. I think he'll find them most enchanting."

Vincent and Tiny snicker. Leonard leads the way while his goons follow behind, dragging Ax. They take him down a flight of stairs, causing his feet to bang down every step. Ax yells out with each bump. They proceed around a corner and stop in the middle of a room where there appears to be a well of sorts. It is eight feet across and has a three-foot rock lip that stands above ground level.

Leonard encourages his boys. "Now come on, Tiny and Vincent. Don't be rude. Show Ax his accommodations."

Leonard's men hoist him up to the edge of the well. Looking down into its cavity, Ax sees pitch-blackness. Suddenly, he is shoved and falls into the well. The pipe man's voice trails him. "Hope you like your new room."

From above, Ax hears the four men laugh and attempts to right himself as he falls—bending and twisting—so his feet will hit first. They do. Upon impact, his right tibia breaks—the jagged end ramming its way through his skin. He collapses to the ground, howling in pain.

Next, Ax hears two items hit the ground. He can barely focus through the blinding pain. He strains his eyes to see what has been thrown down with him. He hears the men's laughter receding, as they ascend the stairs to the cabin above. Closing the door behind them, they leave him in total darkness.

What did they throw down here with me?

He gropes the ground, drags his body across the floor of the well and locates one of the items—a stale loaf of bread. Although his teeth are throbbing, he is ravenous and tears off a hunk. Placing it gingerly in his mouth, he allows it to dissolve. He holds onto the loaf with one hand, while continuing to make his way around the floor, until he comes across the other item—a plastic bottle. He unscrews the lid and sniffs—no odor. He puts it to his lips and takes a tentative sip—water. He greedily gulps the contents of the small bottle. The cool liquid sends electric shocks of pain to the exposed nerves of his broken teeth. Lying on his back, he rips off another chunk of the bread and eats it. After devouring a few morsels, he struggles to sit up.

Gotta see how bad this break is. Motha fuckas are gonna pay for this! No one treats me this way!

He touches the skin on his lower leg. Pulling his fingers away, they are wet with blood.

Gotta stop the bleeding.

Ax takes off his shirt, rolls it up and wraps it around his leg just above the wound. Tying it tight, he manages to stop his blood loss. He collapses on his back, exhausted from the effort and closes his eyes.

I'll just rest a minute. Gotta stay alert. Don't know when they're coming ba….

Ax jerks awake.

How long was I out. Minutes? Hours? Can't tell. Goddamn motha fucka, I hurt! They're gonna pay—especially the son-of-a-bitch who pushed me down here. Gonna enjoy fucking him up.

An evil sneer contorts Ax's face. He reaches for his bread, his stomach growling, but cannot find it. Realizing he must have dropped it in his sleep, he rummages around and locates it. He rips off chunk after chunk, allowing them to dissolve in his mouth, until there is nothing left. His hunger satiated, he closes his eyes.

I'll just rest for another minute.

Ax awakes to the sounds of something heavy being rolled above him and hears men's voices. His knees and leg throb incessantly. He hears the sound of a motorized winch above. With his good eye, he can make out the silhouette of someone being lowered.

"Wakey, wakey, Sleeping Beauty," comes Lenny's voice. "Wouldn't want you to miss your ride out of here."

Ax pulls himself into a sitting position, looks up and calls, "Yeah, come down here, you motha fucka."

He hears Vincent chuckle and respond, "Ha! What you gonna do to me?" He reaches the floor of the pit, walks over to where Ax is sitting and shines a flashlight on him. "Man, you look like shit." He shrugs and continues, "No matter, the boss wants to see you." He places the flashlight in his rear pocket and attempts to hoist Ax, who fights him as best he can, over his shoulder. His energy spent, Ax slumps and Vincent carries him like a sack of potatoes to the platform, where he motions to be brought up.

The men carry Ax up the stairs, his legs dangling. In the cabin, they sit him in a chair where they bind his arms and legs as before. Leonard circles Ax's chair, sizing him up. "Had a rough night down there?"

Ax replies, "Had better."

"Looks like you took a nasty fall into our pit. Got your leg all busted up."

Ax growls through clenched teeth, "Stop. You're gonna get me all choked up with your concern."

"Now, there you go again. Here I am trying to be all civilized and you're dripping with sarcasm."

"Civilized?! You call this civilized? Fuck that!"

"I can only work with what I've got. And I have to tell you, I'm disappointed." Leonard pauses to allow his words to sink in.

Ax asks, "Yeah? What you disappointed in?"

Leonard's face erupts into a sadistic grin as he replies, "Why, you, motha fucka. Thought you'd be more of a challenge. But no—you're just a coward who likes to shoot people in the back because you don't have the balls to face 'em." He pulls out a gun and places its muzzle against Ax's temple. "Not me. Don't have a problem looking someone in the eye as I kill him."

Ax looks defiantly at Leonard. "Go to hell!"

"You first, motha fucka!" Leonard states, as he pulls the trigger.

Back in Pasadena, Doc gets word of Ax's death. His face illuminates with a satisfied grin and he scrawls, "solved" on the file. He and Dan celebrate that evening over steaks and beers.

The next morning, Doc calls Sally in Las Vegas. The phone rings and is picked up. "Hello, Sally?"

"No, this is Angel. Just a minute, I'll get her."

"Thanks."

Doc hears footsteps growing distant, and then he hears another set approaching. There is fumbling of the handset. "Hello?"

"Hi, Sally, this is Doc."

"Hey, Doc. What's up?"

"I have some great news."

Sally's heart skips a beat.

"What?"

Doc's voice exudes enthusiasm when he says, "I just got word that Ax is dead."

"What? How? When? You got him? Oh, my God, I never thought you'd get him…but dead…you said he's dead?"

"Slow down. Let me answer your questions. I put word out that we were looking for Ax. Seems some 'others' got to him before we could." Doc pauses for a moment before continuing. "Eric Angel got his justice."

Sally is speechless, overwhelmed with emotion. As the full meaning of Doc's news sinks in, she begins sobbing. Doc is patient and allows her to express her relief. Regaining her composure, Sally manages, "Thank you, Doc…for everything."

"My pleasure. It's been an honor solving your son's case and bringing his killer to justice."

With nothing else to say, they both hang up.

Angel enters the room and Sally fills her in on the conversation with Doc. "He's gone, Angel. He's really gone! We don't have to worry about him finding us…. We're free!"

"Sally girl, I can't believe it's over…that he's really gone." Angel pauses for a moment before continuing. "We're free? We're really free?"

"Yeah."

CHAPTER 13

The next morning, Sally and Angel take a walk around their gated neighborhood, still processing the news about Ax. They mindlessly walk where their feet take them, lost in conversation, and enjoy the slight mist the fountain by the main gate casts off. Sally stops and cocks her head. "Did you hear that?"

Having walked a few feet ahead, Angel turns and walks back. "Na. What did you hear?"

"Not sure. It was so quiet—muffled. Shhh, there it is again."

"I hear it! Where's it coming from?"

Sally and Angel search for the sound's source. They follow it to its origin, a sealed box with holes cut in it, just outside the gate. Kneeling beside the carton, not knowing what to expect, Sally carefully opens it. "Oooh, it's a puppy. Someone must have left it."

The girls scan the area, but see no one. Sally scoops the puppy out of the box and holds it up to get a better look. A yellow lab, with oversized ears, a wiggly tail and a perfect black button nose looks back. "She's adorable! Can't be more than six weeks old." The pup squirms in Sally's hands, trying desperately to find solid ground for its paws, and makes whimpering sounds while its tail spins like a propeller for balance. Both girls fall under the spell of puppy love-at-first-sight. Sally nuzzles its soft fur against her cheek. "She's so soft and has that wonderful puppy smell."

Its pink tongue eagerly licks her face, causing her to giggle. The girls leave the box and head back to their condo, a spring to their step, cuddling the new addition to their family.

* * * * *

Sally had always loved and needed animals. She shared a kindred spirit with them. Always the first to rescue injured animals—even insects—it physically pained her to see them in distress. If there was a wounded bird, she had mended it. If she saw an insect stuck in a body of water, she would gingerly remove it, lay it on dry ground and gently blow on its wings until they were dry, and it could fly away. The creatures that didn't make it ripped a hole in her soul. She mourned their loss like a mother would a lost child.

When Sally spotted an animal struck by a car, she cringed inside—feeling their pain. She swerved to avoid road kill while others callously drove over it.

She recalled how, as a child, she had deemed that animals could be trusted more than people—making them more valuable in her eyes. They never took advantage of or hurt her. All they wanted was approval. In return, they gave her the undying affection and acceptance she yearned for. Had it not been for the stray animals she encountered while growing up, Sally knows she would not have come out of her childhood intact.

She had never been allowed to have pets of her own. Her father had forbid it. After he left, the family barely existed without the added responsibility and expense of owning pets.

Thus, Sally found herself locating and nurturing stray animals. They were drawn to her. There was Raleigh, the longhaired collie who for years was a stray in her neighborhood. She wore a collar with her name but no address. No one ever claimed her. Whenever things were particularly bad for Sally at home, Raleigh would appear from nowhere and they would seek each other's comfort. Sally poured out her heart and soul to Raleigh who patiently listened hour after hour, occasionally licking her salty tears. The dog disappeared after Sally's father left.

* * * * *

"I know you think the pup smells great," Angel says. "but she needs a bath."

Angel rounds up towels and the gentlest shampoo/conditioner they have. In the meantime, Sally turns on the warm water in the kitchen sink, places the squirming puppy in the basin and lathers her with shampoo. She uses a gentle voice to calm the wiggling bundle. "Settle down. No one's gonna hurt you. Need to get you all cleaned up." Shooting a glance at Angel and chuckling, Sally continues, "*Some* people think you smell." Her tone relaxes the puppy.

When Sally is done, she hands the dog over to Angel, who rubs her with a fluffy towel. "Hey, girl, let's get you dried."

The girls feed leftovers to their new friend. Smelling like lavender blossoms and with a full tummy, the lab pup sleeps soundly in Angel's lap. When she awakes, the girls play with her. She crawls over them, tugging at their hair and licking them mercilessly.

Angel ties a knot in one of her old socks and donates it as a play toy. Both girls enjoy playing tug-of-war with her. Sally fetches a plush comforter from the linen closet and arranges it as a bed for their feisty four-legged friend. All the while, they toss around names, unable to settle on one.

Later that afternoon, Sally and Angel head to the club with their new family member. Desmond, the doorman, melts at the sight of the puppy. The girls tell him how they found her abandoned in a box.

Inside, preparations are being made for the evening show. Several of the girls are getting dressed. Mama Pearl, reviewing the dance schedule, looks up. "Well, hey, there, little darlings." She motions to the squirming bundle Sally is carrying. "What you got there?"

Sally draws back the blanket to reveal the irresistible face of the puppy within. Mama Pearl squeals with delight. In answer, the puppy lets out a yip. "If that ain't the most adorable little creature…. Give it here." Sally hands her over. "She's so sweet. Where's her mama?"

Mama Pearl's squeals attract the attention of Randy the bartender and several dancers who gather round. Drawn by the commotion, Luigi comes up from behind, his thick entanglement of neck chains clanking together. He wags a chubby finger at them while gnawing mercilessly on his cigar. "Okay, what's going on? Don't you have something to do?" he says. Reaching the center of the circle, he spots the puppy. Immediately turning to a pile of goo, he reaches out and cups the little lab in his hands. "A puppy. I <u>looove</u> puppies! Who does she belong to?" He holds her up to his face and nuzzles her shiny black button nose against his own. She responds with a lick. A broad grin spreads across his face, as well as those around him.

Sally and Angel share how they found the orphan earlier that day and ask if it would be all right to keep her there.

"No problem, darlings," Luigi says. "We can all keep an eye on her for you." Looking around, he questions, "Everyone okay with that?"

Heads nod in agreement.

Mama Pearl asks, "Got a name for her yet?"

Angel answers, "No. Been tossing them around all day."

"How about Princess?" Luigi offers. "If she's gonna rule this place like a princess, she might as well take the name."

"Princess," Sally says, allowing the name to roll off her tongue. "I like it. How about it, Angel?"

"Me too."

Luigi, still holding the puppy, says, "Just gotta fly it by her and see if she likes it." He lifts the pup even with his face. "How about it? You like, Princess?"

She yips her approval.

"That settles it. Princess it is. No more boxes for you—you'll have only the best."

The girls get ready to perform. At their first break, they check on Princess and are surprised to find her lying contentedly in Luigi's office on a plush dog bed. She is sporting a new pink collar and is surrounded by quite an assortment of dog toys. Off to one side are a new ceramic food and water dishes. Both girls look at Luigi, who shrugs. He affectionately scratches behind the pup's ears. "Consider it a gift from her Uncle Luigi."

Both girls rush and give him a big hug. "Thanks, you old softie. Who knew you were such a sucker for a puppy?"

Luigi shrugs again. "What can I say? Don't tell anyone, though. It would ruin my tough-guy image."

Sally responds, "No worries, Luigi, your secret's safe."

The girls bring Princess to work, daily. Everyone enjoys her and she becomes the club's mascot. When she is three and a half months old, Sally and Angel begin leaving her at the condo when out for short jaunts. They still bring her to work—no one can bear to not see her.

CHAPTER 14

A few months later, Sally and Angel run errands on a Friday night, happy the week has ended. It is dark out and Angel is driving. After passing through one of the intersections, Sally sees it—a lone dog crossing from the other side of the road. The dog is grey and mottled with dark colored patches, which camouflage it in the darkness. It is not hurrying, just traveling at a happy gait. A thousand phrases scream in Sally's mind.

No! Stop! Be careful! Oh, my God!

The dog holds its course and their truck speeds straight towards it. Angel never sees the dog.

The only words that manage to escape Sally's mouth are, "Oh shit!" She watches in horror as the dog disappears in front of the truck, and then hears it—the sound she knows she will never forget— the horrible *thunk* as the bumper strikes the dog. From the second *thunk* she knows they have driven over it. Attempting to block the horrifying images now flooding her mind, Sally's hands cover her face. Hidden, she shakes her head from side to side endeavoring to undo what has just transpired.

Angel exclaims, "Oh crap!" but continues driving, as if in a daze.

Sally says, "Go back," in a monotone. "Turn the truck around. We have to go back."

Angel, horrified, snaps out of her shock. "I know." She pulls the truck into the center lane and waits to make a u-turn, reaching for Sally's hand. "Are you all right?"

Sally shakes her head. Unable to speak, she tries to pull herself together. They pull to the side of the road where they think the dog is. Unable to locate it at first, they notice it further beyond the red light. Sally watches in agony as a steady line of cars approaches the fallen dog. She cannot tell from her distance if it is dead or alive.

Please don't let anyone else hit it. Please....

She picks up her cell phone and calls the police.

A woman picks up and is abrupt with her. "Can't get someone out there 'til tomorrow."

"Tomorrow?! But the dog is here now, in the middle of the road. It may get hit again or cause an accident."

"I'm sorry, ma'am, but the soonest we can send someone won't be until tomorrow."

"I'm sorry too," Sally curtly responds, as she hangs up the phone.

The light turns green and they pull up just in front of the dog. Sally hurries to see if it is alive or dead. It is not moving and its tongue is hanging out—motionless. Sally fears the worst.

Looking up, she blinks from the oncoming headlights and realizes that another stream of cars is approaching the fallen animal. Sally positions herself in front of the dog, like a human barrier. She directs the row of cars to the next lane over. Several angry drivers shout comments at her as they pass. "Get out of the road." "You're really hard to see in the dark." "Can't believe you hit that dog." Their words sting. Once the cars pass, Sally returns her attention to the still-motionless dog. Suddenly, Sally sees the dog raise its head—eyes unblinking.

She's alive?

The light turns green and another group of cars threatens the wounded dog. Bristling, Sally feels she is on a mission now.

Fuck that! No one else is gonna to hit this dog.

She guards it from the oncoming traffic. A police car approaches and pulls to the side. Angel walks over and explains that they have just hit the animal, and that it is still alive. One of the officers radios animal control, while the other approaches Sally. "Ma'am, please don't stand in the middle of the road."

"But if I don't stand here, someone else will hit her."

"Ma'am, it's not safe. *You* might get hit."

"No one else is going to hit this dog!" Sally growls at the officer. "She's dying.

The least I can do is respect her dignity. I'm *not* moving!"

The other officer finishes his call and reaches into his vehicle to retrieve a canvas strap. Angel looks at him, puzzled, while Sally shakes her head in disgust.

Damn coward! Afraid of a dying dog. Thinks she's going to bite him.

Sally turns her attention to the dog. She is still breathing—barely. She gingerly places a hand on the canine's side and tells her how sorry she is. It shudders and stops breathing. Sally looks into her eyes— they are fixated, open and unresponsive. She watches as the pupils dilate. So wrought with emotion that she can barely speak, Sally looks at the officers and Angel. "She's gone."

The policeman approaches with his strap. Sally squares her shoulders and challenges him. "What were you planning on doing with *that*?"

"I was going to wrap it around her legs and drag her to the side of the road."

Horrified, Sally says, "The strap is unnecessary. I'll help you carry her."

Undaunted, the officer begins to wrap his strap around the animal's rear legs. He watches Sally kneel down beside the dog and lovingly rub the side of her face, telling her again how sorry she is. Sally gently takes hold of the canine's front legs and looks towards the officer for help. Following her lead, he removes his strap and takes the rear legs. Together they carry the dog to the side of the road where they gently lay her. Sally cringes, in pain herself, as she feels its broken bones shift. She kneels beside her and pets her. "Goodbye."

She gets up after a bit and walks back to where the officers are standing by their unit with Angel. "Thanks. Couldn't get anyone from the local police department to help. Said they couldn't send someone until tomorrow."

The officer shakes his head, understanding. "Got hold of animal control. Someone's on the way."

After the officers leave, Sally and Angel walk back to where the dog is lying and look down at her. Sally squats down to stroke her soft fur. She looks up at Angel, tears in her eyes. "Nothing we can do now. Guess it's time to leave." She walks listlessly to the truck and gets in, followed by Angel. Both sit in stunned silence for several long minutes before leaving. Sally turns to view the body as they pull away. Something deep inside her begins to unravel.

Too much pain...so much death...I can't take this.

Sally withdraws as she and Angel run their last errand before driving in silence to get a bite to eat. She pushes her food around on her plate with her fork, unable to block the images of the collision and the dying dog. Neither girl has an appetite. They have their food boxed and head home. Princess greets them at the door. Sally falls to her knees and wraps her arms around her lab's neck, burying her face in her soft fur. The floodgates open and she begins to sob.

Several weeks pass. Time has helped to soften the memories of the accident, although neither girl can bring herself to drive by the scene.

Sally and Angel perform their joint act on the main stage. They apply neon body paint to one another under the blue stage lights, by rubbing up against one another. Their act, always a crowd pleaser, has the men drooling. The girls perform to a slow song. The hooting and hollering dies off when they strip to nothing but their g-strings and begin painting one another's bodies. They gyrate and apply the paint, slowly outlining each other's chests while drawing painted lines from their cleavage down—low. Sally and Angel hear the men collectively intake air when they rub their paint-covered rears against each other.

The stage's many black spotlights make the smeared paint shimmer, shine and change color, giving them the appearance of iridescent chameleons. Both enjoy that the men are almost melting off of their seats with all eyes locked onto their every move.

Someone in the audience catches Sally's attention. Half-blinded by the spotlights, she is fairly certain she knows the man. Although sixteen years have passed since she last laid eyes on him, she recognizes the face and eyes—they have plagued her nightmares. The man is in his early fifties and now has snow-white thick hair. Sally's stomach cinches up and for a moment, she freezes. She catches herself and resumes dancing. Angel flashes her a puzzled look. Sally's eyes never leave the man as he makes his way through the crowd towards the main stage.

She scrutinizes his mannerisms, certain now that she knows him. His hooting and hollering is out of place in a room full of drooling men, who are in a trance-like state. Some of the men snap out of their funk and encourage the girls. The man addresses Sally and Angel. "That's right. Show daddy what you've got."

Although Sally feels the bile rise in her throat, she masks the effect the man has on her. She continues with her act as a true performer—a sweet smile plastered on her face, her mind racing.

When is this song going to end?

The man finds an empty stool centered before the girls. Up and down the stage, one- and five-dollar bills rain down—the stage littered with them. When the song ends, the girls gather the strewn money as customers eagerly slip still more bills into their g-strings. Sally approaches the area where the man is seated. He holds out a large bill, indicating that he wants to tuck it into her thong. She tries to have Angel approach the man instead, but he calls to her, "Hey, there, baby, don't be shy. Papa just wants to show you some love."

A switch flips inside Sally, and she walks over—zombie-like—allowing him to deliver his bill. She has to choke back and swallow the vomit that fills her mouth. Like a dam bursting, a thousand memories flood her mind, and a barrage of questions spills through the floodgates of her psyche.

Why him? *Why now? Why this club? What are the odds...?*

Sally walks away silently counting down the seconds before she thinks he will call out her name. He never does. She realizes that he does not recognize her. Knowing who he is, she fears she might faint or begin to throw up and runs from the stage to the safety of the dressing room. Perplexed by her friend's peculiar behavior, Angel follows and finds Sally on the floor wrapped in a tight fetal position, shaking uncontrollably.

Sensing that something is terribly wrong with one of his girls, Desmond tails Angel and Sally. He knocks on the door. "Angel, Sally, you okay? Which bastard caused you to run like that, Sally? I'll fix it so he don't ever bug anybody ever again. Nobody messes with my girls!"

Angel opens the door a bit and assures Desmond that no one has done anything to Sally—that she will be fine. Unconvinced, he looks past Angel at Sally, who is still on the floor. With a little gentle prodding, Angel assures him that everything is cool. He relents and plants himself outside the door with his arms crossed over his massive chest, like a Chow dog guarding the Chinese Palace.

Angel returns to Sally, kneels beside her still-shaking friend and wraps her in a tight embrace. "Girl, what happened? Never seen you react to a customer like that. Who is that man?"

No response.

Angel tries again. "Come on. Who was that guy?"

Sally looks up at Angel with vacant eyes as tears roll down her cheeks. In a voice barely above a whisper, she utters a name.

"I'm sorry, Sally. Didn't quite hear. Who is that guy?"

"Lee...Lee McFee. He's...my father," Sally replies in an emotionless tone.

CHAPTER 15

Following her dad's appearance at the club, Sally struggles with her feelings and goes on a three-day crack binge. She neither sleeps or eats—her only sustenance is the chemical she inhales. It exhilarates her and blocks reality—most of the time. Angel remains by her side and listens to Sally's random ramblings.

"How the hell did he find me?" "No, Daddy. No! Stop." "Fuck, what does he want?" "Please stop." Tears silently escape her eyes. "I swear I'll be good." "He always finds me." "Not safe anywhere." "Didn't mean to make so much noise, Daddy. I'm sorry. I'm sorry!" "Didn't even recognize his own daughter." "I swear I'll play quietly next time. Just please stop—please don't hit me anymore. Pleeease...."

Sally shakes and cries. She lights her pipe and inhales deeply. Within seconds, her father's face, eyes and the memories that haunt her meld into a euphoric fog.

Angel agonizes over watching her tormented friend.

Hate seeing her like this. Her father was a piece of work—just like mine. Bastards! Big men—yeah, they're so tough they have to beat and rape little girls. Cowards! Someone needs to beat the shit out of 'em.

Sally's binge ends with her a wreck—weak from lack of food and exhausted from her drug-induced insomnia. Paranoid from the effects of the drug, she turns to Angel. "Everything's okay, right? He didn't find me. He's not looking for me, right? Just a coincidence? Tell me everything's going to be okay?"

"It'll be fine."

Angel helps her friend come off the effects of the drug—hydrating and feeding her nourishing meals. She calls Mama Pearl and tells her that Sally is sick and unable to be left alone or come into work. Mama Pearl understands and tells Angel to take as much time as needed.

Sally is depressed and sleeps most of the first two days. When she awakes on the third, Angel suggests that they go for a hike.

The girls explore Chantry Flats in silence while Princess runs ahead, searching for something to chase. Every so often she returns to check in. Farther along Angel spots a hawk flying low. It gracefully swoops down from a branch, crossing right in front of them. "Sally, look how the sunlight shines on its wings."

Sally, normally unable to resist a hawk, barely looks up. She nods her head with the greatest effort.

Angel stops to admire the magnificent bird as it climbs high into the sky, circling, soaring the thermals. "What's up? Why can't you shake this funk?"

Sally does not respond right away. She continues walking—deep in thought. "What am I doing with my life?"

Angle has to jog briefly to catch up. "What do you mean?"

Still walking, Sally kicks at the dirt. "Look at me, I'm twenty-six, have been stripping for a year and a half and using crack for what seems like forever. When the hell did everything get so messed up?"

"It's not such a bad life."

Sally stops and turns to face Angel. "Really? My own father came into the club the other night and tried to hit on me. You don't find something wrong with *that*?"

"Well, that part sucks. But the rest of it ain't so bad. We're supporting ourselves, don't have to turn tricks anymore, have an excellent boss and have great friends."

The hint of a smile livens Sally's face. "Well, you got me there. I can't keep doing this forever. Don't you want more?"

"Like what?"

"A normal life—husband, kids, a family. Hell, a little house with a white picket fence might be nice."

"You serious?"

"Yeah."

Angel toys with the concept. "Sounds kind of appealing. But we're having fun. Isn't that enough?"

Sally faces Angel while a gentle breeze rustles the leaves on the trees—a pained look on her face. "No, it's not...not for me. Think I need to get away. Start over. Start fresh."

"Where would you go?"

Sally sighs. "Back to California. Only left to get away from Ax. He can't hurt me anymore. And I'm sick of using crack to hide. I want off this fucking shit! I'm done running. Feel like I've been running my whole life. It's exhausting. Time to stop—go back."

"And your dad?"

Sally bristles at the mention of her father. Her voice drips venom. "He can go to hell for all I care."

"You sure you're not running from him?"

Sally softens. "I'm sure. It really sucked to have him come into the club and all, but I've been thinking about this for a while now. I'm done wasting my life. It's time to grow up. The only way is to go back."

Angel searches her eyes. "And you're serious about getting off crack?"

Sally doesn't hesitate. "Yes! I've wasted enough years. Every time something bad happens I hide behind a crack fog. It's stupid. I need to learn how to deal with my life."

Angel takes Sally's hand. "Let's do it! Blow this joint."

Sally's overcome. "Really? You'd come with me?"

"Absolutely! Sisters 'til the end—remember."

Sally gives her a bear hug. "I don't deserve you, especially with all the shit I've put you through."

Angel pulls away. "Stop it! Don't want to hear any of that crap! We stick by each other—end of story. I'm not the easiest person either."

"For sure," Sally responds, whistling for Princess.

The following day, Sally and Angel go to the club to talk with Mama Pearl and Luigi. Sally tells them about her father coming into the club and how it caused her to review what she is doing with her life. She tells them it is time for her to move on. Everyone has tears in their eyes. Luigi takes one of Sally and Angel's hands in each of his. "I want you both to know I think of you as family."

"We feel the same way, Luigi."

Putting up a finger, he continues. "If there's anything you ever need, give me a call—it's yours. If you need me, I'll be there in a heartbeat." His voice chokes with emotion. "To the depths of my soul, you're both my daughters. I'll do whatever you need or ask of me." Tears begin to leak out of the corners of his eyes and roll down his pudgy cheeks. "I take care of family."

Sally openly cries. "Don't know how to thank you for everything you've done for me: the job, your friendship, love, protection and what you did for," her voice catches on the next words, "...my son." She leans in to whisper in his ear. "I can never repay you for all your kindness—it's meant the world to me. I'm a better person for having met you."

Luigi wraps her in a tight embrace.

Next, Angel bids farewell. "Hey, big guy. You're the father I wish I'd had. I'll never forget your warmth—how safe and loved you've made me feel."

They hug.

Mama Pearl opens her arms to Sally. "There, there, little darling. It's time for you to spread those beautiful wings of yours and fly to new heights. You're gonna do fine. I just know it." She pulls away and looks Sally in the eye, smiling. "Now go and make your Mama proud."

Both smile through their tears.

Wiping her eyes, Mama turns her attention to Angel who is also crying. "Tsk, tsk, little miss. That won't do. Where's my fighter?"

Angel gruffly wipes away her tears with the back of her hand. "We both know I'm just a frightened little Chihuahua in a pit bull's body."

Knowing it is true, the foursome laughs.

Sally lets out a deep sigh. "God, I'm gonna miss you two."

"Me too," Angel says.

Smiling, Mama Pearl asks, "Now whereabouts in California are you planning to go?"

"Hopefully near where we used to live," Angel replies.

Mama claps her hands. "I have a sister who rents places in Arcadia. How's about I give her a holler and let her know you're coming? She could set you up in a nice place."

"Really?" Sally says. "That would be great."

"I think you'll really like my sister. She'll love you."

Mama places a call to Nadine, her sister, and makes arrangements for the girls to meet up with her. Nadine has a perfect condo available for them right on Orange Grove, and they can bring Princess along.

The girls say a final good-bye to Luigi, who tucks a roll of money in each of their hands. "For traveling expenses and proper food for that Princess of mine."

They hug him and head out into the club to say, "farewell" to the rest of their friends.

The next night, they get together with Jasper, Honey and Cinnamon one last time to sip wine, share stories and enjoy each other's company, as they pack for the move.

CHAPTER 16

The following morning, Sally and Angel load their truck and then drive to the cemetery so Sally can say good-bye to Eric Angel. They stop along the way to purchase yellow daisies—his favorite.

Sally walks towards her son's plot, her eyes brimming with tears. They spill down her cheeks. Her pace slows as she approaches his gravesite for the last time. She lovingly polishes his headstone. Taking a step back to inspect her work, she realizes that she missed a spot and goes about cleaning it until she can see her reflection. Satisfied, she places the daisies in the holder, kneels and places a hand on the earth above where her son rests. She feels a lump in her throat and chokes. "Hey there, sweet boy, Mamma's gotta go. It's time. You won't be alone, baby. The girls, Luigi and Mama Pearl said they'd come by and visit you. Don't know if I'll be back. We gotta be brave." She brushes away her stream of salty tears with the back of her hand. Next, she lays down on his grave and closes her eyes—remembering the times she had held him close while he slept. Her voice catches again. "You stay here while Mamma tries to put her life together. Sleep peacefully, baby. You'll always be in my heart."

Wanting desperately to hold her son one final time, but unable to, Sally wraps herself into a tight ball as silent tears spill down her cheeks. When her crying stops, she gets up and walks back to the car.

Angel looks at her friend. "You gonna be okay?"

Sally glances over her shoulder, steadies her resolve and says, "Let's go."

Angel and Sally drive the first hour in silence—each lost in her own thoughts. They pass through a spectacular desert rainstorm where Angel comments on the brilliant lightning bolts that streak their way across the sky like tracer missiles.

They drive through Mother Nature's show. A little while later, Sally points off to the side and gasps. "Oh, my God! Look at that. Do you see it? It's *huge!*"

Angel looks to where Sally is pointing. "That's the biggest rainbow I've ever seen! It stretches from one side of the sky all the way to the other. Cool!"

The girls continue to talk until they descend the Cajon Pass. Filled with mixed emotions about the life they left behind, each falls silent as they remember their youth and their time spent with Ax. Sally breaks the silence. "Can you believe all we've gone through?"

"Been a helluva ride."

Sally takes hold of one of Angel's hands and looks at her. "No one else I would have wanted to share it with."

"Me either. Wonder where the journey will take us now."

"Don't know. Guess we'll have to wait and find out."

Neil Diamond's *Sweet Caroline* comes on the radio, and the sky erupts into a periwinkle blue, dotted with fluffy white clouds tinged with grey on their underbellies. Both girls grin widely at the song— one of those feel-good oldies that need the volume cranked. Sally and Angel produce imaginary microphones and boisterously sing into them while leaning their heads in towards one another. Drivers in passing cars look at them and laugh. The girls smile in return— unembarrassed. Their performance is corny and goofy, their singing off-key, but they care not. They are having the time of their lives. Dancing in their seats. Undulating against their seatbelts to the beat of the music. By the time the song ends, both are belly-laughing. Catching her breath, Angel comments, "That was great! I love these road trips!"

Angel sees familiar cities pass by and realizes they are nearing Arcadia. "Gonna need you to navigate, now." She hands Sally a piece of paper. "Here are the directions to Nadine's place."

Sally takes the paper and studies it. She looks up at the freeway signs. "You're gonna need to get off in…three exits."

Angel delivers them to Nadine's place. They park and go to the door where Angel rings the bell. There is no answer. Angel asks,

"She knew we were coming, right?"

"Yeah. Mama told her."

They hear footsteps from within accompanied by a woman's pleasant voice. "Be there in a minute. I'm a coming…I'm a coming. Don't give up on me."

The girls hear the lock as it is turned, moments before the door is opened. Standing before them is a slightly older version of Mama Pearl, in every respect—same striking large hourglass figure, sparkling eyes and warm smile.

Sally says, "Nadine? We're Sally and Angel."

At the mention of their names, Nadine becomes animated. "Why, aren't you just the sweetest little things? Pearl said you were pretty, but she didn't mention you were gorgeous!"

Both girls blush a deep crimson. Nadine looks past them, confused.

Sally asks, "Something wrong?"

"Well, now, I don't rightly know. My sister said you had the most perfect dog—a yellow lab, Princess. Isn't she with you?"

Angel answers, "Yeah. She's in the truck." Whistling to her, "Hey, girl."

Princess's head pops up.

A brilliant smile brightens Nadine's face, and she says, "Well, don't make her stay out there in the truck all alone, bring that sweet thing in here."

Angel fetches Princess, and Nadine opens the door wide for them. "Come in, come in." She leads the way into the front sitting room. "You must be tired after that long drive. Want some ice-cold lemonade? I might even have some cookies lying around."

The girls chuckle at Nadine's enthusiasm and warm disposition. She is everything Mama Pearl had told them she would be.

Angel responds. "Lemonade sounds great!"

Sally's stomach growls. "Cookies sound good."

Nadine hurries off to the kitchen, leaving the girls to look around the eclectic assortment of trinkets that adorn the walls, curio cabinets and every spare surface. Sally walks over to one of the display cabinets and spies its contents: a plethora of every imaginable ceramic, wood and plastic cheesy Disney character ever made. Their hostess returns with tall glasses of homemade lemonade and a platter of fresh-baked molasses cookies. She hands each of them a glass while placing the treats on the table. "Let me know if the lemonade isn't sweet enough."

The girls each take a sip. "Mmm, it's perfect."

Pleased, Nadine goes to the kitchen and returns with a bowl of water for Princess. Motioning to the sofa, she says, "Sit down. Sit down. Let me tell you about the place I've got." She sets the bowl of water down in front of Princess and grabs a couple of cookies from the platter. "Is it okay—"

"Sure."

Princess eagerly accepts the treat, Hoovering up every last crumb while wagging her tail. Nadine pats her on the head and then sits in a chair next to the sofa. Princess laps up some water before laying her head in the lap of her new best friend.

Both Sally and Angel smile. Nadine scratches Princess behind her ears and answers their unasked question. "My whole family is crazy about animals."

She proceeds to tell them about the fully furnished place she has for them. Both girls agree it sounds wonderful. Nadine, satisfied, hands them the key and gives them directions. "If there's anything you need, don't hesitate. Pearl considers you family. So do I."

Sally is struck by this stranger's kindness. "Thank you. You've been so helpful."

Nadine gets up. "You must want to get settled. I'll stop by in the morning to make sure everything's okay."

Sally and Angel meet up with Nadine in the morning and ask if there are any good places to go hiking locally. She tells them about a place located up in the mountains above Arcadia. They spend the day unpacking. When done, Angel suggests they hike the location Nadine had told them about.

As they descend the steep hill into Chantry Flats, Angel notices that Sally seems troubled. She lets Princess off leash before saying, "Penny for your thoughts."

Sally lets out a deep sigh. "Being back here makes me think about Eric Angel. My ray of sunshine, he could brighten the cloudiest of days." She looks off into the distance, her eyes growing moist. "That grin of his…. It was so contagious. Didn't know I took it for granted until it was gone."

"What? You never took him for granted—not once."

Sally clarifies. "No, not him…his smile. I'd do anything to see it again."

Angel wraps an arm around Sally's shoulders and gives her a hug. "Girl, I know you miss him. Me too."

The girls walk in silence for a bit. Arriving at a fork in the road, they follow a sign towards a waterfall. They wind and twist their way over bridges and water crossings. Two miles later, they arrive at the falls.

At the base of the cascading water is a charming lagoon deep enough for Princess to swim into as she fetches the sticks Angel throws for her. Off to the side are large rocks. The girls select two to sit upon. Princess brings the stick back to Angel, who tosses it again. Angel looks at Sally, who has fallen quiet. "You okay?"

When Sally looks up, there are tears in her eyes. Angel puts an arm around her and Sally melts against her. "It hurts so much, Angel."

"What does?"

"Eric Angel's death. I've tried so hard to put it to rest." She cries harder. "Can't do it. I can put it aside for awhile, but then…."

"I know."

"Should have been there for him. I was his mother. Should have been able to protect him." She pulls away from Angel and looks at her. "What kind of mother can't protect her own child? He didn't deserve to die—alone—so violently."

Angel looks intensely in her eyes. "There was nothing you could've done to save him. Nothing! You *were* a good mother—the best!"

Sally gets up and begins pacing. "I've asked myself these questions a thousand times. 'Did he know?' 'Did he see it coming?' 'Why didn't he duck?'" She stops and looks at her friend. "Angel, I have to know. Did he suffer?" She pleads. "Please tell me my baby didn't suffer." Not waiting for a response, she resumes pacing, wringing her hands together. Princess shadows her. Sally sobs uncontrollably—the agony she is feeling dripping from her every word. "He was all alone. Must have been so scared. God, I hope he didn't suffer! Did he cry out for me? Angel, pleeease tell me my baby didn't suffer." Sally cannot catch her breath—her body wracked by her tormented emotions.

Angel pulls her into a tight embrace. "He didn't suffer."

Hearing the reassuring words, Sally leans against Angel and repeats, barely above a whisper, "He didn't suffer...."

CHAPTER 17

While at breakfast the next morning, Angel takes a bite of her eggs. "Girl, were you serious when you said you were done with crack?"

Sally cups her coffee mug with both hands, brings it to her lips and allows the steam to warm her lips before taking a swallow. "When we were hiking, before we left Vegas?"

"Yeah."

"Yeah, I'm done. That shit's killing me. I used to take it to get high, then to escape my pain. Now, I take it to avoid the torment of not being on it—I think about it *all* the time, Angel. It scares me—the line is beginning to blur. I use crack to fill the holes in my soul, but nothing plugs them anymore. I don't want crack to swallow me."

Angel finishes the last bite of her toast. "If you're serious, I'll be beside you."

Sally falls silent while pushing the eggs around on her plate. Angel sits, patiently allowing her friend to collect her thoughts. After a couple of minutes, Sally looks up and continues, "I'm scared."

"I know, girl."

"No, I'm *really* scared. I don't think I'll be able to quit on my own."

"Don't have to. I'll be there with you."

Sally puts down her fork and looks at Angel. "I know. You'll support me. And I'm grateful. That's not what I mean. Don't think I'm strong enough to go through withdrawals on my own. You've seen me—I've tried before and have never managed to stay off it for more than a few days. Maybe I need to check into a program this time."

The girls research drug addiction treatment facilities. They find one that has a twenty-eight day inpatient plan. Sally places a call and makes arrangements with the director to arrive first thing the next morning. Meanwhile, they busy themselves with unpacking and getting settled in. They eat an early dinner and call it a night.

The next morning, Sally rolls over—eyes still closed—and smacks the off button hard enough to send the clock flying when her alarm blares. She struggles to wake up.

Did I get any sleep last night? I swear it feels like I just laid down.

Anxious and irritable, she wakes Angel and they begin getting ready. Angel notices Sally's edginess. "Sally girl, everything's gonna be okay. I know you can do this!"

Sally's hands are shaking so badly she can barely apply her makeup. She gives up for the moment and goes to stand before the open closet. Angel, noticing her frozen stance, tries to initiate small talk. "So, what you gonna wear today?"

Sally's shoulders slump forward. "Wear? What am I going to wear? Hell, I don't know." Her anxiety transforms into anger, and she turns to confront Angel. "You want to know what the hell I'm gonna wear. I can't seem to make a fucking decision." She throws her hands in the air. "Hell, you might as well ask me the meaning of life."

Both girls get ready in silence, the tension hanging in the air like mid-August humidity in Florida. Sally finds it harder and harder to breathe as the time to leave approaches. Her rapidly beating heart threatens to rip its way out of her chest. Ten minutes before it is time to depart, she becomes immobilized with fear.

I can't go through with this. Detox is gonna be a living nightmare. What the hell was I thinking?

When Angel indicates it is time to leave, Sally's internal coach kicks in.

Just get in the car and start driving. Everything will be okay.

Somehow she manages to ambulate herself out the door and into the waiting car. But all is not right. Never has a car ride taken so long or been so debilitating. By the time they arrive, Sally feels exhausted. She gets her bag and lurches towards the ornately forged iron double gates at the entrance, beside which she notices an intercom. She looks at Angel who nods and then pushes the button. The minute she does, a thousand thoughts crowd her mind.

Turn and run! I can't do this! What the hell? Using crack isn't so bad. I can handle it. I'm scared to death! Run! Run, stupid, while you still have a chance! Why the fuck are you still standing here?

The buzzer rings once, twice, three times. Each unanswered ring seems an excruciating eternity. It is answered mid-fourth ring.

"Hello?"

"Ah, it's me, Sally McFee. I have an appointment."

Sally pictures herself walking back to the truck, getting in and making a run for it just as the gate is opened by a pleasant-looking woman in her early fifties, who has shoulder-length wavy brown hair graying with age, a robust figure and a warm smile. She unlatches the barrier for them. "Hello, I'm Sylvia. If you'll follow me, I'll take you to meet the doctor."

It'll be okay. Just walk through the gate. Don't back down now. It's now or never. Walk—one foot in front of the other. Come on, you know how to do it. You've been walking for years—don't tell me you forgot how—it's just like riding a bike....

Sally manages to pass through the gate, past a lush courtyard planted with an abundance of green ferns softly swaying in the gentle breeze, and accompanies Sylvia through the main door. Angel follows, foiling any thoughts of escape.

They walk a short distance down a hallway painted in soothing pastels and stop before an office whose door is open. Within, they spy a tasteful space decorated in rich masculine colors of burgundy, camel and black. A compassionate-looking man with a slight receding dark hairline greets them. He is six feet tall with an athletic build, appears to be about thirty years old and emits a sense of strength and confidence. His penetrating gaze is genuinely kind. Sally feels self-conscious when he states, "Hello, I'm Dr. James Whitmore. I'll be Sally's doctor during her stay here."

Angel, noticing Sally's frozen posture, steps forward and takes his hand. "Hi, I'm Angel and this," motioning to her silent friend, "is Sally."

He shakes both girls' hands then stands aside, allowing them entry.

The room is furnished with a burgundy antique sofa upholstered in stripes with complementing paisley cushions and throw pillows. There is an adjacent dark distressed leather overstuffed chair and a rich mahogany desk, behind which are several bookcases lined with an impressive collection of books.

The doctor indicates for them to take a seat, looks at Sally and gets right to the point. "I understand the courage it's taken for you to come here. We each have a role to play in your recovery. You have taken the first step by acknowledging that you have a problem."

He directs his gaze to Angel. "You must realize that you can support an addict in her recovery, but you cannot do it for her. Al-Anon has a saying, which they call the three C's. 'You didn't cause it, you can't control it and you can't cure it.'"

He looks back at Sally. "You, however, have it within yourself to heal if you are willing to apply the tools I'll give you. I won't kid you, it's going to be tough—most things worth undertaking are." His eyes bore through Sally with intense scrutiny. "Do you believe that you are worth fighting for?"

Sally avoids his gaze. "I think so."

"There's no thinking about it; either you believe that you are worth the battle or you don't. Now is the time to decide. If you cannot commit, then you might as well leave."

Sally rises to the challenge and sits a little taller in her seat, looking Dr. Whitmore in the eye. "Yes, I'm worth fighting for!"

"Good, I believe you are as well." He stands. "Well, let's get you settled in."

Dr. Whitmore explains that the girls will need to say their farewells prior to Sally checking in and assures them that they will be able to see each other at group session on the weekend. Sally puts down her bag and turns to face Angel, who hugs her in a tight embrace. Sally allows herself to sink against her friend. In a voice so quiet Angel has to strain to hear, she says, "I'm so scared. Don't leave me here. I don't know if I can do this."

Angel tightens her embrace. "It'll be okay, girl. You can do this. You're stronger than crack. Where's my fighter? Remember, don't let this shit win!"

Sally straightens, bolstered by her friend's confidence and supportive words. "Okay, I'll give it my best."

Pulling away, Angel looks at Sally and smiles. "That's my girl. There's the fighter I know and love."

Sally squares her shoulders. "I'm ready to do this. The sooner I get started, the sooner I get better. Right?"

"Yeah."

The girls hug again before Angel turns and leaves. Dr. Whitmore, who has been standing off to the side during the girls' farewell, picks up Sally's bag. "Shall we?" They walk without speaking down the hall to a small office where Sylvia is waiting for them. Dr. Whitmore stops and hands Sally her bag. "Once you're settled in, I'd like for you to come and see me."

"Okay."

He turns and leaves. Sally sits across from Sylvia who takes her bags, explaining that they need to be searched for contraband. She is given a stack of papers to fill out and when she completes them, is asked a barrage of questions concerning what drugs she is taking, how often, how much, and on and on. As Sally answers each question, she is brought face-to-face with the severity of her problem. Sitting here, responding to Sylvia's incessant queries, she cannot hide from the overwhelming facts of her dependency. The experience proves to be emotionally exhausting.

When she is done, Sylvia takes her to her room, which is average-sized with matching twin beds and a small private bathroom. The space looks like a modest hotel room. Sally unpacks and then reports to Dr. Whitmore's office where she finds his door open. He is sitting behind a desk piled with neatly stacked files, and looks up. "Oh, Sally, come in. Please." He rises and motions for her to have a seat on the sofa. She does, as he closes the door. "Can I offer you a cup of tea? I was just going to get one myself."

"No, I'm okay."

"Let me guess, not a big tea drinker?"

"No, I'm a coffee girl."

"Oh, well, I can get you some coffee if you'd like."

"No, really, I'm okay."

The doctor walks over to a parson's table to make a cup of tea before joining her.

Sally chuckles under her breath.

Here we go. Let the good times roll.

Dr. Whitmore sits in the leather adjacent chair. Holding his teacup in one hand, he raises and lowers the tea bag rhythmically. "What's so funny?"

"Just thinking how weird this is. The last time I sat in a shrink's office I was a little girl. Doesn't seem that long ago. Yet it's been a lifetime. So much has changed and yet so little. Here I am, still messed up, sitting across from a shrink."

"How do you feel about that?"

Sally lets out a nervous laugh.

Oh, God, how cliché.

"Scared. Tired. Anxious," Sally answers.

The doctor places his cup on the table and leans back in his chair, where he meticulously rubs the back of one hand with his long slender fingers and traces his cuticles before repeating the process with the other. "That's fair enough. I can imagine that this has got to be hard for you. The first week of detox is going to be the hardest. We'll try to make you as comfortable as possible, but your body and mind will suffer the effects of withdrawal. We're going to start out slow and easy with our sessions for the first week and then delve deeper during the second week." He pauses to see how Sally is absorbing the information. Leaning forward to retrieve his tea, he notices that she has visibly shrunk into the sofa where she sits.

She reminds me of a helpless child who needs to be protected.

He raises the cup to his lips and blows on his tea before taking a tentative sip. "I can imagine that this is overwhelming for you and probably pushing some triggers right now. How are you feeling?"

"Honestly?"

"Yes."

"I'm thinking about walking out of here and not looking back."

"Hmm."

She's a frightened child who wants to bolt. She's obviously been hurt. I want to shield her from the world. I need to tread lightly here.

He takes another sip. "Fair enough."

Maddened by his calm response, Sally continues, "I'm thinking about how quickly I could score some crack and have its fog wash over me."

"Okay, that's how you are *feeling*. Now, what are you going to *do*?"

Sally slumps on the couch. "I'm gonna stay. I promised Angel. I owe it to myself."

The doctor dunks his teabag again. "I find it interesting that you placed your promise to your friend higher than your obligation to yourself. Why do you suppose that is?"

"I don't know—you're the fucking doctor—you tell me."

Dr. Whitmore takes another sip of tea and then stands, indicating that their session has ended. "Actually, I am going to let you figure that one out."

Over the course of the next week, Sally suffers through a dry detox program that includes exercise, sauna sweat-outs and increasing specific amounts of effective nutrients, oils and vitamins in her diet. Her body and mind torment her with vomiting, muscle pain, lack of motivation, angry outbursts, depression and disturbed sleep. Angel comes up on the weekend to see her for a family group session. They embrace as if it has been a year, not a week, since they last saw each other. Angel notes Sally's improved appearance. She has more of a glow to her, is calmer, more focused and appears positive. "So, tell me, how is it here? How are you? Do you think it's helping?"

Sally can't help but chuckle at her friend's enthusiasm. "Whoa, slow down. Give me time to respond." Sally looks around at the other patients, many of whom are also visiting with friends and family. "I'm meeting all kinds of people who, like me, have drug problems. In group discussions and private sessions with Dr. Whitmore, I'm learning a lot about my addiction."

Angel smiles broadly.

"What are you grinning about?"

"Addiction. Do you know that's the first time you've ever admitted to having a problem?"

Sally shrugs. "Like I said, I'm learning a lot here. I won't kid you though, the detox is hard."

Angel grows serious. "Worse than you thought it would be?"

"Yeah, much. Sometimes all I can think about is checking myself out and getting high." Noting the concern on Angel's face, Sally rushes on, "Don't worry. I won't. I told you I'd give it my best shot and we McFees don't back down from a challenge."

Angel smiles, noticeably relieved.

Sally begins her second week in rehab in a session with Dr. Whitmore. "Okay, Sally, I want to start out easy today. Why don't you tell me a little about your drug-of-choice—crack?" He stops rubbing his hands and folds them in his lap. "Tell me what it means to you." He watches as Sally scooches to the back of the sofa, pulls her feet up in front of her and wraps her arms around her knees before resting her chin upon them.

Dr. Whitmore notes her childlike attempt to make herself smaller.

She's like a wounded animal retreating. She's irresistible. I just want to embrace her and let her know that everything's going to be all right.

Looking down, Sally lets out a deep sigh. "I think about it all the time. When I'm not on crack, all I can do is think about my next fix." Her voice takes on an excited tone. "When I'm riding the high, I experience anticipation, fear and an intense adrenaline rush. After, when I'm coming down, I see things *sooo* clearly. Things are revealed to me that I don't get the meaning of any other way." She hides her face by placing her forehead on her knees and lowers her voice— disgusted with her own weakness. "But then the ride ends. Reality kicks in, and my body needs another fix—it's all I can think about. Then comes the depression. I ask myself how I got this way. *Why* I handed control of my life over to something I'm dependent upon— something I would be willing to do anything to get." She raises her head, revealing salty tears that cascade down her cheeks. Shaking her head, she continues, "That's when I see how fucked up I am—how crack is ruining my life and yet, I can't stop. I don't want to stop." Her crying mounts to sobbing. She gulps huge intakes of air and wraps her arms around herself, doubling over into a tight ball. "My need has surpassed my desire. They are so intertwined that I can't tell where one starts and the other ends." Her voice cracks. "I *need* crack. God help me, I know it beats the shit out of me, but I want it more than anything! Fuck, why does this have to hurt so much?"

Dr. Whitmore's breath catches as he notices the beautiful color of her eyes. He leans forward to offer her a box of tissues. "Sally, you have to understand that in order for you to enjoy the good and beauty in life, you must first bear pain. Asking questions is part of that painful process." He pauses to look at her compassionately, noticing how her auburn hair drapes over her shoulder like a shawl, shimmering as the light catches it. "Are you willing to ask questions?"

Sally retrieves a tissue from the box, blows her nose and then allows herself to retreat to the corner of the sofa where she curls into an even tighter ball. She covers her face as an endless stream of tears spills from her eyes. Great waves of despair erupt from deep within her. Their intensity is frightening.

Sally, lost somewhere between self-pity, humiliation and self-loathing, hears the soothing rhythmic tempo of his speech. His words wash over her like a calming wave. "Sally, I think Kahlil Gibran's counsel is appropriate here. 'Your pain is the breaking of the shell that encloses your understanding. It is the bitter potion by which the physician within you heals your sick self. Therefore, trust the physician and drink his remedy in silence and tranquility.'"

As the eloquent words bathe her, Sally's sniveling slows and then ceases. She looks up, her nose red, eyes puffy. "I hear what you're saying, but I feel like I'm kicking and flailing in all directions. Every time I try to take the potion it feels like someone is reaching down my throat to the pit of my stomach, in an attempt to turn me inside out. I'm so scared. What if I can't do this?"

Dr. Whitmore fights the overwhelming urge to enfold her in his arms.

What the hell? What's wrong with me? She's my patient. I've never experienced feelings like this towards a patient before. Get a grip, man. Where's your professionalism?

To Sally he responds, "Don't allow what you cannot do to interfere with what you can do. Open yourself to the possibility of success. Only then do you stand a chance of recovery." He looks at the clock on his desk. "I think we've covered enough ground today. I'd like to call the session early. Is that all right with you?"

"Yeah."

"You have a couple of hours before group session this afternoon. Why don't you go outside? Go for a walk. It might help you to process what we've discussed. Are you okay?"

Sally, more composed, gazes out his window. "Yeah, I'll be all right. It would be nice to feel the sunshine on my face."

"I'll see you at our next session, then."

CHAPTER 18

When Sally meets with Dr. Whitmore the next morning, he hands her a steaming cup of coffee. "I wasn't sure how you take it." He motions to the parson's table. "Anything you might need you'll find over there."

A smile warms Sally's face. "Mmm, coffee does sound good. Thank you."

She crosses to the table where she adds creamer and sugar to her drink. From behind her Dr. Whitmore states, "Sally, from our session yesterday I surmised that it's difficult for you to voice your feelings. Would you say that is a fair assessment?"

Slowly stirring the contents of her mug, she does not answer right away. Taking her coffee, she sits on the sofa, where she is unable to get comfortable and repositions herself. Finally, she stops fidgeting. "Yeah, you pretty much called it."

She allows her eyes to wander to the bookshelves behind his desk where they travel across an impressive collection of leather-bound and hardback books. Dr. Whitmore's voice is soft. "For things to work here, I'm going to take you outside your comfort zone."

Hearing this, Sally stiffens in her seat. "What does *that* mean?"

"Well, when we are in session, I'm going to have you verbalize what's bothering you. We are going to take a look at the triggers that cause you to turn to your drug-of-choice, bring them to the surface, address them, mourn them and then I'm going to help you put them to rest—once and for all." He pauses to sip his tea, allowing his words to sink in. "Does that sound like something you think you can do with me?"

Suddenly unable to drink her coffee, Sally places her mug on the table and reaches for a pillow to hug. She remains silent for a long while, resting her chin on the cushion, deep in thought. "Not sure. You called it. I'm not real good with expressing my feelings. Don't like to feel pain."

Dr. Whitmore begins absentmindedly dunking his teabag. "Pain is the most effective medium through which we learn. We must not run from it, but face it, endure it and gain release from it if we are to be saved. If we are willing to embrace it, then we will be rewarded with an unparalleled wealth of knowledge and a better self."

Sally mulls over his words. "Not promising anything, but I guess I can try."

The doctor nods his approval. "This will be tough—probably one of the most challenging things you have ever had to do. But you won't have to go through it alone. There are two of us. I'll be right beside you the whole while. I can't do it for you, however. You are going to have to reach down deep within yourself to succeed." He drains his drink, places his empty cup on the table and looks deeply into her eyes. "You're going to have to want to succeed more than you want your crack."

"I'm scared," Sally says, as she begins nervously playing with the corner of the pillow, tracing her fingers over the piped edging.

"I know. Opening up to the world is a difficult thing to do, but there is so much to gain when you do. If you'll conceive of treatment as an ongoing process rather than a cure, a different, more optimistic and far more realistic notion of success can emerge. Being scared is an excellent place to begin."

He hands her a spiral-bound notebook and a pen, which she takes while questioning, "What are these for?"

"Journaling. I want you to write in it every day. What you scribe doesn't need to be neat, in order or make sense. I just want you to write down whatever comes into your head in whatever order it presents itself. Three pages per day—that is your assignment. I don't care if you're angry and fill the pages with, 'This is a stupid idea. I hate this assignment.' Just so long as you get in three pages, daily. Will you do that?"

She pushes the pillow off to the side. "I'll try."

"Excellent. Each day we'll look at your entries and address

whatever needs to have a closer look. Remember, you're not alone. We're going to do this together. I want you to be brutally honest in your entries. Write whatever you're feeling or whatever comes to mind. We can only hope to reform your behavior if you are willing to acknowledge your feelings and mitigate them."

He gets up, signaling that the session is over. Sally takes her journal and returns to her room. Anxious to write down the thoughts that clutter her mind, she begins writing.

Well, Dr. Whitmore said he wanted me to write-anything-so I will. For the longest time, I've been out of it-dazed, zombie-like and detached from reality. Now that I've checked back in, I must face the problems I've created for myself. Don't know if I can do this. Patients keep walking past my doorway-they seem more zombie-like than I feel. I find myself hiding from and avoiding my downfalls because I simply want to move forward, pick up where I left off and not have to go back into the past. Ah, the past-that black hole, where I'll attempt to do the impossible-to fix my fucked-up deeds. I look back at not too long ago when I thought I was on top of things-a part of it-and then I look at myself now and see nothing but a lost child. I know what I need to find, yet I don't know how to go about it. Is any of this making any sense? Is this the drugs talking or me?

Can't tell. More patients are walking past my open door-like a line of ants. Chaos surrounds me-feels like I'm in the funny farm. Time passes by so quickly. I want to be given the opportunity to redo an event in my past-if only for a brief moment-so that I could change my actions. I wish I were given that moment now, for I'd say, "Fuck off!" to my outside surroundings and concentrate on what I had to accomplish correctly-the first time. How do I go back? I know it's impossible-but what if I could? God, imagine how different things might be. I want to change the way things are now. This is insane. Why am I dredging all of this up? It won't change anything-everything stays the same. Things can't get any worse-or can they? Don't think I could take it if they did. Are things good as they stand now? No!! Maybe all I need is time to dig deeper into this desire to be given just another brief moment. They say that you can't go back in time. I know I can't, yet-what if I could? Wait! I think I've got it. To make things better, I must be determined and stubborn-not give in when the going gets rough. I must conquer *these tough times. Angel's right. Dr. Whitmore's right. I have to be willing to fight for me. Shit! I know I've got it now! It'll be rough, but I know that I can do it.*

Sally smiles and closes her journal, satisfied.

The next morning she brings it with her to her session with Dr. Whitmore, who asks her to read what she has penned. Sure of her words the day before, now she is shy to share. Taking her normal seat on the sofa, she reluctantly begins reading. When she is done, she sees that the doctor is contemplating her words.

Looking up, he states, "According to Francois Duc de La Rochefoucauld, 'We only confess our little faults to persuade people that we have no large ones.'" He asks the tough question—the one she hoped he would not. "You speak of going back, setting right a misdeed. It would seem that your entry is hinting at a larger problem. What is it that you want to go back and undo?"

Sally's eyes well up with tears as she retreats into the sofa. "Damn you! Why did you have to ask that?" Her brilliant green eyes glisten with tears. They seem to change several shades lighter—their vibrant color now almost transparent.

"Because it's what you wrote."

Sally closes her eyes, causing a stream of tears to spill from them. She lets out a deep sigh. Her face contorts in pain. "Eric Angel—my son. If I could change anything—God help me—I would *never* have had him." Realizing the terrible implications of her words, she looks up like a guilty child. "I mean—don'…don't get me wrong—I loved him with all my heart, but he didn't deserve to live that life. If only I'd remembered to take that fucking pill." More tears cascade down her cheeks like a waterfall-come-to-life. "All his suffering could have been avoided."

Dr. Whitmore watches as she retreats to the corner of the sofa and cowers like a wounded animal.

Be careful, James. This is tender territory—tread lightly. God, I hate to see her hurt.

When he speaks again, his voice is soft and tinged with compassion. "Tell me about Eric Angel. What was he like?"

Sally dares to look up from her corner. A rush of motherly pride gushes from her. She sniffles back her tears, and her eyes sparkle. "Oh, he was perfect—the best son a mother could ever dream of. He had such an easy personality. He was always happy—even in the worst of it." She smiles at the memory. "He had this contagious laugh, just like my brother's. It was a kind of chortle and unrestrained giggle mixed together. Everyone who heard it couldn't help but join in." A dark mask overtakes her countenance, causing her eyes to flash with unrestrained rage. "Well, everyone except Ax. He didn't laugh—at anything."

"Who is Ax?"

Sally's voice lowers. Sounding as if it is traveling a great distance to be heard, it is flat and emotionless. "He was my pimp—the one who killed my son."

Dr. Whitmore is shocked.

Wow. That was weird—not what she said, but the coldness with which the words were spoken, as if they were merely fact, not denoting a mother's devastating loss.

Suddenly, Sally bolts up and begins pacing. She has the look of a cornered animal. "I don't want to talk about this anymore!"

The doctor uses a soothing tone. "I understand that this is uncomfortable for you to talk about, but it is something that we need to discuss. I believe it is one of the main triggers for your using crack. The sooner you look at this and address it, the sooner you can move beyond it."

Sally stops pacing and returns to the couch, where she sits sullen. Almost under her breath, through clenched teeth, she growls, "I *have* moved on."

Dr. Whitmore eyes her with his penetrating gaze. "Have you? Have you—really?"

Her bravado unravels, as Sally admits. "Well…no…not really."

"All right then, why don't you tell me what happened."

Angry now, Sally returns to pacing. "Shit! You want to know what happened? Fine, I'll tell you. I was a naive little girl who left home, became a prostitute, forgot to take my fucking birth control pill, got pregnant and had this wonderful little boy—Eric Angel." Her eyes fill with tears at the mention of her son's name, and they tumble down her cheeks. Engulfed in her emotional outburst, she doesn't notice. "To force me to continue working, my pimp, Ax, held him hostage every day of the five years of his life." Sally spits out the next words. "One day there was a shootout with another pimp and my son got hit by Ax's fucking crossfire. End of story—he's dead. There, are you happy? Now I've said it. My baby's dead. And it's my fault." Sally breaks down, overcome by heaving sobs.

Dr. Whitmore, who has remained quiet throughout, interjects. "Your fault? How could it be your fault? You said that Ax was the one who shot him."

Sally hitches so violently that she can barely get the words out. "He did, but I was his mother. I should have been able to protect him—if I had been a *good* mother, he never would have been in that position in the first place. I may not have pulled the trigger, but I sure as hell contributed to his death. I have to live with that."

Sally's sobbing intensifies. Dr. Whitmore comes to sit next to her on the sofa. "I think you have things confused." Placing his hand under her chin, he tilts her head up. "Look at me."

She looks up through a glistening shield of tears.

"Sally, you did nothing wrong. *You* are not responsible for your son's death. You were a helpless victim, as much as he was. You are *not* to blame."

"Don't know what to believe any more. I'm so confused."

"Even in the greatest confusion there is an open channel to the soul. You've been carrying a tremendous burden over your son's death. It was not your fault. You have got to be willing to let go of that guilt. Your most splendid future will always be dependent upon the necessity to release the past. You cannot move forward in your recovery or in life unless you are willing to rid yourself of the unwarranted guilt you have been slave to." He sits with her until her sobbing ceases.

Drained, she mumbles under her breath, "Insanity paves the way to sanity."

Dr. Whitmore cocks his head. "What? I'm sorry, I didn't catch what you said."

"Nothing. I was just thinking out loud. It doesn't mean anything."

The doctor smiles warmly at Sally. "Oft times the things we don't intend to have heard are the things that most need to be heard. Trust me—please. Tell me what you said."

"All right. I said insanity paves the way to sanity."

Dr. Whitmore contemplates the comment before responding. "Insanity often defies meaning." He begins rubbing the back of one of his hands with the long fingers of the other while examining his cuticles. Almost absentmindedly he repeats, "Insanity paves the way to sanity. That's very profound. Where's it from?"

"Nowhere. Just something I thought up."

Dr. Whitmore smiles and looks at her, scrutinizing her eyes. "It's almost poetic. Do you like verse?"

"I do. It calms me."

"Have you ever tried writing any?"

Sally chuckles aloud. "Yeah, a bit. No one knows, though—not even Angel. It's just for me."

"I'd like you to try something for me. In your journaling today, write a poem on what it feels like when you are on crack. Can you do that for me?"

Sally thinks about the assignment. A sheepish smile spreads across her face. "Yeah, I think I could do that, but only if no one else sees it. I mean it's okay if you read it, but that's all. I don't want people to think I've gone soft."

"What's so terrible about being perceived as being soft?"

Sally looks at him, not quite sure if he is serious. Realizing he is, she cannot believe he does not know the answer. "Being soft—it...it

127

means being vulnerable. To be vulnerable leads to getting hurt."

Dr. Whitmore's heart breaks for the patient sitting before him.

God, she's beautiful. She's so frightened—puts up a fierce facade of being tough. She must be so terribly broken inside. All I want to do is wrap my arms around her and protect her. What the hell's the matter with me?!

He shakes his head.

"No, Sally, allowing yourself to be seen as soft shows incredible strength. In order to be strong, you have to learn how to forgive yourself. It is my belief that you are amongst the strong." Having said that, he concludes their session, leaving Sally to mull over his statement. "So, tomorrow I'll be looking for that poem. Okay?"

Sally nods. "I'll have it."

CHAPTER 19

Sally arrives the next morning prepared with her poem—both excited and nervous. She knocks on her doctor's door and hears him say, "Come in."

Upon entering, she observes him taking a sip of tea, a familiar sight that comforts her with its predictability. Dr. Whitmore watches her cross the room and take her usual spot on the sofa. There is a mug of hot coffee in front of her with creamer and sugar already added. He spies the journal in her hand and her heightened confidence denoted by the new manner in which she carries herself. "Hello, Sally. How are you today?"

She answers while settling herself on the couch. "Okay. Thanks for the coffee. Sometimes I feel a little bit better...and...others a little worse. Right now I'm pretty good."

She reaches for the coffee and takes a sip, blowing on it first.

Dr. Whitmore gets up from behind his desk, carrying his tea, and sits in the leather chair beside her. "So, were you able to write that piece for me?"

He notices how she lowers her eyes before responding, "Yes."

Dr. Whitmore is transfixed by Sally.

My God, her shyness is irresistible. I'm mesmerized by it. What is happening to me?! I think I'm falling in love with her. This is so irrational, but I'm at a loss to resist. No—I don't want to resist.

Sally hears him let out a sigh before taking a sip of his tea. A compassionate smile plays across his face. For the first time, she notices his eyes. They are the color of caramel with bright flecks that dance and sparkle when the light catches them. They fascinate her.

Emboldened by his kind accepting eyes, she places her coffee mug on the table, opens her journal and begins reading.

" Spinning out of control

It attacks in a hurry:
The nervous pace
The jumpiness
The inability to be calm.

It sets in:
The feeling of being hyper
The spinning out of control
And yet, it has only just begun.

My emotions are raw.
Unable to be controlled,
They come in waves
Oozing from my every pore.

Incapable of understanding,
The feeling of flight or fight returns.
Fight, resist, deny
Abandon, run, hide

Looking for a distraction,
Something to make the pain stop

Openly daring trouble.
Wanting to be checked-hard.

Frightened to be alone:
Too much trouble to get into
Too many thoughts crowd my mind
Too much time to think things through

So many triggers:
An empty room frozen in time
A mother's greatest loss
A reappearing parent

When will it stop?
When will the pain cease?
When will the tears dry up?
When will self-control return?"

Sally closes her journal before venturing to look into her doctor's eyes—in which she sees what? Sympathy? No—compassion, understanding and longing. Longing? Longing for what?

Over the next couple weeks, Sally notices a deep reawakening within her, fed through her journaling and poetry writing. She begins to reconnect with a part of herself she abandoned as a young girl in order to survive. It is a softer side—one that takes the time to appreciate the subtleties in the world and feels safe enough to permit them to touch her soul. She often finds herself lost in thought.

Feel—it's nice to be able to feel again—it's been so long. I've been so fucking busy running and hiding to protect myself that I'd forgotten what it was like to really experience things. I like it—even *the hard stuff. It's better to feel <u>something</u> than nothing.*

Sally is content most of the time and is surprised to find herself drawn to her doctor. While hiking the grounds one day, she quietly shares her discovery with Angel. Kicking a stray pebble, she says, "For the first time in my life, I feel like I'm at peace. I guess we can find our true love in the most unlikely places. Just look at me. Who would have thought that I'd meet mine here, in a drug inpatient treatment facility." She sees the concern on Angel's face. "Don't worry. Please be happy for me."

"I am, girl, I just don't want to see you get hurt. You've been through *so* much and have come so far. Does he feel the same for you?"

"I'm pretty sure he does."

"Pretty sure?"

"Well, it's not like we can discuss our feelings for one another *in here*."

"I can't imagine that anything good can come from a patient-doctor relationship. Be careful."

"I am. Did I tell you he's a good doctor?" Sally rushes on, not waiting for a response. "The other day, he got me talking about Eric Angel. He's constantly having me talk about how I'm feeling. And you know me. That's *way* outside my comfort zone. He has me bring things to the surface: my father, childhood, being a prostitute, stripping, having Eric Angel and then losing him. He helps me address them, mourn them and then lay them to rest—once and for all."

The girls pass under a canopy of grand oaks. Sloping hills lined with lush ferns draw up on either side of their path. Angel asks, "So, you getting better? I mean, you sound better—different. I don't think I've ever seen this side of you."

A shy smile plays with the corners of Sally's mouth. "You haven't. No one has. I buried her a long time ago. It's nice to get this part of me back. I've missed her. I'm a long way from being healed, but I'm beginning to understand why I reach for my crack pipe. My sessions with my doctor and the group discussions are really helping."

"Are your meetings during the week pretty much the same as what we do during the weekend ones?"

Sally stops to admire a butterfly as it flutters from one plant to another. "Yeah, they're mostly the same, except that there aren't any family or friends there. We talk about what's bugging us, why we do drugs and what causes us to use."

"How does that help?"

"Just knowing that I'm not alone gives me strength. There were lots of times—times I never told you about—when I thought I was losing my fucking mind. Coming here has helped me realize that is normal for an addict, and that I can do something about it—there's hope."

The pathway ends and the girls pause to admire the beauty surrounding them before heading back. Angel looks at Sally for a long while and then smiles. "I can't believe how far you've come. Just one more week before graduation. Do you think you'll be ready?"

Sally stoops down to pick up a stone, pauses and then tosses it into the bushes. "I've been thinking about that a lot. I'm happy when someone else is graduating, but now that it'll be me, I'm scared. I know I've come a long way, but it's safe in here. What will I do when I'm out there faced with all the temptations?"

The girls resume walking. The scent of jasmine is thick in the air.

Angel asks, "Have you talked with Dr. Whitmore about it?"

"Yeah, he says it's a good thing that I just moved here and I haven't had a chance to make a pattern of getting my drugs locally. He says the best chance I have to remain clean is to attend daily Al-Anon meetings and stay in touch with a sponsor—he'll set me up with both." Sally lets out a heavy sigh. "After that, it's up to me."

Angel puts her arm around Sally's shoulder. "Remember, you got me, too. I'll do whatever you need to beat this thing."

Sally leans into her embrace. "Thanks, Angel. I'm sorry."

"For what?"

Sally turns to look at her friend. "For all the shit I've put you through. No matter how fucked up I got, you were always there to pick me up and put me back together again."

"Ah, you'd have done the same for me. Remember, we're sisters-till-the-end. We stick together."

Sally, overwhelmed, tears up and manages a weak, "Thanks."

A few days prior to her graduation, Sally, in session, comments, "I'm getting really worried about when I get out. My life seems to be one never-ending drama. Every time I think things can't get any worse, they do—it never ends. It's as if I'm the main character in a soap opera."

Dr. Whitmore offers a smile. "Sally, don't you know? Life is one continuous soap opera. Each drama outdoes the previous one. The sooner you accept that, the better equipped you'll be to cope." His demeanor becomes more serious. "The trick is to not cause unnecessary chaos. We've talked a lot about that and how you can eliminate a large portion of the drama from your life." He eyes her closely. "Trust in the tools I've given you. If you attend your daily meetings and stay in touch with your sponsor, you will be fine."

Sally slumps on the sofa. "What if I can't do this? What if it's too much, I slip and start using again?"

Dr. Whitmore gets up and sits beside her. "Then we deal with that at the time *if* it happens. But let's not get ahead of ourselves. Okay?"

Suddenly, Dr. Whitmore envisions kissing her.

How did it ever get to this point? How is it that I fell under her spell? I am overwhelmed with longing desire for this broken patient who is an addict and has unresolved issues.

Startled, he gets up. "I think we better call it a day."

In session with Dr. Whitmore the day before she graduates, Sally gushes, "I had to share with you—had to tell you. You'll be so proud of me."

"What's so exciting? What did you do? Tell me."

Sally takes a deep breath in an attempt to slow her speech. "Well, remember how you told me I had to be careful not to allow the feeling of guilt to settle back in once I rid myself of the things that have been bothering me?"

"Yes."

"Well, I did it." She beams. "I stopped them."

"What do you mean? Stopped what?"

"After my group session yesterday, I was feeling sad about Eric Angel. Tried to push away the memories. The more I tried, the guiltier I felt about everything that had happened—and then it hit me. I heard your words and noticed that my mind was trying to put a guilt trip on me. I realized that I *could* think about my son without feeling guilty. I went for a long walk and thought about all the good times we'd shared. Then I came back to my room and wrote another poem." Sally looks up and takes a deep breath before continuing. "Want to hear?"

"Of course!"

She opens her journal. "I call it, Standing Tall.

Setting out to right the past
Seeking peace, wholeness and closure
Wanting to move on

Taking steps on trembling legs
Anxiety grabs hold
Willing to go the distance

Making right a wrong
Rewriting history
A pleasant surprise unfolds

Didn't see it coming
Didn't see the connection
Reclaiming my lost self

Melting snow
New buds sprouting
Understanding blossoms

> *To be unblocked*
> *To let the words flow*
> *To heal*
>
> *Floating free*
> *Despite my skeletons*
> *Let them be revealed*
>
> *Standing tall*
> *No more regrets*
> *Embracing life."*

When she finishes, she sees that her doctor has a wide grin on his face. "What are you smiling about?"

"I'm so proud of the work you've done. How far you've come. That was a beautiful poem. I believe that you understand now. You have to feel and become soft in order to be strong. You're well on your way to becoming useful and making a difference with your life. I'm so happy for you and admire your strength." Dr. Whitmore leans forward, suddenly serious. "I do need to caution you, though. This won't be the last time your resolve is tested. In here it's easier to avoid the temptation to slip up—out there, many things will test your strength. You need to be prepared for such eventualities."

A mask of seriousness strains Sally's features. "I know. I think about it all the time. That's what scares me."

CHAPTER 20

The graduation ceremony is not grand. Instead, it is plain and succinct—focusing on how far Sally has come and the distance she must continue to travel on her endless journey to recovery. Angel is there, of course, as well as Dr. Whitmore. After the ceremony, fellow patients offer Sally their good wishes. Phone numbers are exchanged and hope burns strong amongst the patients with an intensity not understood by outsiders.

Sally is in her room packing with Angel when Dr. Whitmore knocks on her open door. Looking up, she sees him and smiles. Angel gets up from sitting at the foot of the bed. "I'm gonna get some coffee. Either of you want anything?"

"No, thanks," Sally answers.

When Angel leaves, Dr. Whitmore leans against the doorway. "So, are you ready?"

Sally places a folded shirt in her bag. "I'm almost done packing."

He lets out a chuckle. "That's not what I meant."

Sally laughs. "Oh…right, you meant am I prepared to leave." She lets out a deep sigh. "As ready as I'll ever be, I guess. A little nervous, though."

Dr. Whitmore nods his head in understanding. "Mmm, that's to be expected. It's a normal reaction to the unknown. If you forgive yourself for the past and don't forget your triggers and where you have come from, you will be fine."

Sally stops folding the pair of jeans she is holding and looks up, gratitude in her eyes. "How can I ever thank you?"

"Not necessary. This is what I do."

She grows serious and looks at him. "I promise I'll make you proud of me by staying clean."

Dr. Whitmore pushes away from the door jamb and crosses the room to stand before her and looks down into her emerald green eyes, which shine with sincerity. "Don't, Sally. Jean Jacques Rousseau said it best, 'He who is slowest in making a promise is most faithful in its performance.' Take your time. Don't rush. And your assurance should be to yourself, not me."

"But I want to make you proud of me."

"I already am—more than you know."

Sally resumes folding the jeans and places them in her bag. Zipping it shut, she sets the suitcase on the floor beside her and looks up. "Well, this is it. This is where I get off."

Just then, Angel returns and asks, "You ready?"

"Yeah."

Dr. Whitmore reaches for her luggage. "May I walk you to your car?"

"I'd like that."

The three walk to the truck without talking. There is a gentle breeze blowing, causing the leaves to dance and rustle on the trees around them. Once at the vehicle, Dr. Whitmore places the bag in the truck bed. After a moment's hesitation, he turns. "Sally, I'd like to take you to dinner tonight—to celebrate your graduation. Would that be okay?"

She breathes in the crisp air, beaming. "I'd really like that."

She gives him her address, and they agree that he will gather her at 7:00 PM. Before returning to the facility, he reaches for her hand and gives it a loving squeeze.

As Angel gets into the truck, she says, "It was nice to see you again, Dr. Whitmore."

"I'm no longer Sally's doctor. Please, call me James."

"Okay. See you later, James."

James takes Sally to a quaint sushi restaurant where they sip sake, nibble on exotic fish entrees and talk. She is intrigued by the man-of-mystery who sits across from her and the overwhelming feelings of desire that resonate from the center of her being. "James, I feel like you know everything about me, but I know nothing of you."

He places his chopsticks on his plate and gives her his full attention. An inviting smile warms his features. "I am but an open book to you. I will answer any inquiry."

"Tell me about your childhood."

For a brief moment, Sally sees the twinkle she has grown to love leave James's eyes.

"Well, that's a short sad tale, indeed."

Sorry she asked, Sally says, "That's okay, you don't have to tell me. I'm sorry. What the fuck's the matter with me? I didn't mean to pry."

James reaches across the table and covers her hand with his. "You have nothing to apologize for. I told you I would tell you anything, and I meant it."

"You don't have to."

"I know. I want to." He begins. "I was your average all-American kid with loving parents who exposed me to a wide variety of reading from a very young age. Before I could read, they would recite the scribed words of the literary greats. When I began reading, they would help me understand how to read the classic works myself. I was never very good at sports, but I had a passion for the written word. I couldn't read enough. I guess you'd call me an intellectual nerd." He lets out a nervous laugh.

Sally joins in. "You, a nerd? I find that hard to believe—someone as handsome as you—never."

"Have you ever heard the story about the ugly duckling?"

"Yeah, why?"

"Well, you're looking at a living specimen."

Sally scoffs, "You? I don't believe it. I'll bet you were an adorable little boy."

James blushes a deep crimson and then continues. "Oh, you can believe it, my own mother wanted to put a paper bag over my head. Well, not really—but close."

Sally enjoys hearing about how James' childhood contrasted with her own. "It sounds like you had a great childhood—loving parents— a fairy tale every child would want."

"Ah, but not all fairy tales have happily-ever-after endings. When

I was twelve, my parents were driving home from a holiday party. They were hit by a drunk driver—both were killed."

Sally puts her hand to her mouth. An audible gasp escapes her lips. "Oh, my God, that's terrible. I'm so sorry. That must have been horrible for you."

"It was, especially since I had no other family. Both my parents had been only children with my grandparents having passed away long since."

"How awful. What happened?"

"I became a ward of the state and was placed in an orphanage."

Sally shakes her head in an attempt to understand the cruel twist of fate his life took. "Please tell me you were adopted and there was a happy ending."

James shakes his head. "No. Wish I could, but it didn't happen that way. Seemed no one wanted to adopt an older kid—they all wanted irresistible little babies, whom they could blend into their families, seamlessly. Every weekend I'd watch the parade of prospective parents arrive and pass me by."

Sally reaches across the table, takes James' hands in both of hers and holds them lovingly. "How terrible. That must have been heartbreaking."

"It was. I sought comfort from the books in the orphanage's library. The characters and words I encountered on those pages became my family. They nurtured me. I got to know them well—staying at the facility until I was eighteen. By that time, I had read and reread my favorite books many times, memorizing many of their passages."

A smile of understanding awakens Sally's face. "*That's* where your skill of reciting quotes comes from."

Grinning, James says, "I've been discovered! I had an abundance of time to read and absorb the written word. I became passionate about it. It always seemed that just when I needed it the most, I would come across a quote that would inspire me to keep going or reach a little further. I began reciting them to the other kids when they seemed to need a boost. The others seemed encouraged by them. That's when I learned that I had a knack for and received great satisfaction from helping ease others' suffering. I swore that when I grew up, I would dedicate my life to relieving individuals of their pain. And, well, here I am."

Sally swallows her bite of food and reflects for a moment before responding, "So there was a happily-ever-after."

James takes a sip of sake, allowing her assessment to wash over him. "I guess there was. I hadn't thought of it that way." He locks eyes with her before continuing. "A lot of people think you shouldn't dredge up old memories—that they only serve to awaken regret and grief. I disagree. I prefer to visit where I've come from and embrace those experiences, painful though some of them may be, as making me who I am today. I'm a better person because of them. Due to the trials I've undergone, I can empathize with others' adversity. I don't like to see people in torment, so I try my hardest to help them. Now, I've told you all about my childhood and parents. You've told me about your father, but haven't mentioned your mother. Is she still alive? If so, do you have contact with her?"

Sally sits back in her chair and lets out an audible sigh, as James selects and eats a piece of spicy tuna cut roll. "Yeah, my ma is still alive and no, I'm not in contact with her."

"Why not? Her decision or yours?"

"Is this the doctor talking?"

"No, just someone who knows the value of a relationship one can have with their parents and hates to see others miss the opportunities it affords."

Sally suddenly feels tired. She stalls for time before answering his queries. "Well, when I left home and began hooking, I made such a fucking mess of my life that I thought I couldn't go back. Then, when I ran from Ax, I didn't want to place my ma in danger, so I continued to keep my distance."

James drains the remaining sake from his cup. Picking up the carafe of warm rice wine, he pours himself and Sally more. Replacing the decanter on the table, he asks, "What's keeping you from making contact now? You've made a lot of changes, Ax is out of the picture, and you could benefit from her added support."

Sally pushes her plate away and leans forward, her expression softening. "Actually, I've been thinking about making contact with her. She was a great mom. I miss her advice and support. I value your opinion. What do you think I should do?"

"I think you should get in touch with her. I'll bet that she…what's your mother's name?"

"Gloria."

"…would love to hear from you and have the two of you resume a relationship."

Hearing his words, Sally is encouraged and brightens with hope. "You really think she'd be happy to hear from me?"

"Well, I don't know her, but I can tell you that a mother's love is a powerful forgiving force. It's never too late to try. You stand nothing to lose and everything to gain from approaching her. Why wouldn't you attempt to reconnect?"

They finish their meal and leave the restaurant. Sally ponders his words and the potential truth they bear as they walk to his car, holding each other's hand. "If you could, James, would you change your childhood?"

"No."

"Why not?"

"I miss my parents terribly and feel robbed of all the lost time we should have had together, but the experiences I've had since their deaths have made me who I am. I believe I would be a lesser person without having gone through them."

"How do you figure?"

"Well, in the words of Oscar Wilde, 'Nothing that is worth knowing can be taught.' I wouldn't change my knowledge for anything—even though it was hard learned—for it allows me to serve others in a unique capacity and deliver them from their torment."

Sally stops and turns to face the man with whom she is falling in love. She looks into his eyes and picks her next words carefully—speaking them with tenderness. Her eyes glisten with tears. "I don't know what the hell I did right, or who I have to thank for placing you in my life. What you have given me is priceless. You've given me back myself, and hope for my future. From the bottom of my heart, thank you."

She looks into his eyes, scanning them, watching the light as it plays with the flecks of gold within them. He returns her gaze, cupping her face in his strong hands. She closes her eyes and sighs as he brushes his lips against hers, lingering before kissing her passionately. Her lips eagerly meet his own. James and Sally remain locked in an ardent kiss that seems to last forever. When it ends, both are breathless. Sally gives him a hug, and James kisses the top of her head before pulling away to look into her eyes. "I'm genuinely touched by your words of appreciation. But it is not I who deserves the credit. You are the one who has initiated the process of recovery. In the words of Quintus Horatius Flaccus...."

"Enough with the quotes already," Sally says. "Shut up and kiss me again!"

CHAPTER 21

After their date, James drops Sally at her place and proceeds home—his mind tormented with the difficulties that might arise should Sally enter into a romantic relationship too soon. He spends a sleepless night tossing and turning, chastising himself for the dilemma he has inadvertently placed them in.

If I approach her now and tell her that we should wait, I'm afraid that she'll go into a downward spiral and might return to crack. God, I couldn't bear to be the cause of that. What am I going to do? She can't enter into a relationship with me now. It's not healthy for her.

Abandoning all thoughts of sleep, he is up well before his alarm goes off and stumbles into the kitchen to make himself some tea, hoping it might soothe his frazzled mind. James is plagued with what to do about Sally while getting ready for work. He heads to the facility early in the hopes of having some time to ponder his situation before seeing his patients for the day.

Alone in his office, with his door shut, James leans back in his plush leather desk chair and closes his eyes, rubbing his temples.

I can't avoid it. I'm going to have to address this with her. But how? I don't want to hurt her.

He resigns himself to the inevitable—he will have to meet with Sally in person. He knows that trying to explain this to her over the phone would be too impersonal, so he calls and arranges to meet her for lunch. The hours seem to drag by as he works his way through his list of patients and group sessions.

James takes Sally to a quiet Italian restaurant where they are seated in a rear corner booth, affording them privacy. She is concerned by the strained look on his face and asks, "Hard day?"

"A little."

"You seem stressed."

James puts down his menu and lets out a heavy sigh before saying, "I am. I've done something that may compromise your recovery."

Sally scans his face, noting the furrowed brow, taut mouth and the lack of luster in his eyes. "What have you done?"

James looks down and fidgets with the corner of his linen napkin, stalling for time. After several interminable minutes filled with deafening silence, he looks up to meet her gaze. "I'm so sorry. I never should have let my feelings get in the way of my better judgment. But I couldn't help it. I have such strong feelings for you, and they disable my ability to act rationally."

Sally remains quiet and offers him an encouraging smile.

James continues, "I think I may be falling in love with you. I've never experienced such overwhelming emotions towards another."

Sally's heart soars when she hears his admission and confesses, "I have strong feelings for you too."

James puts up a finger. "Shhh, I know you do—that's the problem."

"I don't understand. We both have feelings for the other and want to proceed with a relationship." She pauses. "Oh, wait. Maybe you don't *want* to proceed." She sees the pained look on his face, notes his silence and continues, "If you don't want to see me, you don't need to worry. I'll be okay."

"It's not that I don't *want* to see you. I do, more than anything. But now is not the right time."

Sally bristles. Fearing the worst, she lashes out, "Let me guess. You're involved. Coming out of a bad relationship. Maybe you're married. *Are* you married?"

"No, but I deserve that. I've made this so complicated. That wasn't my intent. Let me try again. You've just come out of an inpatient rehab center and are now at your most vulnerable. Over the next month, your mind is going to be barraged with a plethora of overwhelming emotions and feelings that have been concealed by the drugs you had been taking. Now is not the time for you to enter into a romantic relationship."

"Why not? We both like each other."

"I know, but it's not that simple. I think we should give you a chance to adjust. The first thirty to sixty days following any detox from drugs is complicated. You're halfway through that right now. I don't want to make the process any more difficult than it has to be. I think that we should allow you the next thirty days to readjust to being on the outside and drug-free. That will afford you time to process emotions you're feeling, procure a job and begin pulling your life back together. At the end of that time, I would very much like to enter into a friendship with you, but strictly platonic. I believe that we should follow the teachings of Al-Anon and refrain from pursuing a romantic relationship for a year." He pauses to allow his words to sink in before continuing, "If, after a year, we mutually decide that we want to take our friendship to the next level, then would be the time to do so—not before."

Sally doesn't respond right away. She sits in stunned silence—the menu, the unordered meal and the restaurant forgotten. When she does speak, the pain can be heard in her voice. "A year? A whole year?"

"Yes. I really like you and want to give your recovery and our future every possible chance for success. I've seen it happen too many times before. Patients, who think they're ready to enter into relationships, end up getting hurt and return to drugs as a result. I can't bear the thought of that happening to you because of me."

As she listens to James' words, a warm glow simmers just below the surface. She is touched that the man sitting before her, to whom she is ready to give her heart, is so compelled to protect her. She has never experienced that comfort before. She responds, "A month won't be so bad. I can get through it, as long as I know you'll be there at the end to be my friend. You'll be there. Right?"

James locks eyes with her, penetrating her soul with his intent gaze. "I'll be counting down the days."

Sally looks down momentarily, takes a deep breath and blinks ever so slowly before agreeing, "Okay. I'll do it. I'll take a month off, from us, and focus on putting myself back together." She lets out a heavy sigh.

That night, while walking out to their car, their arms full of groceries, Angel questions Sally, "So, how was your date with James?"

"It was perfect. He took me to a sushi place, where we drank sake and ate, while getting to know one another."

"Sounds like it went well." Angel places her bags in the truck bed.

"It did. And then I saw him, again today, for lunch."

"You did? When are you gonna see him again?"

"Well, I'm not—at least not for now," Sally responds, while placing her bags alongside Angel's. She avoids making eye contact.

"What? But I thought you said it went well."

Sally rests her hands on the truck bed and answers. "It did, but we both decided that it would be best if I took a month to focus on getting myself together."

Angel looks at her. "A month isn't that long."

Sally meets her gaze and adds, "Well, it's a bit longer than that. We also decided that we'd stick to Al-Anon's suggestion and not enter into a romantic relationship for a year."

Angel's eyes grow wide, the look on her face incredulous. "A year? A whole year? What happened to a month? Let me get this straight. You're gonna cool your heels for the next year, not have any contact with James and then *whammo*, pick up where you left off a year from now?"

Sally laughs. "No. We decided to be friends after a month of giving me time to adjust to being out of rehab. If that goes well, then we'll consider dating at the end of a year."

"You say 'we' decided. Is that both of your thoughts or mostly his?"

"Both of ours. I think it'll be good to have him as a friend. He'll help keep me on track. And the points he made as to why we should wait seem to make sense. I really like him and want to give our relationship the best chance. If that means I have to be patient and wait a whole fucking year in the company of a new friend, then so be it."

"But a year? Jeez, girl, that's a long time."

"I know, but I've got plenty to keep me busy during that time what with staying off drugs and pulling my life back together." Sally looks down at her watch. "Speaking of time, we better get going so we aren't late for our interviews."

They make the short drive home while continuing their conversation. Angel looks at Sally and asks, "So, what is it about this guy that you like?"

Sally navigates through the commuter traffic, pulling around a slower moving vehicle, and pauses before answering. Splitting her attention between the cars around her and Angel, she replies, "Lots of things. He's irresistibly handsome, has a kind heart and experienced a similar painful childhood. Best of all, he accepts me—even knowing how fucked up I am."

"I know you probably don't want to hear this but how do you expect this to work out?"

Sally shoots her a quick glance. "Why wouldn't it?"

Angel pauses before answering, "You come from two different worlds. He's a doctor. You're an ex-prostitute, stripper and drug addict. *Our kind* doesn't mix well with his."

"Says who?"

"Well, just about every movie or TV show I've ever watched, especially Jerry Springer."

"Angel, you can't believe everything you see in movies or on the TV. I believe that where there's a will, there's a way and that opposites do attract."

"I don't know, girl. From what I've seen, his kind pays to be serviced by our kind. I just don't want to see you get hurt."

"I appreciate your concern, but James isn't like that. He's different—he cares about me."

CHAPTER 22

Sally and Angel secure jobs as waitresses at a local restaurant. Over the next month, they hike and explore the local foothills on their days off. Sally keeps in contact with her sponsor and attends Al-Anon meetings. The girls are content with their new, slower, normal lifestyle. Just as James had predicted, Sally finds herself experiencing feelings that had been masked by the drugs she had been taking. She is determined to remain sober and turns to her sponsor when those emotions become too intense.

She gives a lot of thought to her conversation with James about reconnecting with her mother. After a month, she decides to give her a call.

The phone rings several times at her mother's house before being picked up. A pleasant "Hello" comes through the line.

Hearing the familiar voice, Sally is time-warped, and the past nine years fade away. "Hello, Ma? It's Sally."

An audible gasp is heard on the other end, followed by a brief pause, and then her mother's soft crying, "Sally? Is that really you?"

"Shhh, Ma, don't cry. Yeah, it's me."

"Didn't think I would ever hear from you again. It's been so long. Are you okay?"

Sally's own tears surprise her. "Yeah. Ma, I've missed you *so* much! I'm sorry for making you wonder and worry all these years. Can I come over? Please." There is a long pause. "Ma, did you hear me?"

There is an icy edge to her mom's voice. "Yeah, I heard. Where are you?"

"Here in town. About fifteen minutes away. Can I come now?"

Her mom replies, "I suppose."

Sally stands in the house of her youth, locked in an awkward embrace with her mother. Both cry tears of sorrow and gratitude for lost years and for the opportunity to reunite. When they pull apart, Sally studies her mother's appearance. Although nearly a decade has passed, she still sees the youthful woman her mom was when she left home. Seeing her mother's nose—crooked from having been broken one too many times by her father's hands—Sally self-consciously raises her hand and traces the raised bridge of her own nose, noting its slight curve. Her mother's compassionate brilliant green eyes—Sally's own—still shine. Her once glowing red hair is now almost completely snow white, not the dull, lifeless grey of most, but the shocking white of freshly fallen snow, and her face bears the lines of wisdom hard obtained. Sally smiles.

She beholds the familiar interior. Its sights, smells and welcoming feeling are just as she remembered. The tabletops are still cluttered with an assortment of framed photos—all of Sally, her brother and her mother. Sally walks around admiring each, reconnecting with memories. Her mother watches.

Sally lingers for quite some time on one photo in particular—the last one taken of her brother. She reaches down and picks it up, gingerly cupping it in her hands, as if she can feel his embrace through it. In the snapshot, Eric's head is thrown back, caught in laughter— that contagious laugh of his. She studies it for a few minutes— remembering—before replacing it on the end table.

Her mother breaks the silence. "Can I get you something to drink?"

Sally looks up. "Some coffee would be nice."

Wordlessly, her mother goes into the kitchen and sets a pot brewing while Sally follows behind and goes about retrieving mugs, spoons, cream and sugar, all of which are still located in the same places. She arranges them on the table, stalling for time, before sitting down. Soon, the sharp acidic aroma of fresh-brewed coffee fills the room, and her mom brings the pot to the table, where she pours some into each of their mugs.

Sally adds cream and sugar to hers and begins stirring it while remembering days-gone-by in this very kitchen: the popcorn her father used to make, the cookies her mother used to bake and the darker times as well.... She looks at one of the upper cabinets and remembers....

* * * * *

Sally was terrified. She could never recall seeing her father so angry. As he continued to slap and punch her, she kept wondering.

Why? What did I do? Why does he always have to beat on one of us?

He slapped Sally face hard—hard enough to spin her head to the side. Rubbing her cheek, she dared to look back at him. As their eyes locked, she saw it, the look of glee on his face, the moment before he pounded his fist into her nose, shattering the cartilage and sending a splattering of blood across the upper kitchen cabinets. Sally fell to her knees, cupping her hands over her throbbing nose, as white stars flashed before her eyes.

Her father had grabbed her ponytail and yanked her up, yelling, "You'll clean up that mess, or I'll beat you some more."

* * * * *

A shiver runs down Sally's spine at the memory, and she forces herself to look away from the cabinet. She takes her spoon out of her coffee, places it beside her mug and then looks up. "I always wondered.... Why did you stay with Daddy?"

Her mom lifts her mug to her lips and blows on it before taking a tentative sip. Deciding it is still too hot, she puts down the mug and begins toying with its handle before answering, "Oh, honey, it's complicated. There are a hundred reasons—none of them the right one, I'm afraid. I loved him. He loved me. He could be so kind and gentle.... I didn't want to be the one to destroy our family. Your father had broken my self-esteem, my self-worth and me. There wasn't any of me left. I thought it must have been my fault. That if I tried harder to be a better wife/mother, he wouldn't get so angry and beat us. I couldn't fathom how I would be able to support us on my own, so I stayed with him. I know it probably doesn't make any sense to you, but at the time I thought I was doing the right thing. I'm so sorry for what I put you and your brother through. You didn't deserve that. I should have protected you more."

Sally locks eyes with her mother. "Ah, Ma, you have nothing to apologize for. You did the best you could."

Her mom looks away. "Maybe. But I can't help but wonder if you might have stayed longer, not been in such a rush to get away from here—me—if you hadn't been so exposed as a little girl."

Sally reaches across the table and places her hand over her mother's. "Ma, don't…. You're not responsible for my mistakes. I am. I had this stupid idea that I had to get out and see the world, on my terms—my way. Turns out it was the hard way. It's what I had to do, though. You didn't cause me to leave. I left because everything here reminded me of Eric, and the memories surrounding his death were too painful. I wasn't running from you. And I didn't leave because of what Daddy did to us. There are a lot of things I can blame that bastard for, but me screwing up my life isn't one of them."

Her mother takes a moment to appreciate the sentiments her daughter has just spoken. She swallows hard and chokes back tears of gratitude. Once composed, she asks, "Where did you go when you left? What have you been doing all these years?"

Sally takes a deep breath before saying, "Do you remember that group of friends I began hanging out with after Eric died?"

"Yes…."

"Well, I made a great friend there—Angel. She's still my best friend. Back then, she introduced me to a man in Pasadena who took us in."

"Why would he do that?"

Sally does not answer.

Her mother's gaze bores through her with intensity. "You're telling me that a total stranger—a man—took you in, just like that?"

Sally still remains silent.

Her mother's voice is laced with frustration and years of concealed hurt. "Do you plan on answering me, or are we just going to sit here, locked in silence, like old times?"

Sally's eyes flash. She meets her mother's gaze and nearly spits out, "He was a pimp! Are you happy?"

As if she's been struck, her mother leans back hard in her chair, a shocked expression upon her face. "Don't tell me you became a prostitute."

Sally wishes she could spare her. Knowing that she cannot, she continues with sadness in her voice. "Yeah, I did. We were young and stupid. Our pimp, Ax, fed us drugs. They helped to take away the pain of losing Eric. He made prostitution sound so appealing— fucking bastard. We believed him and thought it would be fun and exciting. It wasn't. It was a nightmare."

"How long did you sell yourself?" Her voice drips with sarcastic venom. "Or are you still?"

Sally does not recoil from her mother's attack. "No, not any more. I quit after seven years."

Her mom gasps, "Seven years?! You did it for seven years? Until you were…twenty-five?" Her mother's sarcasm returns. "Why so long? I thought you said it was horrible."

Sally refills her mug, adds more cream and sugar, and stirs, choosing her next words carefully. "I didn't have a choice. I had to stay. Ax was…. He could be violent. No one left him."

Her mother does not respond.

Sally rushes through the next part of her tale, knowing it will cause her mother great pain. "After a year of hooking, I became pregnant with my son, Eric Angel."

Her mom looks astonished. "You have a son? *I* have a grandson? Where…where is he? Tell me all about him. When will I get to meet him?"

A dull monotone edges Sally's voice as she explains, "You won't—get to meet him, I mean." She notes the hurt expression on her mother's face.

"Why not?"

Sally remains silent, as if she has slipped into a catatonic state. The room falls silent, and a million memories flash through her mind.

* * * * *

Sally had played with her son, Eric Angel, that very morning. They had laughed and giggled with one another before it was time for her to begin selling her body to the johns, during which time, her five-year-old son was to sit obediently in the back of Ax's car.

The argument between Ax and the other pimp had been frightful. They had spat venomous words at one another before Ax had begun savagely beating the man. Breaking free, the other pimp had fled for his life. Ax calmly followed and shot him dead, before departing the scene.

When the swarm of police had dissipated, Ax had returned to gather his prostitutes, Sally amongst them. She had wondered where her son was. As she sat in the exact spot of Ax's car where her son had been, only hours earlier, the full meaning of her premonition dream revealed itself, and she knew.... Her son had been killed by one of Ax's stray bullets during the battle with the other pimp.

* * * * *

Sally barely hears her mother's barrage of questions in the background. She resurfaces from her painful memories and responds, her voice dull. "My son is dead."

Her mom cannot conceal her shock. "What? When? How did—"

Sally goes about the arduous task of telling how Ax had held Eric Angel hostage, about the shootout, her son getting hit in the crossfire and how she and Angel escaped to Las Vegas. As Sally speaks, her mother sits back in her chair, recoiling from each new tidbit of information. By the end, both are tired and worn.

Long minutes pass with neither saying anything. Then Sally smiles. "Ah, Ma, you would have loved Eric Angel." Her voice resonates maternal pride. "He was perfect—the most beautiful little boy in the world. He had Eric's brilliant green eyes. Bore right through you. And that laugh of his.... Just like Eric's—so contagious that you couldn't help but laugh along with him." Sally becomes reflective.

* * * * *

Sally and her brother, Eric, had conceived the game of silly dance one night while dancing at will to the music emanating from her stereo. When their father had appeared in the doorway, both children had ceased dancing, fearful that they had somehow upset him, and that he would unleash his wrath upon them. He hadn't, though. Instead, he encouraged them to continue and, in a rare moment, had joined them. Soon, all three were laughing so hard that their mother came and joined them. Both parents mimicked their childrens' dancing. In no time, the four had been reduced to fits of uncontrolled belly laughter. Thus, the game of silly dance had been invented.

* * * * *

Sally recalls the times she had silly danced with her son and how his laughter reminded her of her brother's. She contemplates the profound impact her son had on her and tries to explain to her mother. "I saw the world as a better place through his eyes." She lets out a sigh. "God, I wish you could have met him—he made the world shine brighter."

Sally stirs her coffee. Both women sit in silence, each lost in their own thoughts. Sally breaks the stillness. "About Daddy…. I don't blame you. God knows, I've had my share of bastards who have abused me." She pauses to let her words sink in before continuing, "Why did I let them? Like you, there are a hundred reasons—none of which make any sense now. Guess you and I are alike. Have to learn things the hardest fucking way possible."

Her mom flashes her a pained smile. "Why didn't you ever call or write? I've spent so many sleepless nights wondering…. What you did—disappearing without a trace—was cruel. Especially since I'd already lost your brother."

Sally cringes at the anguish in her mother's voice. "I'm so sorry for causing you to worry. I never wanted to hurt you."

"I know. I've got to ask though, did you ever think about coming home? Calling? Dropping me a note?"

"I did early on, but I was so ashamed of what I'd become…of what I'd allowed men to do to me…. When Angel and I ran away from Ax, we couldn't risk having any contact with anyone back here or he would have found and killed us. If Ax could have, he would have found and hurt you as a way to get to us. I'd made such a fucking mess of my life by then that I couldn't face bringing that upon you."

"Las Vegas? Why did you go there?"

Sally tells her mother about her life of stripping at Luigi's and the close relationships she forged while there. Again, she sees her mother's shocked countenance and hurries through the last part. "Ma, I saw him—Daddy—he came into the club while I was stripping one night."

Her mother looks as if she's seen a ghost. "He saw you? Tracked you down? What did you do?"

"No. Don't think he was looking for me. Just a coincidence. Didn't even recognize me. Really messed me up, though—sent me on a three-day crack binge."

"Crack? Oh, Sally, you still do drugs?"

"Not anymore. Just finished an inpatient program." Sally peers down, unable to look at her mother for fear of seeing disappointment in her eyes. "You must be so ashamed of me. I've fucked up in every possible way."

Her mom raises Sally's head by gently placing her hand under her chin. She looks directly into her eyes, which brim with tears. "Honey, don't you know? No matter what, I could never be ashamed of you. Upset and angry, yes. But you're my little girl…. Lost though you may have been, I'll *always* accept you—that's what mothers do. Time and actions don't alter that."

Sally dares to look into her mother's eyes. She sees acceptance instead of the rejection. Tears of gratitude and understanding stream down her face, as her throat clenches on a choked sob.

Later that night, Gloria, alone in her bed, pulls out a journal from her nightstand drawer and begins writing.

I heard from Sally today. Called out of the blue. She looks the same except for the lines etching her face, denoting the passage of time. They've come at a great expense. She's adopted a world of hard knowledge, exposing herself to many of my worst fears. But she's still my little girl, and I love her despite what she's done. Can't believe it's been nine years-nine years. There she was sitting before me-just like that. How often have I hoped for this? Prayed for this day? My little girl has come home.

Sally shocked me with the news that I had a grandson. Imagine, me, a grandmother. But I'll never get to see him, or hear his voice. I wonder what he was like? What were his favorite games or toys? Did he have toys? Was he allowed to play? Did Ax abuse him? I wish I could have spared Sally from the pain of losing her child. That's one thing I never wanted to have in common with her.

Gloria closes her journal with mixed emotions. She replaces it in the nightstand drawer and clicks off the light as she draws the covers over her. She closes her eyes and falls asleep. A multitude of images and questions plague her mind.

CHAPTER 23

Following her meeting with her mother, Sally is euphoric and anxiously awaits Angel's return from work. The minute her friend walks through the door, Sally begins talking a mile a minute. "Oh, my God, Angel! Can't believe how well my meeting with my mother went. I was so nervous going over there. Thought she might be distant—or worse, reject me once she found out what a fucking mess I'd made of my life."

"Whoa, girl," Angel says. "Slow down. Let me put down my jacket and you can tell me how it went."

"I've got a better idea. Come in the kitchen. I made dinner. Had so much energy when I got back.... Had to do something."

Angel's eyes grow wide. "So you cooked? From a package or from scratch?"

Sally's face screws up into a mock frown. "From scratch. Wanna make something of it?"

"I'll let you know after I eat...*if* I survive."

"Shut up. You can't spoil my good mood. Come in and help me serve."

Obvious surprise can be seen on Angel's face as she rounds the corner and spies the meal. "Wow! This looks...good!"

Sally beams. "Wait 'til you taste it."

During the meal, Sally tells how, although her mother had been angry and hurt, she accepted her. "God, Angel, it was so good to see her again. Didn't realize how much I'd missed her."

"I'm happy it went so well."

Sally grows serious. "I want to introduce you to her."

Angel chokes. "Me? Why?!"

"Because I want the two most important people in my life to get to know one another."

Angel lets out a sigh and scrutinizes Sally for a minute before responding, "Okay, if it means that much to you."

A few days later, Sally sits in her mother's kitchen, sharing a pot of coffee. There is a palpable tension between the two. Sally looks at her mother and states, "Can't believe we're back to this?"

"What?"

"This." Sally gestures between the two of them. "The awkwardness. It won't serve any purpose, except to make both of us miserable. Besides, I thought we worked everything out the other night."

Her mother penetrates her with her gaze for several long moments before exhaling heavily. "You're right. We're both adults. Maybe we should just agree to leave what happened in the past and start afresh."

"I'd like that. Can you do that? I know I hurt you."

"Ah, honey, we both made mistakes. Let's move forward."

Sally smiles. "Agreed." She takes a sip of her coffee then lowers her mug, stalling for time, and tilts it in a circular motion to swirl the liquid. After what seems an eternity, she summons the courage to proceed. "Ma, if you're willing, I really want you to meet Angel. We've gone to hell and back together. She shored me up every time I faltered."

Her mom takes a sip of coffee and states, "She sounds important to you."

"Couldn't have made it through half the crap I've faced if she hadn't been by my side."

"Well then, why don't we have a bar-b-cue here tonight, so I can get to know her?"

"You'd do that?"

Little crow's feet crinkle the corners of her mother's eyes, and she lets out a gentle laugh. "Yes."

Sally gives her mom a warm hug and then calls Angel to make the arrangements before heading off to work.

The nervousness in Angel's voice can be heard as they drive to dinner. "You think she's gonna like me?"

"What's not to like?"

"What if she hates me?"

"Well then, I guess we won't be able to play together any more," Sally says, grinning.

Angel relaxes. They arrive at Sally's mom's house a few minutes later. Angel surveys the neighborhood. "This isn't too far from where I grew up. Can't believe we never knew each other until high school. What's up with that?"

Sally shrugs. "Traveled in different circles."

Sally lets them into the house of her youth and goes to the back patio where she finds her mother taking the last of the meat off of the grill. Sally introduces the two. Dinner is served and they gather at the table. Passing the corn on the cob, Gloria asks Angel, "How did you two meet?"

Angel looks at Sally and reflects for a moment before replying, "Well, I guess it wasn't too long after Eric died. One day she was...just there—hovering around us. I'd never noticed Sally before."

"I used to hang with my friends, but after the divorce and my brother's death, they dumped me. I was a loner until I found you guys."

Angel suddenly laughs. "Remember the initiation Grease dared you to do?"

Sally grins. "Yeah, I remember. Wasn't so funny at the time."

Gloria joins the conversation. "I've got to admit, back then I was horrified that Sally had been arrested. Later, I found it amusing that she had shoplifted dried fruits." Gloria grows serious. "Sally tells me you two have always stuck together."

"Yeah. Like sisters—blood's thicker than water...."

To Sally she asks, "Gone through a lot, haven't we?"

"I'll say. Couldn't have made it through half of it without you."

"Yeah, you could. You're stronger than you think."

Sally locks eyes with her friend. "Don't you know? *You're* where I get my strength."

Gloria smiles, witnessing the affection the girls share. "Angel, thank you for being there for Sally all these years. She's lucky to have found a friend as loyal as you."

Angel shifts uncomfortably in her seat. "It's nothing. She's bailed my sorry ass out plenty of times."

Over the following month, Angel, Sally and Gloria often get together to hike with Princess or have bar-b-cues at Gloria's. A strong bond forms between the three.

Meanwhile, James soul-searches whether he should or should not pursue a relationship with a former patient. He seeks the advice of his good friend and colleague, Alexander, over lunch at a local diner. "What am I setting myself up for? I've gone over this a thousand times and have weighed all the pros and cons. It doesn't make any sense to pursue Sally, and yet I can't get her out of my mind." He pauses to take a bite of his club sandwich.

Alexander sips his iced tea before responding, "You know the facts. The struggles that lay ahead of her with recovery. How she might use sex, love and a relationship to manipulate her mind as she seeks euphoric chemical release in her brain. And I know that you're aware that her infatuation with you could be nothing more than transference. But where does yours stem from? Why are you drawn to her despite all you know?"

James lets out a heavy sigh. "I know the medical jargon. Believe me. I know this is insane, and yet I'm still drawn to her."

"But why?"

James pushes his plate away and combs his fingers through his hair. "I wish I knew."

Alexander leans back in his seat. "I think you know, but are unwilling or unable to admit the reasons to yourself. I'm sure you don't want to hear it, but I wouldn't be a good friend if I didn't mention it. Your job as her therapist was to assist her in fashioning a healthy relationship with herself by establishing trust and boundaries. By showing her your feelings, you crossed a line—ethical and professional. If you chase her and something goes wrong—say she relapses—it could end your career. Are you prepared for that?"

James looks at the ceiling, as if the answers he is seeking will be written there. "You're not telling me anything I haven't pondered a million times already. That's one of the reasons I suggested to her that we just be friends and wait a year before pursuing a romantic relationship. I want to give her a chance at sobriety."

"That's a step in the right direction. Can't I convince you to look elsewhere for romance?"

"Afraid not."

"You're really stuck on her, aren't you?"

James slumps in his chair. "Yes."

Alexander reaches over and places his hand firmly on his friend's shoulder. "Well then, we're just going to have to find a way to make this work."

CHAPTER 24

James returns to his office to see the remainder of his clients. He struggles to concentrate, however, his mind distracted by his conversation with Alexander. The hours seem to drag by, an interminable painful test of his endurance marked by shadows falling across the walls of his office as the sun dips in the sky. Finally, his last patient leaves, and James bolts out of his chair. Grabbing his coat and briefcase, he races for his car.

On his drive home, he barely takes notice of the wide boulevards lined with mature trees. He passes older mansions, many of which have been converted into multi-unit dwellings. As he rounds a bend, there is an abrupt change to the lay of the neighborhood. Older apartment buildings outnumber houses. He drives in a funk while the anchor of the news station he has tuned into drones on—an unrecognizable static in the background.

James arrives home and waits, engine idling, for the secured gate to rise and grant him access to the underground parking garage. While paused, he notices the 1960s architectural features of his building and smiles to himself, marveling at how plain and simple they are. He pulls his car into his slot, gets out and is affronted with the dank smell associated with older subterranean garages.

Ah, the smells of home. They remind me of the orphanage.

As soon as James thinks the words, his mind flinches at the assault of memories that threaten to surface. In an attempt to stave off the traumatic recollections of his youth—the ones he had not told Sally about—he gathers his briefcase from the backseat and proceeds to the uninviting utilitarian-looking elevator, which delivers him to the ground floor.

Walking a short distance, he arrives at his front door, puts the key in the slot and twists extra hard to make it release. He muscles the door with his shoulder, the damp weather having caused the wood to swell, and is granted entry to a cold and sterile atmosphere devoid of any personal touches, knick-knacks or creature comforts. The maroon faux-suede blackout drapes are pulled closed over the main window, creating an almost cave-like environment. A frown tugs at James' mouth as he notices the sharp contrast between the well-appointed masculine furnishings that adorn his office and his own plain uninviting living space.

I'm a boring down-to-earth guy whose life is mundane, predictable and sterile, complete with my ritualistic routines.

A small smile plays at the corners of his mouth as thoughts of Sally enter his mind.

Now, Sally.... There's someone who could brighten my life. So full of energy. She makes me want to try to be better than I am, if not for myself, then for her. And I'm intrigued with the way she deals with her chaos.

He sheds his coat and tosses it, along with his briefcase, onto the coffee table on the way to the kitchen, where he fetches a highball glass, plunks in a few ice cubes and proceeds to fill it with tequila.

I'll only have one drink tonight.

He takes a swig of the liquor and is instantly gratified as the liquid makes its way down to his belly. Loosening his tie and unbuttoning his shirt, he kicks off his shoes and plops down on the sofa—an old relic with a store-bought slipcover—before placing his feet on the coffee table, a solid piece of dark wood. He pushes his briefcase and coat off to the side with his foot, takes another sip and sinks farther into the sofa, closing his eyes.

Several minutes later, he opens them, his gaze falling upon a narrow bookcase filled with an eclectic collection of books—each highly treasured and well read. Unlike the neatly organized leather-bound books in his office, the ones that adorn these shelves are placed haphazardly—a veritable cornucopia of varying bindings leaning against and supporting one another as if an earthquake had attempted to disshelve them.

He drains the contents of his glass in one swallow and his stomach voices its hunger. He gets up and makes himself a second drink.

Just one more.... The last one went down so fast.... I'll savor this one.

* * * * *

He remembered being introduced to the numbing effects of alcohol in high school at parties his friends threw, where they raided the adults' liquor supplies. He recalled how, at first, a few beers dulled the memories of the grisly automobile accident that forever altered the course of his life. When a few beers no longer had the desired effect, he progressed to six-packs before being introduced to Jack Daniel's— that helped....

* * * * *

James takes a sip of his drink, goes to the refrigerator and surveys the meager contents sparsely decorating the shelves. He pulls out a white to-go box, opens it, sniffs and flinches from its acrid odor before tossing it in the trash. He selects another and, upon opening it, recoils from the scientific experiment covering the once-recognizable food in a fuzzy orange coating. He scores a two-pointer as that container joins the first in the trash. Taking a long sip from his drink, he removes the final doggie bag and opens it slowly, hoping for the best, fearing the worst.

So far so good, no alien life forms.

He takes a tentative whiff and cocks his head at the lack of rancid odor.

Hmm.... Wonder how long <u>this</u> has been residing in my fridge?

Unable to recollect, he closes the door, takes another sip of his drink before placing it on the counter, and puts the food, holder and all, in the microwave.

Nuking it should kill enough of the bacteria....

When the buzzer sounds, he retrieves his meal and returns to the sofa where he flips on the television. He lowers the volume, creating ambient background noise so he won't feel alone, and pokes at his leftover meatloaf and mashed potatoes. Having lost his appetite, he pushes the plate to the side, gets up, leaves the uneaten food on the table in true bachelor fashion, and pours himself a third drink.

This is the last one. Needed to freshen this drink since the ice cubes melted and diluted the last one.

He sighs and returns to the sofa where he slumps.

My drinking doesn't affect my life. No one has to know.

No sooner does his rear connect with the cushions than a barrage of thoughts bursts through the dam of his psyche.

Alexander asked why I'm drawn to Sally. Well, let's see. She's like me. We're kindred spirits—drawn to one another by forces outside our control. We understand each other, can empathize with the other's pain and speak the same language of broken souls.

He marvels how, although his youth had been straight out of a fairy tale up until the deaths of his parents, his final childhood years had left him disemboweled and forever altered just as Sally's abusive and troubled youth had with her.

I feel like a knight in shining armor riding in on my white steed to save the day. Sally is my damsel in distress.

James recalls how he had learned early on, in the orphanage, that if he busied himself with helping others eradicate their troubles, then he could avoid being affected by his own. Of course, that had only lasted so long. Eventually, his memories of the horrible accident began to spread through every fiber of his being like a malignant cancer cannibalizing his mind.

* * * * *

As his thoughts screamed their way into his childhood, he remembered leaning forward and hearing his father cry out just as he spotted the headlights of the oncoming vehicle directly in front of them. His father swerved severely at the last second in an attempt to avoid hitting the other car, but their bumpers clipped, sending his family's car careening off the highway onto the soft shoulder. The moment the tires hit the sand, the car flipped and rolled—once, twice, three times—before slamming into a retaining wall.

No one had been wearing seatbelts.... James remembered the blood—it was everywhere. He could still hear his mother screaming his father's name over and over, receiving no response. It was then that he noticed his father. The car had landed upright and he was slumped over the steering wheel like some macabre marionette at rest, doused in blood.

James remembered the smell of gasoline and could still feel the heat of the flames as they seared upholstery, clothing, flesh and hair indiscriminately. The shrill animalistic screaming that had filled the car still rang in his ears. None of them could escape. The doors were crushed in, the windows closed. He remembered feeling like he was sealed into the center of a volcano, flames burning his family and him alive.

Suddenly, he heard animated voices coming from outside, heard the whining crunch of metal being forced and then felt hands reaching in to extricate him from the inferno. The memories ended abruptly when he blacked out.

* * * * *

James winces at the memory and subconsciously traces his fingers over the scars on his chest and thighs. He thoughtfully inspects the contents of his glass, swirls the ice and takes another gulp. Setting his glass down, he rubs his temples in an attempt to mollify the throbbing in his head. A merciless parade of queries marches through his mind, invading every hidden recess. He leans back on the sofa and attempts to stifle them by squinting his eyes shut tight. His effort is fruitless, however, and he surrenders to his mind's relentless cryptic interrogation.

Sally doesn't like to face her pain any more than I do. And yet, bravely, she has forged ahead while I....

James reclines on the sofa and allows himself to be enveloped by the deep pillows.

Sally and I have quirks and vices. She enshrouds herself in a tough-girl facade, while I go to extremes to impress others. I'm so proud of her. She's learning how to remove her barriers and deal with her triggers. Perhaps I'm drawn to this like-minded creature so that I can save her. Who knows—it's conceivable that by rescuing her, I can extricate myself from my own demons.

He drains the contents of his glass and looks mournfully at the bottom of his empty tumbler. Exhaling heavily, he sets it on the table beside the remains of his dinner and heads to bed.

The following morning he drags himself out of bed when his alarm invades his slumber and passes through the living room on his way to the kitchen for some tea. Pausing, he takes note of the bleak décor and allows himself to view it as Sally might.

What does my place say about me?

He shakes his head.

My life is a mediocre existence at best.

He scrutinizes the room with a judgmental eye.

Track lights might warm the place up.

Catching sight of the time, he forgets about decorating and hurries to make tea. He spies the tequila bottle.

No need to start drinking now. A hot mug of tea will help relax me.

He goes to the cupboard where he rummages around for his favorite travel mug.

Reluctantly turning away from the tequila that calmed him last night, he pours heated water into his mug, adds an Earl Grey teabag, one level spoonful of sugar and a splash of milk, and heads out the door.

It's not like I'm an alcoholic, just sometimes....

Making the short drive, he arrives a few minutes early to his 6:00 AM yoga class, where he drains the last of his tea before going in.

In class, James' mind is cluttered with an incessant chatter of static about Sally.

Just let me get through my asanas in peace—please.

He progresses through a series of yoga stretching positions beginning with the Bridge Pose, working his way through the Sleeping Vishnu, the Flying Crow and then the One-Legged King Pigeon poses. Focusing on the relaxing postures, his mind begins to relent and grant him sanctuary from its interminable niggling.

James enjoys the de-stressing effects of his class and heads to work an hour later feeling relaxed and able to face the day. He drops his coat and briefcase in his office before hurrying down the hall. He stands just outside the door and sighs before knocking. A muffled "Enter" is heard from within.

James infiltrates the room and smiles warmly at the stately middle-aged woman sitting behind the desk. She is of Indian descent, has aquamarine eyes and a mane of wavy jet-black hair that hangs loosely, framing her olive-toned face with its flawless complexion. "Hello, Dr. Stykes," James offers.

The woman looks up, a smile warming her face as she recognizes her patient and fellow colleague. She motions to a chair across from her. "Please, have a seat, Dr. Whitmore," she says in a soft-spoken voice.

James closes the door, crosses the room and takes a seat in the proffered Queen Anne-style chair. Dr. Stykes closes the file she had been reading. "So, how have you been?"

"All right, I guess."

"Well, which is it? You're all right, or you think you're all right?" Dr. Stykes asks, pushing her glasses farther up the bridge of her nose.

James glances off the side before answering, "Well, I've been a little troubled since last we spoke,"

"About what?"

"Why I'm intent to pursue a relationship with an ex-patient of mine."

Dr. Stykes shifts in her seat. "You're referring to Sally?"

"Yes."

"It's good you've been thinking about it. What conclusions have you come to?"

"Unsettling ones, I'm afraid. I believe I've fallen in love with her. I think the triangle is at work here."

Dr. Stykes replies, "Ah, the triangle. We psychiatrists know it well."

James shakes his head. "Perhaps a little too well. I put it into action, by rushing in to save others, so often that I actually end up enabling them."

"Why do you suppose you do that?"

"So that I'll feel needed. It always backfires, though."

"How so?"

"Those I help eventually tire of being rescued and push me away. How many of my relationships has the triangle ended?" James grunts a disgusted chuckle before continuing. "There's something different about Sally, though. I'm not drawn to her for her weaknesses, but her strength. Not sure if she's cognizant of her own intestinal fortitude. I am. It shines like a beacon—calling to me—drawing me in."

Dr. Stykes laces her fingers together and raises both index fingers like a church steeple. "Hmm, why do you suppose her strength appeals to you?"

James, not wanting to reveal his own hidden troubles, lies, "I'm not exactly sure."

Dr. Stykes looks across her desk at him. "Then I suppose that you'll need to do some more soul searching."

"I know. I've got to be careful with my decision. I could lose everything by pursuing her. Am I prepared to risk all? What if I do, only to discover that it's nothing more than a transference infatuation on her behalf...or perhaps mine?"

"Do you think it could be?"

James rubs the back of his fingers of one hand with those of the other and contemplates the doctor's question before responding. "I don't think so, but maybe. Too soon to tell."

Dr. Stykes looks at the pocket-sized clock on her desk. "You'll need to enter this relationship with your eyes wide open and be aware of warning signs that would indicate if it isn't healthy for one or the other of you." Dr. Stykes rises, indicting that the session is over and, smiling, offers him a parting thought, "Take it slow and you'll be fine."

CHAPTER 25

James awakes on the one-month anniversary of Sally's graduation from the drug rehabilitation center both euphoric and as nervous as a teenager preparing to ask a girl to a dance. He readies himself for work and then calls Sally in the hopes that he can catch her before she might have to leave. As the phone rings on the other end, he breaks out in a cold sweat.

What if she doesn't remember me? What if she's a mess, back on crack or her feelings for me amount to nothing?

Each unanswered ring is an interminable test to his tenacity.

Can't believe the rollercoaster ride I've been on for the last month.

Sally picks up on the fourth ring. "Hello?"

The sound of her voice washes over him like a warm spring breeze. "Hello, Sally. This is Dr. Whitmore...I...I mean, James from the rehab center."

Sally responds without a moment's hesitation. "Hey, James. Glad you called."

"How are you doing?"

He can hear Sally's smile as she replies, "Great! Haven't used since before I checked into the center. There were times I was tempted, but then one of your goofy quotes would pop into my head, and I'd tough it out."

James, realizing that he's been holding his breath, exhales. "I'm glad. I've been hoping that you were moving forward. Sounds like you have."

"Had a good teacher who taught me to take baby steps, one day at a time and sometimes one fucked-up hour at a time." Her voice trails off. "Thanks."

"No thanks necessary. Your sobriety is enough. Whatever

171

happened with you and your mother? Did you make contact?"

Sally's joy literally dances through the line. "I did. We've worked through a lot of stuff and are having a ball reconnecting."

"That's great! I'm so pleased. I'll bet you're gaining immeasurable strength from your reunion."

"I am. Ma's been awesome."

"That's good." James pauses for a few awkward moments, pacing his living room like a caged animal, while summoning courage to forge ahead. "I was wondering. Are you still interested in being friends?"

Sally's response wraps around him like a warm embrace. "Yeah! I'd like that. Thought about you lots over the past month."

A wide grin spreads across James' face. He stops pacing, does a victory dance and punches the air while whispering, "Yesss!" under his breath.

Sally questions, "Did you say something?"

Panicking, James fibs, "I...I was just saying that I think we could have a good friendship." He takes a deep breath and boldly continues. "You've told me how fond you and Angel are of hiking. Perhaps I could join you sometime?"

"That would be neat. We're planning a hike this weekend. You're more than welcome to join us."

James, not a huge nature enthusiast, but eager to spend time with Sally, brightens at the invitation. "What day?"

"Probably Sunday. That would give us time to get all our chores and errands done. Does that work?"

"Yes, Sunday would be fine."

"Great! Call you later this week, and we can decide when and where to meet. Gotta go to work now."

James' facial muscles, having smiled so broadly for so long, begin to twitch, and he responds, "All right. I look forward to hearing from you."

Sally and Angel pull into the Chantry Flats parking lot where they find James waiting. He gets out of his car and comes to greet them. Looking around, he comments, "This is beautiful."

Angel asks, "Directions okay?"

James offers her a fetching smile. "Yes, very easy to follow." Turning to Princess, he comments, "This must be the famous Princess I've heard so much about."

Beaming like a proud parent, Sally responds, "Yep, this is our baby girl, the most beautiful and smartest dog in the world."

Princess, at the mention of her name, wags her tail. James leans down and rubs her sides.

Sally smiles and remarks, "Well, come on. We can talk while we walk."

They exit the parking lot and begin the steep descent into the canyon. At the bottom of the hill, they cross an antiquated wooden footbridge, spanning free-flowing water, and traverse the valley floor where they pass intermittent cabins frozen in time. Smoke billows from the chimneys of several, while well-attended gardens frame others. They come to a fork in the trail and Sally opts for the one to the left. James asks, "Why this way?"

She looks back at him and comments, "It's a better workout and you can look down on the falls from above."

James grows concerned. "From *above* the falls? We're ascending *higher* than the top of the falls?"

Sally stops and turns to look back at him. "Is there a problem?"

"Well, that all depends on how high up you're planning on taking me. I don't do well with heights."

A devilish smile curls the corners of Sally's mouth, and she teases, "The great Dr. James Whitmore has a fear of heights? Perhaps we should schedule weekly sessions, where I'll take you outside your comfort zone by having you examine and face your fears. You know, like you did with me."

They all laugh, and then James grows serious. "Very funny. But really, how far up are we talking?"

Sally wipes the grin from her face and answers, "Not far."

James notably relaxes and says, "Lead the way, then."

They navigate a series of steep switch-backed narrow trails that are, at places, no more than two feet wide with up to a thousand-foot drop off the edge. James, pale and stressed, makes it to the location where they peer down at the waterfall and its lagoon. He looks at Sally and remarks, "I've got to be frank. Those were the most death-defying trails I've ever hiked. One false step—you're dead."

He directs his attention to Angel. "You know your friend is crazy. I mean, anyone who thinks this is fun has got to be certifiable. Right?"

Angel smirks, "Ain't gonna get me to agree with you. I like hiking these trails."

James lets out a soft laugh, warm and heartfelt. His eyes sparkle with mischief. "Then it's official. I'm surrounded by crazy people."

He looks at Sally. "Tell me, why do you like this?"

She doesn't hesitate before responding, "Because it relaxes me and lets me think about things."

James nods. "Fair enough."

They take in the spectacular view for a bit before turning and heading back. On the valley floor, Princess runs ahead looking for squirrels to chase. The group makes its way back to the steep hill, which they climb to the parking lot. James walks the girls to their car and comments, "That was fun."

Sally jokes, "Even the crazy trails?"

James laughs in spite of himself. "Well, that part I could have done without. Maybe we could admire the falls from the ground next time?"

They girls load Princess and themselves into their truck. Rolling down the window, Sally looks at James. "Give me a call?"

"Will do," he says.

Sally and James' friendship grows. She is determined to create in him the same love of nature that she possesses, while he resolves to broaden her cultural horizons by taking her to museums, art shows and the theater. The two, with such varying tastes in what constitutes good entertainment, do agree, however, on suspenseful movies and watch them often. Encouraged that their friendship is going well, Sally wants to introduce James to her mother, but he contends that it would be better to wait. Sally, disappointed, accedes to his wishes.

Trees with new leaves unfurling in numbers too plentiful to count replace bare winter branches as buds open. The arrival of spring brings signs of new life and birds busying themselves with making nests. Looking out her window, Sally knows that the baby birds leaving their nests will signal the upcoming anniversary of Eric Angel's death.

Although she continues to faithfully see her sponsor and remain drug-free, each passing day that Sally watches the tiny eggs tests her intestinal fortitude to remain sober. On the three-year anniversary of Eric Angel's death and eight months into her sobriety, the eggs begin to reveal their hidden treasures. Each peck of the miniature birds' beaks breaking through their tough shells reminds her of nails being hammered into a coffin—Eric Angel's. She calls her sponsor and arranges to get together to talk.

Sally arrives at the coffee shop a few minutes late and finds Claire already seated sipping a hot beverage. As she approaches the table, she notes her sponsor's aristocratic features: pale skin, high cheekbones and dirty blonde hair pulled back into a ponytail. Concern-filled hazel-green eyes greet her. "Hi, Sally. Everything all right? You seemed upset on the phone."

"Yeah...well, not really. Give me a minute to order and then we can talk." She goes to the counter to place her order and waits for her drink. Adding a packet of sugar and some cream, she returns to the table. She tells Claire about the baby birds heralding the anniversary of Eric Angel's death. She looks across the table at the woman who has been where she is, can empathize with her pain and has been her rock. She confesses, "Don't know if I can resist the urge to use."

Claire's face is filled with compassion. "Have I mentioned how proud I am of you?"

Sally's face wrinkles up in confusion, and she asks, "For what?"

"For doing so well with your recovery. Believe me. I know it hasn't been easy. I'm proud of your courage."

Sally smiles demurely.

"You're considering using again. Why?"

"Feel like I've had a handle on this, up until recently. But when that damned mother bird began making her nest outside my window, I don't know. Each passing day, I'd think about crack more and more, until I was practically thinking of it every waking moment of every miserable day. I want to numb the pain of Eric Angel's death so badly. It's eating me alive. And when I saw the eggs begin to crack...."

"So that's it?" Claire asks. "You want to get high and throw away everything?"

Sally exhales, takes a sip of her coffee and slumps in her chair. In an act of defeat, she throws her hands in the air and states, "Yes! I want to get fucking high and screw up everything I've worked so hard to overcome. There. Happy? Now, I've said it."

Claire reaches across the table and clasps one of Sally's hands in her own. "No, I'm not happy that you want to use. I am happy that you're here talking with me instead of holed up somewhere getting high." She offers a reassuring smile. "It's a step in the right direction."

Sally looks down at her watch. "Ah, shit! I better get going or I'll be late for work." She drains the last of her coffee and gets up to leave.

Claire mimics her motions and, scrutinizing Sally, asks, "Are you going to be all right? I could drive with you and we can continue talking if you need to."

Sally returns her sponsor's smile and says, "I'll be okay. Thanks for being here."

"No problem. Promise to call after work? We can grab a bite to eat or something. I don't want you to be alone."

Sally agrees. The two part and Sally goes about the rest of her day bolstered by Claire's support. On her drive home, she looks forward to having dinner with Claire.

Arriving home, Sally parks the truck and walks to her front door, feeling the weight of her son's death bear down on her. She spots a plain brown package, her name written upon it, on the doorstep.

Wonder who it's from?

She picks it up and enters the house. Smiling, she tosses her things on the kitchen table and turns the package over in her hands.

Probably from Claire.

She tears the wrapper off the box and opens it. Suddenly pale, she sits down heavily. Her hands shake and she drops the box, causing its contents to spill onto the table. There, before her, is a brand new pipe and enough crack for a three-day binge. Sally gets up and begins pacing. Thoughts rapid-fire their way around her head, colliding into one another like careening bumper cars.

What the hell?! Is this a sick joke? Who would send this to me?

Sally, unable to move, stares at the opened package and its strewn contents. Thoughts of her dead son overwhelm her tormented mind. After what seems like an eternity, she gathers up the box, its contents and heads out the door.

Sally, haggard-looking, finds Claire already seated at a table, nursing a frozen margarita, when she arrives. Sally orders her own and downs nearly half of it in a single gulp, plagued with sudden brain freeze.

Looking on, Claire's voice is tinged with concern. "What's wrong?"

Sally tells Claire about the package. Both discuss who would have done such a hateful thing. Claire questions, "Where's it now?"

"In my car. Didn't want to leave it at home."

Claire assures Sally that she has done the right thing and suggests that they stage an immediate intervention-of-sorts with her mother, Angel and James. Sally agrees to the meeting. She and Claire pay their tab and then leave the restaurant without eating. They drive to the nearest isolated dumpster where they toss Sally's mystery package. Next, Sally drives while Claire calls the others to set up a meeting.

In her living room later that evening, Sally sits surrounded by her mother, James, Angel and Claire, who takes the floor. "I suggested this meeting so that we could all understand what's happened, voice any sentiments each of us might have and offer our support. I'd like to start. Then I'll open the floor to each of you. Is that agreeable?" Claire looks around and is answered by a unanimous show of nodding heads.

She fills the group in on the appearance of the mystery package.

There's a general disruption as everyone questions who would have done such a hateful thing. Claire regains control and directs her attention to Sally. "I'd like you to express what you were experiencing when you opened the box."

Sally takes a deep breath before responding, "It felt like my head was an overactive pinball machine. Thoughts of Eric Angel's death swirling everywhere." She winces when his name leaves her lips. "Fighting the pain for so long, I felt burned out—rubberized. And then that damned package appeared. Can't imagine it coming at a worse time. I was desperate to numb my sorrow."

Claire's response is measured. "But you didn't." She turns her attention to the others. "At this time, I'd like to open the floor for each of you to let Sally know how her using affects each of you. We can start with Gloria."

Gloria wrinkles her brow and wipes away the tears that have fallen down her cheeks. She turns to look at her daughter. "Sally, it breaks my heart to see you in so much pain. I wish I could have been there all along to help you—perhaps things would have turned out different."

Sally crosses the room to sit next to her mother and, choking on her words, says, "Ma, don't. I'm so sorry for dragging you into this mess." She wraps her arms around her mother.

Gloria embraces and pulls her in close. Both sit sobbing for a bit. Sally melts against her mother's bosom, comforted by the beating of her heart.

Claire continues officiating. "Angel, what does seeing your friend like this do to you?"

Angel, normally not one for public displays of emotion, is reduced to tears. She faces her friend and says, "Ah, Sally girl. How you look when you're on a high or bingeing...it tears me apart. You're a different person. Paranoid, lost, fragile—not the Sally I know and love. I feel so helpless.... You promised you'd reach out to me instead of that damned crack pipe. Never have. Why won't you?"

Sally gets up and goes to sit next to her lifelong friend. Looking sincerely into her eyes, she responds, "Want to, but can't."

Angel's words catch in her throat. "Why not?"

Sally responds, not wanting to hurt her friend, but knowing that she must be honest. "The pull of the drug.... It's not that I don't love you or appreciate all that you've done—all the times you've been there to pick up the broken pieces of me. I hate it every time. No, I hate myself for putting you through that. I'm sorry."

Both girls embrace and, forgetting those around them, sob unabashedly, their bodies wracked by their bawling. It takes a while, but they expel all of their emotion-filled tears.

Claire turns to James and asks, "How does it make you feel to see Sally like this?"

He leans forward and gazes in Sally's eyes. "Unlike your mother and Angel, I have seen the destructive path crack paves many times in my profession, but never have I been so affected by its wake. Never before have I had to watch someone I am close to self-destruct. Although we've only been friends for seven months, I feel as though I've known you forever. We're so similar. I can offer support, but cannot do this for you. I believe in you. According to Blaise Pascal, 'The strength of a man's virtue should not be measured by his special exertions, but by his habitual acts.' I'm willing to stand by your side and help you create a pattern of healthy behavior."

Angel, Gloria, James and Claire express to Sally how pleased they are that she resisted the urge to use, and that they are willing to support her rehabilitation. Sally, overcome with emotion and relief, goes to James and folds herself against him. In a voice barely audible, she whispers, "I don't deserve you or your acceptance, but am grateful for both."

CHAPTER 26

Over the course of the next four months, Sally remains sober with a vengeance. Always at the back of her mind is the niggling question, *"Who sent me that package? And why?"* Her mother, Angel, Claire and James remain steadfast in their support and she is honest with them, confessing when things become overwhelming instead of trying to internalize her feelings. Her friendship with James continues to deepen with every passing day. He becomes a base rock in her newly formed foundation, and she gains immeasurable strength from seeing him often.

On a clear day, five months after the anniversary of her son's death, James places a call to Sally, where they talk about everything and nothing all at the same time, as is oft the case. Suddenly, there's an uncomfortable pause on the line as James tries to decide how to proceed.

Just do it, man—ask her.

"Ah…Sally…I was wondering."

"Yeah?"

"I've enjoyed our friendship over the past year."

He can hear the smile in her voice when she responds, "Me, too."

"When we went on that date we seemed to have pretty strong feelings for one another. I was wondering if…well…do you still have any of those feelings?" He rushes on, not wanting to sound desperate. "Of course, I'd completely understand if you didn't. I'd be perfectly content maintaining our friendship as is."

Sally's voice jumps through the line full of enthusiasm and affection. "I've got feelings for you, too. I talk about you constantly to my mother, Angel and Claire. Think they're sick of hearing about you. You're definitely under my skin."

James, his heart beating uncontrollably, takes a deep cleansing breath in an attempt to gain courage. "So, you'd be agreeable to go out with me…on a real date?"

"Of course, but only if you agree to kiss me every time you consider quoting one of your damn sayings."

James chuckles—warm and seductive. "Agreed. How about tonight?"

"That would be great!"

"Seven o'clock?"

"I'll be ready. Sushi again?"

Wow! She remembers.

James laughs, "I can't believe you remember we had sushi last time."

Sally's voice is sultry when she responds, "Some things are worth remembering."

On the inside, James is doing backhand springs. His good mood resonates through the phone. "Sushi it is."

Immediately after hanging up, Sally's phone rings. Thinking it might be James, she picks up. "Miss me already?"

Her mother's voice comes through the line, "What?"

Sally laughs softly. "Oh, hey, Ma. Thought you were James."

Gloria feigns mock hurt feelings. "Well, I can hang up if you don't want to talk with me."

"Don't be silly. I've got amazing news to share! Wait 'til you hear." She proceeds to chatter about James' call and their decision to take their relationship to the next level.

That evening, James and Sally return to the quaint sushi restaurant they had dined at on their first date. They leisurely enjoy the other's company, slurp miso soup, eat edamame and enjoy the artistically cut sushi rolls they order. Towards the end of the meal, Sally says, "I'd like you to get a chance to get to know my mother and she you. How would you feel about me setting that up?"

James thinks for a minute before answering, "Well, seeing as we have decided to take the next step in our relationship, I imagine it's only natural. Sure. Go ahead and set it up."

Sally calls her mother the next day and schedules an afternoon at Descanso Gardens in La Canada where the three of them amble across crushed gravel pathways and paved avenues lined with trees adorned in a colorful palette of fall colors. They wind their way through lush gardens, under arbors canopied with blooming rose vines and past ponds teaming with fauna and flora.

The threesome traverses a crushed clay path. As bits of red clay crunch under their feet, Gloria smiles. James and Sally's fingers are interlaced. "James, my daughter tells me the two of you met at the facility. You were her doctor?"

"That's right. I never would have believed that's where I would meet my soul mate."

"I guess there are stranger places to meet one's partner," Gloria says.

Around them, the air is perfumed with the scent of thousands of blooming roses. Sally stops to appreciate a magnificent crimson-red Mr. Lincoln. She leans over and gently cups her hand behind the flower, closes her eyes and inhales deeply—a smile of contentment spreads across her face. Sally straightens and, enchanted by the man who stands before her, is filled with love and admiration. She wraps her arms around James, placing an affectionate kiss on his lips.

From behind, Gloria grins while remarking, "You're a special man, James. You have the heart of my daughter. She's lucky to have found you and that you accept all that she has been through."

James counters, "It is I who am the lucky one, to have someone so full of integrity. In my profession, I have often found that those who have no vices are lacking in virtue. Sally has made a choice. She is wiser."

The three head back to the parking lot. Sally and James bid farewell to Gloria, then get in the car so James can drive her home. On the way, Sally turns in her seat to face him. "Well, what do you think? That wasn't so horrible, was it?"

James shoots her a quick glance, a smile upon his face. "No. I enjoyed getting to know your mother. She's very compassionate."

Sally says, "I'm lucky that she has accepted me despite all I've done." She faces forward, and they drive in silence for a bit.

A short time later, she turns back to face James. "Something's been bugging me."

James takes his eyes off the road momentarily to look at her. "What?"

She takes a deep breath before continuing. "If I didn't know better, I'd think you were trying to avoid having me see your place."

"That's not true."

"Really? Why is it every time I come to pick you up, you meet me at the gate instead of having me come in?"

"I don't know. Thought it was easier that way." He pretends annoyance. "Pardon me for trying to be considerate."

Sally's voice takes on a singsong quality. "A-void-ing."

James grows defensive. "I am not. And to prove it, I'll take you there now."

"Really?" Sally teases. "Are you sure you don't need to call in a toxic clean-up crew first?"

"Ha! Ha! Very funny."

They arrive at James' place a short time later, where Sally stands in the middle of his living room scrutinizing his sterile environment: the almost bare walls, slip-covered sofa and pulled drapes all washed out by harsh lighting. "Wow."

"What? I'm a bachelor and like to live simply."

Sally does not respond.

James tries to defend his living space. "If you think this is bad, you should have seen where I lived when I was in college. It was decorated in modern beer cans and pizza boxes—some of them not even empty." He smiles fondly at the memory and laughs. "Of course, that made finding something to eat or drink so much easier."

Sally's eyes widen a bit, and her face contorts into a grimace. "Well...then...I guess this is an improvement." She looks around, a mischievous smirk on her face. "Frat boy décor to modern mental institution. Who's your decorator?"

James laughs. "Now, that's just plain mean."

Sally raises an eyebrow. "It could be worse. You could be a thirty-year-old bachelor still living with his mother."

James grins playfully. "Okay, now you've cut me to the bone. See if I ever bring you back here again."

"Now, don't go getting all worked up. I'm just kidding. You know I'm kidding—right?"

James winks at her. "Yeah. Got that."

He tells Sally of his plans to spruce up the place, and she listens intently while watching the light play with the caramel specks in his eyes. Looking around the room, she spies pictures poking out from behind the sofa. She crosses the room and pulls them out. Holding first one and then the other at arm's length, her gaze falls upon the two dramatic black and white photos. "James, these are beautiful. Where did you get them?"

He answers nonchalantly, "On one of my trips abroad."

One depicts a sprawling English countryside with ancient stacked rock walls that hug the curve of the land and are covered with a thick layer of lichen. The other captures historic buildings lining the waterways of Amsterdam. Sally leans them against the back of the sofa and stands back to admire them. "You should hang these. They're too nice to have hidden."

"I plan to." He playfully winks at her. "Now that I'm not afraid to show you my place, perhaps you'd like to come over this weekend and help me."

Sally smiles. "I'd love to."

That weekend, she and James take on the task of warming up his place. They paint the walls an inviting tan and install track lighting that they use to highlight his European black and white photos now prominently hung. While redecorating, they have fun sneaking up on one another to dot wet paint on each other's noses and paint love notes on the walls before painting over them. They giggle and laugh their way through the endeavor. When done, they stand back, covered in paint, arms around the other's waist, pleased with their handiwork.

Sally sits in her mother's kitchen sipping coffee. "So, Ma, what did you think of James?"

"I like him," Gloria answers. Tiny smile lines frame her eyes. "You're fortunate to have found a man as loving and gentle as he appears to be. It's obvious that he adores you."

Sally blushes and giggles like a schoolgirl. "He is amazing! I can't believe that he's stood by me." She grows reflective. "I'm falling in love with him."

"Be careful. Listen to what your heart tells you, but be willing to listen to any truths your mind reveals. Don't allow love to make you blind." The intensity of Gloria's gaze penetrates Sally to her core.

Sally, understanding the implications of her mother's words, hugs her and responds, "I won't, Ma. I'll keep my eyes wide open. Promise."

CHAPTER 27

Over the next two months, Sally and James become almost inseparable. They attend the theater, go to art exhibits and hike the local mountains. One day, while they are hiking Chantry Flats, Princess pulls on her leash and Sally releases her.

Princess runs from one plant and tree to another until she locks on the scent she is looking for—a squirrel. She follows the odor that leads her right to her prey, which is hiding under heavy underbrush.

Flushed out, the squirrel takes off, running for its life towards the nearest tree. Princess, hot on its trail, snaps and barks enthusiastically. She narrowly misses catching a bit of its tail, as it makes a desperate leap for the nearest tree—a sapling with flimsy branches. The squirrel jumps from one branch to another in an attempt to locate one strong enough to hold its weight. Princess, having worked herself into a frenzy, tracks it from beneath. Sally and James look on and hold their breath.

The squirrel, realizing the tiny branches offer little safety, makes an Evel Knievel death-defying leap through the air. Princess follows below as it sails through the air. When it hits the ground, the squirrel takes off running just in front of Princess. Escaping, it scurries up the nearest towering trunk. Princess stands on her hind legs and stretches the length of her body up the tree. Wagging her tail, she barks wildly. The squirrel turns—ten feet up the tree—and faces its predator.

It chatters angrily as if to say, how dare you chase me. Who do you think you are? Ha! Think you're so good. Look who's laughing now. It does a victory dance and swishes its bushy tail before climbing higher.

Sally and James are nearly beside themselves, wracked with laughter. Princess barks as if to reply, come back down here and say that to my face, you little fleabag. I dare you!

Sally whistles to Princess. "Come on, girl. It got away fair and square."

Princess barks at the escapee then turns and returns to Sally, who reaches down and pets her. While clipping on her leash, she notices the distant look in James' eyes. "Penny for your thoughts," she says.

James looks at her. "I was thinking how similar you and that squirrel are."

Sally laughs, soft and easy. "So, now I'm a squirrel? How so?"

"The squirrel represents you. Chased and oppressed by evil forces, you draw upon your inner strength and turn to confront your persecutor in an attempt to gain control of your life." James pauses for a minute, smiling at Sally before continuing. "In the beginning, that's what attracted me to you. Your inner strength. I was impressed that in the most trying of circumstances, you never gave up. You run, but only to allow yourself extra time to call upon your reserves and fight back."

Sally looks up and searches his eyes. "You think I have inner strength?"

"I *know* you do."

Soon, Christmas lights adorn houses, carolers stroll the boulevards and people frantically rush to complete their holiday shopping. James is among them but takes a break from his hectic schedule to have dinner with Alexander. They choose a local Italian restaurant and are seated at a rear table. Soft music plays in the background and the clinking of glasses can be heard. The ambient noise of diners enjoying each other's company fills the air.

Over the course of their meal, James shares with Alexander how his feelings for Sally have grown and that he is thinking of proposing. Alexander stops eating and looks at his friend. "Are you sure? Have you thought this through? You've only been dating a few months."

James takes a sip of wine. "I know. But I feel as though I've known Sally all my life. She's my rosebush."

Alexander raises an eyebrow.

James continues, "When I first met her, she was a bare bush of twigs with a multitude of thorns placed around her as a shield of protection. As time wore on, she sprouted leaves of new life, followed by buds of hope."

"A rosebush. Really? Is that the analogy you want to use?"

"Yes," James responds, undeterred. "As I nurtured her and tended to her broken self, her petals began to unfurl. Her once-prominent thorns no longer stood out, replaced by the beautiful bloom emerging. Once she felt safe enough to open up, her beauty became resplendent and irresistible."

"Have you thought this through? Unique and challenging obstacles might accompany a relationship with her."

"I'm aware of that. I also know that some roses are short-lived. Sally may be one of them. I'd rather risk getting pricked by her thorns than to not appreciate her beauty."

Alexander pushes his plate away and places his folded napkin on the table. "It just seems so…soon."

James grows serious. "Perhaps the tragedy of losing my parents can be transformed into joy after all these years."

"What?"

"Losing them taught me to savor every moment of a meaningful relationship. One never knows when it might end."

"I couldn't agree more, but don't you think it would be more prudent to slow things down a bit?"

"Perhaps. But I'm not going to."

"Why not?"

James chuckles. "The best way I can answer that is with a quote."

Alexander rolls his eyes. "You and your quotes."

James ignores him and proceeds. "Franklin P. Jones said, 'Love doesn't make the world go round. Love is what makes the ride worthwhile.'"

"Good Lord! What are we going to do with you?"

James looks at his friend and laughs. "I'm going to propose to Sally and enjoy the ride. I know you have your doubts, but I'd like you to stand by my side as my best man after she says, 'yes.'"

Alexander shakes his head. "You mean *if* she says, 'yes.' Hopefully she's got enough good sense to see what a pompous windbag you are."

Just after the holidays, James and Sally hike through the Los Angeles Arboretum in Arcadia. They wind their way through pathways lined with an abundance of plants. Trees once robed in colorful foliage now stand naked against the brisk winter sky. A few straggling geese mill at the waterways and peacocks randomly display their colorful tail plumage. The couple walks hand in hand, circling the lake in front of Queen Anne's Cottage. James motions for Sally to sit on a bench. He looks down at her, noticing how the sunlight dances across her face and sparkles within her eyes.

"Sally, you once told me that you didn't know what you did right or who to thank for having put me in your life. Now, it is I who must say the same to you. You make my life complete. Your smile warms my heart. My life shines brighter for you being a part of it. And your compassion warms my soul." Their eyes meet. He kneels on one knee and takes each of her hands in his own. His eyes never leave hers. "You are the soul mate I've been searching for my entire life, Sally McFee. You complete my life. Because of you, I awake every day wanting to be a better person—for you. I would be honored if you would do me the honor of becoming my wife and allow me to spend the remainder of my days attempting to make you as happy and fulfilled as you have made me."

Sally's chest heaves with the greatest joy. She looks at the man before her, still unable to comprehend the amazing good fortune that brought him to her. Her eyes glisten with tears, her face erupts in a broad smile and she replies, "Yes! Of course I'll marry you!" as she throws her arms around his neck.

He rises to his feet and they embrace and share a passionate kiss before an audience of peacocks, geese and ducks.

Sally shares her good news with her mother, who offers her back yard for the ceremony and with Angel, whom she asks to be her maid of honor. Next, she calls Luigi and Mama Pearl to share her news with them. Luigi is overcome with emotion when she asks him to give her away. Finally, Sally places calls to Cinnamon, Honey and Jasper. All squeal with delight at her happy news.

On a beautiful day in early May, James stands, prepared to take his wedding vows in Gloria's back yard. An arbor, adorned with yellow daisies in honor of Eric Angel, arches over him. Alexander is by his side. An intimate ceremony—only a few of the bride and groom's closest friends and family are present. As a gentle breeze picks up, leaves of dark crimson, bright orange and warm yellow gently rain down upon the guests, who rise at the beginning of the Wedding March.

The back door opens, revealing Sally standing resplendent in her wedding gown, holding Luigi's arm. She sees James and beams a radiant smile. The love the two share is palpable in the air.

James watches as Luigi escorts his bride-to-be towards him. He sees her beautiful hourglass figure with its tiny waist accentuated by her flowing gown. The sunlight plays on her auburn hair that flows freely, cascading over her shoulders in soft waves. As she draws closer to him, he sees her porcelain doll face, with its sprinkling of freckles across her nose and cheeks like those of a little girl whose skin has been kissed by the summer sun. Her brilliant iridescent green eyes never waver—locked on his. Sally and James' eyes shine with the hopes and dreams of a brilliant future together.

As Sally approaches her soon-to-be-husband, her gaze falls upon the familiar faces in the audience: Mama Pearl, Honey, Cinnamon, Jasper, Nadine and, of course, her mother. As she passes each, her heart swells with unbridled rapture, and she gives Luigi's arm a loving squeeze. Although she told herself she wouldn't cry, tears of joy leak from her eyes. Luigi leads her to stand beside James. Gently lifting her veil, he places a fatherly kiss upon her cheek and whispers, "I'm so proud of you. Be happy!"

Sally hands Angel her bouquet. Their eyes lock and they cup one another's hands. A thousand unspoken words pass between them. Both have tears in their eyes. Princess, who is sitting beside Angel, lets out a joyful series of barks. Sally laughs and bends down to pat her faithful companion.

That night after making love, Sally lays in bed contentedly, her husband curled around her. Princess yips and runs in her sleep, presumably chasing squirrels. James kisses the top of Sally's head and whispers, "Good night, Mrs. Whitmore."

Before closing her eyes and drifting off to sleep, a smile warms Sally's face. "Good night, my husband."

* * * * *

The ocean of red rises and falls rhythmically. Enormous waves, which began as the slightest hint of a ripple on the water's surface, gather momentum. As each grows in intensity, Sally spies a lone figure just behind the swells—struggling, fighting. She dives into the surf and swims frantically, unaware of the pain each new wave causes as it crashes over her. She cries out to the figure but is unheard. Although her body aches from fighting nature's forces, she is desperate to get to the individual—to save him. No matter her effort, he remains just outside her reach.

* * * * *

Sally awakes in a pool of sweat. Her mind is a jumble of fragmented images.

One of my dreams? Of all nights.... Why now?

Although she knows it is useless, she tries to reconstruct the fractured components of her vision.

The ocean. It was red. So much pain—blinding pain. Someone needed me...no...I needed to reach someone...to save them. Is this about my brother—Eric? I couldn't save him. Why was the water red? Red water—all around—it surrounded me, engulfed me.

Sally's head pounds with the onset of a headache. She looks at James who is asleep by her side.

What does it mean? What next? God, what next? Just let me be happy—pleeease. No more pain.

She lies down and closes her eyes, hoping the images she has seen will not materialize.

CHAPTER 28

Sally and James settle into married life relatively easily. They learn the trials and tribulations of what it means to give oneself to another for better or worse, and enjoy getting to know the intricacies and idiosyncrasies of living with one another. James learns that Sally never screws the cap back on the tube of toothpaste, while Sally realizes that her husband doesn't seem to notice the globs of toothpaste he leaves behind in the sink basin. They learn how to compromise on their bigger differences while laughing at the smaller ones.

Five months into their marriage, James takes advantage of a relatively new convenience. On his way home from work, he decides to stop at an ATM to get some spending cash for their dinner date that evening. After getting the money, he marvels at how times are changing and the relative ease with which things are being made available to people. Smiling to himself, he heads to his car. He hears, from behind him, a sudden shuffling of feet. Before he can turn, he feels it—the blinding pain to his skull.

James awakes some time later in the hospital, his head pounding. His face hurts like hell. Sally is there, holding his hand, a concerned look upon her face. "Oh, James. Thank God! I was so worried."

"Wh...where am I?"

"In the hospital. You were mugged."

James reaches up. "My head hurts."

Sally smiles compassionately. "You took quite a blow."

James' brow knits into a furrowed expression. "I vaguely remember being hit." His hand travels to where the side of his face is experiencing a heartbeat of its own. "What's wrong with my face?"

"It was cut."

James struggles to sit up. "What?! How bad?"

"Bad. They called in a facial plastic surgeon, who stitched it up."

"How many?"

"Thirty-seven."

James closes his eyes and flops back on his pillow.

Discharged from the hospital, he returns home, plagued by a recurring nightmare, one where he is repeatedly mugged. His stitches are removed, and in their wake is an angry jagged scar that travels from his left eye down to the corner of his mouth. He attempts to pick up where he left off, and gains strength from his newlywed life.

Drawn by the delightful smells, James stumbles down the stairs into the kitchen. As he rounds the corner, his eyes come to rest upon Sally, who is frying maple bacon and eggs. He leans against the doorway, absorbing the vision of his wife and openly undresses her with his eyes, noting her slight figure, tiny waist and sensuous hips. He smiles, thinking of her voluptuous breasts. He knows they are well rounded beneath her T-shirt. Her auburn hair alluringly cascades down her back to her waist. Aroused, his eyes roam her body noting every curve, dip and canyon. He is intimately familiar with each. His desire mounting, he longs to caress her velvet skin and run his fingers through the silky waves of her hair.

Pushing away from the door jamb, James goes to her and embraces her from behind, whispering in her ear, "Have I told you how beautiful you are?"

Sally allows herself to lean against him. "I'm not beautiful."

"Oh, but you are. You're perfect."

She sighs and turns in his arms, looking up at him. "Perhaps—in your eyes."

Sally looks intently at him. Their gazes lock momentarily, as their lips meet in a passionate kiss. His powerful arms lift her off her feet, backing her up against the refrigerator. She wraps her legs around her husband's waist and trembles. He feverishly kisses her while his hands caress her body, hungry for its treats. She responds, running her fingers through his thick, black hair and wraps her arms and legs more tightly around the musculature of his frame in a desperate attempt to fuse with him. Soon they are in a race to see who can moan the loudest. He lowers her onto the cold kitchen floor. Neither seems to notice its chill as they roll entangled as one on the icy tiles. The sizzling of forgotten frying bacon and eggs can be heard in the background, the smell of burnt food filling the room. When they finish making love, James helps Sally up. Cupping her face in both hands, he looks deep into her eyes and remarks. "You're the most beautiful woman in the world."

Sally smiles but does not respond.

Later that day, Angel jokes with her friend over lunch at a curbside bistro. "So, how's married life? Any hot sex scenes lately?"

"As a matter of fact," Sally begins, the color rising in her cheeks, "we had a rather intense encounter this morning—in the kitchen."

"Really?" Angel chuckles. "That must have been hot."

Sally looks down and pokes at her food, a sigh escaping her. "What the hell's the matter with me, Angel?"

"What do you mean?"

Sally looks up with sorrow-filled eyes. "I've got the world's most perfect husband, a man who adores me and treats me like a queen, but I'm not happy—no, I'm bored."

Angel stops eating and focuses on Sally. "Bored? I'm not following. Why are you bored?"

Sally shakes her head and looks off into the distance. "I don't know. I guess I was so used to living outside the box and on the edge for so long, that this new normal existence seems so...plain...so ordinary." She looks at Angel, troubled. "Do you ever miss our old life? All its weirdness?"

Angel nods. "Sometimes I do. It was a wild ride. Easy to get hooked on that kind of excitement."

Sally looks down and without thinking secures a stray strand of hair behind her ear. "This is all I've ever wanted. Now that I've got it...." Noticing the look on Angel's face, she shakes her head. "Listen to me, I don't know what I'm talking about. Forget I said anything."

She changes the subject. "What time are you coming over for Thanksgiving tomorrow?"

"When do you want me there?"

"How about late morning? We can have a cup of coffee before you help James and me wrestle that unruly-looking bird we've got into the oven."

"Done." Angel motions for the check.

The next day, Angel shows up and lets herself in, calling out as she enters. "Knock, knock, if you two are having wild sex on the kitchen floor, now's a good time to stop."

She enters the kitchen where she finds James, embarrassed and red-faced. "Oh, you heard about that?"

"Yeah. Got all the juicy details from my number one source."

Sally, as if on cue, enters the room. "What juicy details?"

James wraps his arm around her small waist and pulls her close to him. Placing an affectionate kiss on her cheek, he states, "Apparently, Angel got the details of our lovemaking in the kitchen." He continues, his eyes twinkling. "What can I say? With a bride this beautiful, I just can't keep my hands off her."

Angel responds, "Ah, how sweet! Do you have any nice handsome friends?"

Shaking his head, James grins broadly. "Nope, I'm a one-of-a-kind, the last of the old-school chivalrous men."

Angel lets out a disappointed sigh. "Guess I'll just have to settle for hearing about your unbridled sex life through my friend."

The three laugh and begin preparing the food for the day's feast. Princess shadows them in the kitchen, hoping for handouts and is not disappointed. Gloria arrives a few hours later to the aroma of cooking turkey and delicious side dishes that fill the house. Sally washes the yams and then goes to the cupboard where she noisily rummages through cans and jars, unable to find what she is looking for. "Ah, shit! I forgot orange marmalade." Shooting a glance at the wall clock, she adds, "I have just enough time to run to the store before they close."

James offers, "I'll go."

Sally grabs her keys. "That's okay." Walking past him, she gives him a chaste kiss on the cheek. "I'll be back before you know it."

"Don't leave me alone too long with these gorgeous Venuses, James says. "Who knows what might happen?" He winks at Angel and his mother-in-law. They beam.

Gloria and Angel crack jokes with and enjoy James' company while setting the table. Once finished, it looks as if Martha Stewart herself has done the deed. James compliments them on the beautiful setting, then checks his watch and comments. "Wonder what's taking Sally so long?"

Sally arrives at the market and heads straight for the aisle with the marmalade. She locates the spot where it should be. It is empty.

Damn! They're out.

She checks her watch while heading back to the car.

I should make it.

She drives the short distance to the next nearest superstore and, arriving just prior to their closing, is able to secure the item she seeks. She heads to the front of the store and finds herself amongst the traffic jam of other last-minute shoppers. Choosing a line, she settles in behind a man to wait....

When the timer rings, indicating that the turkey is done, Angel, Gloria and James busy themselves with taking the bird out of the oven and adding side dishes to be heated. Just as the last dish is being placed in the oven, Sally returns. Upon entering the house, she is drawn in by the irresistible smells of cooked turkey and delicious accompanying dishes. She hurries to the kitchen and whips together her candied yams in the electric skillet.

Thirty minutes later, the kitchen becomes a flurry of activity. The women pull steaming food items from the oven and transfer them to ornate serving dishes to be placed on the table—Sally's yams amongst them. James proudly places the golden turkey to a serving platter and parades it into the dining room.

After every one is seated, James clears his throat and says, "Since this is our first Thanksgiving, I would like to continue with a tradition that I loved while at the orphanage." He thoughtfully looks around the table. "Before we ate, we would go around the table, each of us stating what we were grateful for."

Gloria beams at her son-in-law. "How sweet. I think that's a great tradition. I would like to start." She looks first at James and then at Sally. "I'm thankful that my daughter is back in my life, and that I have a wonderful son-in-law."

To her right, Angel says, "I'm grateful that my life seems to be headed on the right track now, that I'm free of Ax and can live a more normal life." She looks expectantly at Sally.

"I'm thankful that I've reconnected with my mother, have found the man of my dreams, haven't managed to alienate my best friend," she winks at Angel, "and that I'm managing to stay drug-free, despite anonymous people trying to trip me up."

James looks thoughtfully at her. "I'm grateful to be surrounded by the people who mean the most to me—my family."

Having said his piece, he stands to carve the turkey. The minute the knife slices through the perfectly bronzed skin, tiny rivulets of juice cascade down the side of the bird. The four enjoy a meaningful meal. Several hours later, they manage to laboriously extricate themselves from their chairs and meander into the living room to enjoy a crackling fire.

Later that evening, after their guests leave, James takes Sally's hand and leads her to the floor in front of the fireplace. He gently lowers her to the plush area rug and makes love with her. After, he spoons Sally from behind and they nestle—entangled as one.

CHAPTER 29

Sally and James host Angel and Gloria to ring in the New Year. Dick Clark can be heard counting down the final ten seconds to 1998 from the television. When the apple drops in Time's Square, signaling the beginning of the New Year, Sally steals a private moment with her husband. "Can't believe we've been married eight months. I'm so lucky to have found you. Don't deserve someone as wonderful as you."

James encases his wife lovingly in his arms, drawing her close. "What are you talking about?"

"You've been so incredible." Sally stands on her tiptoes and places a loving kiss upon his lips.

James looks down at her child-like face and ardently kisses her.

On Valentines Day, Sally prepares a romantic dinner for James and herself. When James enters the house, the air is tinged with their meal cooking. The lights, dimmed low, add to the idyllic setting. James, armed with two-dozen long-stemmed red roses, calls out as he crosses the living room and enters the kitchen. Sally, upon hearing him, turns. Her face livens when he hands her the flowers.

James and Sally become embroiled in a passionate kiss, each taking in the other's enticing taste. Lost in one another, they intertwine as one on the cold kitchen floor. A blanket of rose petals, as if the heavens themselves had opened and rained down the velvety-scented flowers, covers the floor. The petals cling to their naked bodies as Sally and James make love.

Sometime later, they disentangle themselves. The multitude of candles lighting the room have burned down low, each decorated with streaks of melted wax that pools on the table beneath. Sally takes

James' hand and leads him to the beautifully set table. She guides him to his chair, kisses him deeply, and then goes about serving their special meal—a content smile upon her face.

Just prior to her one-year anniversary, Sally sits in her mother's kitchen, fidgeting. Her mother looks over and asks, "Something wrong?"

"No...well.... Not really. I mean...."

"Wanna talk about it?"

Sally hesitates. "Maybe.... I'm.... Well, I'm pregnant."

"Oh, honey, that's excellent news! James must be so excited."

Sally looks down, unable to meet her mother's enthusiastic eyes. "That's the problem. I haven't told him yet."

"Why not? Doesn't he want children?"

"Someday.... I'm not sure how he'll react." She looks up at her mom. "When Ax found out that I was pregnant with Eric Angel, he beat me."

Her mother comes to sit beside Sally and wraps an arm around her shoulders. "James is nothing like Ax. He loves you and will be thrilled."

Sally brightens. "You think?"

"I do."

Sally turns to look at her mother. "How did Daddy react to you being pregnant?"

Her mother scoffs, "That was different."

"How? The two of you were in love and hadn't planned on getting pregnant."

"That's true. But your father could be a selfish violent man. James is a good husband, who adores and supports you. Tell him. You'll see."

Sally and James dine at a restaurant on their one-year anniversary. All through the meal, James is unable to take his eyes off his bride. Halfway through, he asks, "What?"

Sally tries to look innocent.

He puts down his fork and scrutinizes her closely. "There's

something different about you. You're beaming…no, glowing."

Sally reaches across the table and clasps one of his hands in her own. "James, I don't know how to tell you…. Not sure how you'll react." She takes a deep breath and exhales slowly in an attempt to stall. "I'm pregnant."

"What?! When?! How?!"

Sally laughs nervously, unable to read if he is happy or angry. "Well, I could draw you a picture."

James is on his feet and around the table in a blink of an eye. He swoops her up and twirls around the table. Nearby diners eye them. Seeing the broad smile on James' face, Sally relaxes.

Oh, my God! He's happy. He's really happy.

Both cry and laugh. Suddenly, James' face is marked with grave concern. He stops whirling and gently places Sally on her feet. "I shouldn't be doing that. What if I hurt the baby?"

Sally can't help but laugh through her tears. "You can't hurt the baby by spinning me around."

"Really? Are you sure? Do you need to sit down? Is there anything I can get for you? You must be tired."

What a contrast. This is the way I dreamed it would be. Ma was right. James is a good man.

She shudders, remembering Ax's violent reaction to her pregnancy. Shaking off the memory, she takes James' hand and guides him back to the table. "I'm fine. And the baby's fine. Remember, I've done this before."

James' cheeks flush. "That may be, but I haven't."

Sally's smile can be heard through her gentle laugh. "In that case, how about you let me have the baby."

Numb, James responds, "Okay." Regaining his composure, he asks, "When did this happen? How far are you?"

Sally blushes. "This is the third month I've missed my period, so I think it happened on Valentine's Day."

"Weren't you on the pill?"

Her heart skips a beat, as fear clutches it. She meekly replies, "Yes."

James smiles wickedly. "Then I guess, Mrs. Whitmore, that our lovemaking is just too powerful."

Relieved, Sally returns his grin.

Over the next few days, the couple shares their news with friends and family, who express congratulations. James walks around like a proud peacock, displaying his plume of feathers for the world to see. Sally's body settles into being pregnant. By her fifth month, her skin has a warm glow, and she looks like a basketball is tucked under her shirt. Sally, accompanied to her prenatal appointments by James, delights in his excitement and thrives under his attention.

On a warm August evening, in the beginning of her sixth month, Sally is awoken by terrible pains—instantly recognizing them for what they are.

No! This can't be! I can't be in labor. It's too soon.

She reaches over and shakes her husband. "James! Wake up! There's something wrong."

Startled, he sits upright and, rubbing the sleep from his eyes, asks, "What? What's the matter? Are you okay?"

Sally begins crying. "No. I'm in labor."

James is awake in an instant. "What? Are you sure? How can that be? You're only six months along."

Sally protectively holds her stomach as she is overcome with another sharp pain.

James calls her doctor, whom they meet at the hospital. Dr. Tanner checks her and then delivers the bad news. "Sally, you're dilated to an eight. There's nothing we can do to stop your labor."

Sally, seeing the concerned expression on her doctor's face, begins to cry, as her body is wracked with another contraction. When it passes, she pleads, "No, it's too soon. My baby won't make it." Sally grabs Dr. Tanner's arm with a vise-like grip. "You have to stop my labor."

The doctor places her hand over Sally's. "It's too late. We've got one of the best neonatal facilities in the country. What I need you to do now, is relax and focus on delivering your baby."

Sally, reassured by her doctor's encouraging words, calms down. Two hours later, with James by her side, she delivers. She hears no baby crying and struggles to prop herself up. She dares to ask, "Is... is my baby—alive?"

Dr. Tanner answers, "Yes. You have a handsome son."

Sally allows herself to collapse back against the bed relieved.

Although he is tiny and struggles, James Charles, Jr. is alive. Upon seeing his son, James bursts into tears of relief, joy and worry.

God, he's so tiny and flawless and fragile.

He leans down and gently kisses the top of Sally's head. "He's perfect. Just like you."

Sally gazes into the eyes of her husband. Her face flinches and she begins hemorrhaging. Try as she might, Dr. Tanner can't stop the bleeding. James is escorted from the room by her and asks, "What's wrong? Is that much blood—normal?"

"No, Dr. Whitmore, it's not. Your wife is hemorrhaging as a result of DIC, disseminated intravascular coagulation."

"What does that mean?"

"Simply put, your wife is going to bleed out if we don't get her into surgery to perform a hysterectomy."

I could lose her? A hysterectomy? She won't be able to have any more children? James cringes, backs away from the doctor and leans heavily against the wall. He opens his mouth and hears an animalistic gut-wrenching wince emanate from deep within him.

Dr. Tanner watches him. "Dr. Whitmore, I know this is a hard decision. But if we do nothing, you *will* lose your wife. We're running out of time. Do I have your permission to do the surgery?"

James looks past the doctor into the delivery room. He sees that Sally is being sustained by blood that is being pumped into her via an IV. He looks back at the doctor and replies, "Yes."

Before turning to leave, Dr. Tanner places her hand on his arm and gives it a gentle squeeze. "It's going to be all right. I'll take good care of her." She turns and leaves.

James finds himself standing alone in the hallway, watching the doors to the delivery room close. Moments later, they reopen and James Charles, Jr. is wheeled out, in a tiny bassinette. James looks beseechingly at the nurse. "Where are you taking my son?"

"To the neonatal department."

"But I thought he would go to the nursery."

The nurse's expression softens, and she explains, "We need to have him where we can closely monitor his vitals."

James is torn.

I don't want to leave Sally, but....

A cold dread grips his heart and he asks, "Can I come?"

"Yes."

They arrive in the neonatal department, and James stands beside his son's infinitesimal form, viewing him through the Plexiglas hood of his bassinette.

God, there are so many wires and tubes going in and out of him. It looks so...so painful.

James watches as his son's chest labors to rise and fall with each breath.

What happened? Yesterday I was on top of the world. Today I'm watching my son struggle to breathe, as my wife lies on a surgical table fighting for her life. What the hell happened!

He drops his face into his hands in an attempt to block out the unimaginable possibilities that lay before him. His heart shatters as waves of emotion effervesce from deep within him. Tears of despair pour down his face, and he slumps into a chair beside his son, doubled over with fear.

A while later, a nurse finds him in the same pose. She gently lays a hand on his back. "Dr. Whitmore?"

James looks up, his face etched with deep worry lines. "Yes?"

"Your wife is out of surgery and in recovery. You can see her now. Would you like me to take you to her?"

He looks back at his helpless son. "But...."

The nurse says, "He'll be fine while you're gone. We'll take good care of him."

Reluctant to leave, James follows the nurse, passing a final glance over his shoulder at his namesake.

Over the next few days, James travels between Sally's and his son's rooms. He personally breaks the news to Sally about her hysterectomy and is in the room when Dr. Tanner comes in to check on her. Sally looks at her doctor and questions, "What happened? Why did I deliver early?"

"I believe that your premature labor was caused by an incompetent cervix."

Sally remarks, "But I didn't have any problems with my last pregnancy."

"I know. I believe that your cervix may have been damaged due to years of rough intercourse. And the membranes ruptured prematurely, thus placing you in labor."

Sally looks from her husband to her doctor. "So, I did this? *My* actions caused this? And the only way for you to stop the bleeding was a *complete* hysterectomy?"

"In your case, yes. Normally, we'd try to go in and stop the bleeding and get out as quickly as possible. With you, there was too much damage—we had no choice but to do the procedure." Dr. Tanner looks from Sally to James before offering, "I'm sorry."

Sally is strong enough to be wheeled in to see her son, on the third day following his birth. Although James had tried to prepare her for what to expect, she lets out an audible gasp when she sees her baby.

He's so tiny... and helpless!

An intricate webbing of tubes and wires invade his body in an attempt to maintain his immature lungs and keep his frail form alive. Reaching through one of the gloved openings, she touches her son for the first time. The minute she does, an electric surge of maternal bonding passes through her.

You are my son—a McFee Whitmore. Fight, little man, with everything you've got. Fight! Don't make Mommy lose another son. I don't think I could take that.

Through the gloved arm, she strokes the side of her son's face, taking notice of his features. "You have your daddy's long slender fingers. How many times have I watched him rub the back of one hand with the other, while lost in thought? Will you do the same? And look at those eyelashes—those you get from your Uncle Eric." She chuckles aloud. "I'd know those full pouty lips anywhere, they're those of your father's." She spies his tiny button nose. "Would you look at that? You've got my mother's nose. Ah, little man, there's so much history wrapped up in you. We have so many hopes for you. Fight! Fight to stay alive, so you can have the normal childhood I didn't and the one I couldn't give to your brother."

A lone tear falls from her eye. She leans in close, presses her free hand upon the glass hood of his bassinette and whispers, "Mommy just wants you to live—that's all—just live."

The next day, Angel and Gloria meet Sally and James at the hospital. While the two are in with their son, the monitors and machines around him begin to buzz and blare their warnings. Hospital personnel descend with an arsenal of IVs and stethoscopes. Nurses check the machines. One calls a code blue, while another asks Sally and James to step outside, where they join Angel and Gloria, who are motionless with fear. James wraps his arms around Sally in a protective gesture. Gloria asks, "What's going on? What's wrong?"

Encased in James' arms, Sally turns her head and responds, "Don't know, Ma. All of a sudden the machines started going crazy and making noise. No one's told us anything, except that we had to leave."

They watch a crash cart get rushed into the room. An army of hospital personnel takes control, with a mix of hurry and calm, as they struggle to save James Charles, Jr. For the next forty minutes, Sally, James, Gloria and Angel are tormented as more and more heroic measures are taken.

As suddenly as it all began, the nurses and doctors step away from the infant, who lies motionless—James Charles, Jr. is dead. The pediatrician approaches his parents. James can barely pull together sentences. He gasps out his fear in staccato. "Baby? My son? Please, God…. No!"

Sally, overcome with grief, collapses into Angel's arms moments after hearing her husband's guttural despair. She looks into Angel's eyes and cries, "No! Not again—not another son. I've failed another son!"

CHAPTER 30

Sally is discharged from the hospital—no newborn to cradle in her arms. Her baby, left behind in the hospital's cold morgue, is unable to be warmed by his parents' loving embrace. In a cruel twist of fate, on the day she is released empty-handed, Sally accompanies James to make arrangements for their son's burial. A thousand thoughts crowd her mind as she bides her time in the funeral home's waiting room.

If I hadn't been a prostitute.... My son would still be alive. All I ever wanted....

My sons—my beautiful sons.

Closing her eyes, she places a hand on her stomach.

I can almost still feel James Charles, Jr. inside me, kicking, rolling from side to side—the flutter of his heartbeat. How can he be gone if I can still feel him?

James runs on autopilot, an emotionless robot, going through the motions.

He had been allowed to hold his son for the first and only time, once the life-supporting tubes and wires had been removed. As father cradled his son's lifeless form in his arms, something deep within him shattered. The overwhelming pain and agony he had felt when his parents died washed over him, threatening to consume him. He lifted his son's body and gently brushed cheeks with him, marveling at the coldness. It was at that moment his mind had shut down. He had listened to Sally wail inconsolably, while he shed no tears.

James and Sally sit zombie-like, waiting to handle the business affairs of their son's funeral—James' face void of expression, his countenance stoic. Their name is called. They are led to an office where a pleasant middle-aged woman gets up from behind a desk to greet them. She is plump, with shoulder-length hair turned under at the ends, and wears an empathetic smile.

"I'm sorry for your loss. My name is Catherine. I'll be helping you with the arrangements."

Sally and James cringe. Catherine motions to the chairs across from her desk and then returns to her own. They discuss the particulars of the funeral, after which she leads them into a showroom displaying an array of caskets ranging from very affordable to elite. Spotting the infant caskets from across the room, Sally is unable to take another step.

They're so—small.

James takes her arm and gently urges her to continue walking. Together, they approach the lit display shelves holding the small coffins—indeed, beautiful works of art. Instinctively, Sally lays her hand atop one of them, appreciating the craftsmanship.

My son will be safe and protected in one of these.

James looks at the cold coffins and painfully remembers the ones that took his parents from him. He notes the contrasting nanoscale of these.

No one that minute should have to be placed in a casket. Nothing that small should have to be buried. Why must these boxes rob me of my heart's greatest passions?

Sally and James select a powder blue casket and manage to muddle their way through James Charles, Jr.'s funeral. By the end, both are hollowed-out shells of what used to be comprehensive individuals.

James and Sally are removed and distant following their son's funeral. Physically, Sally recovers from her hysterectomy. Her state of mind, however…. At home, although it stands empty, she seeks comfort in the nursery. She allows her eyes to wander over the collection of teddy bears—her son will never hug them. She spots a handmade blanket and crosses the room to pick it up—it will never offer him warmth. She closes her eyes and brings it to her cheek—he won't feel its velvety fabric.

Her feet carry her to the closet filled with miniature clothes that will never be worn. Sally, in a trance, lovingly runs her fingertips across the diminutive garments. Her hand lingers on one in particular—a sailor outfit—her favorite. She remembers how she had planned to bring her baby home wearing the ensemble. When he was buried, James had suggested that they place him in it, but Sally could not bear to part with the attire.

She takes the suit out of the closet and holds it up. An image of her son dressed in it flashes in her mind. She drops to her knees, clutching the outfit to her bosom and doubles over, in a tight ball, overcome with grief, sobbing uncontrollably.

Suddenly, her mother is behind her and helps Sally. "Come on, honey. Let's get you up."

Sally looks at her with beseeching eyes, her face tear-streaked. She tries to speak but fails. She tries again. "Ma— When...when will it stop hurting so much?"

Her mother looks at Sally and tells her the truth. "Ah, baby, never, completely. Every day gets a little easier, though. You just have to take it one hour at a time."

She assists Sally to her feet, hangs the sailor outfit in the closet and heads towards the door. They leave the room, sealing it behind them. "I think it's best we keep this room shut for awhile."

Sally looks up. "Like Eric's?"

Her mom offers a pained smile. Unspoken words of grief and understanding pass between them.

James, stuck in a perpetual state of mourning, becomes obsessed with using alcohol as a form of self-medication. Sally cannot stand to see him this way.

Where is my rock? Where is your strength? Your courage? Your bravery? I can't do this without you. I need you to be strong.

James is regularly too intoxicated to drive himself home and so his cronies chauffer him. They attempt to understand what he must be going through. As friends, they make allowances for his excessive drinking. They know he just needs to get through this rough time, so they cover for and keep a watchful eye on him.

Over the course of the next months, James' drinking affects his ability to work, causing him to have frequent run-ins with his boss, Clyde Stimmons, who can only be so flexible.

James barely manages to drag himself out of bed in the morning. The night before, two of his buddies, Alexander and Steven, drove him home. Although they managed to get both him and his car home safely, they worry about his depression and are at a loss of how to help him.

James pulls himself from bed and stumbles into the bathroom. He showers and dresses, in a manner less than befitting a professional of his stature, before getting in his car. Halfway to the office, he rubs his chin and realizes....

Ah, shit! I forgot to shave.

He looks at the display on the clock and groans.

No time to go back.

Arriving at work, James is an hour and a half late. He manages to navigate his way to his office, bumping into the wall along the way. He enters, closes the door and slumps into his executive leather chair. That is when he sees it—the note Clyde left earlier on his desk. Unequivocally, it states that he is to report to his boss's office upon his arrival. Letting out a heavy sigh, James struggles to stand and heads out the door.

Today marks his fifteenth consecutive day of being late. His co-workers, like his boss, are sympathetic to his plight, yet know that this cannot continue. In a position to help others, they realize that James is incapable of doing that now. Despite being put on probation, the list of his missed appointments has been growing by the hour. They watch him pass their offices, knowing what is in store for him.

James stops in front of Clyde's door and attempts to straighten his sloppy attire. Knocking, he hears his boss' voice tell him to come in. James opens the door, steps inside and closes it behind him.

The meeting is direct. Clyde is kind, yet unyielding—James is fired. He tries to soften the blow by stating, "Perhaps you can use this time to seek some help. Talk to Dr. Stykes?" The two stare at one another—Clyde gravely concerned about James's state of mind, James reserved and sensitive. Both know that although James is broken inside, he will accept no assistance for his suffering.

Emerging from his boss' office thirty minutes later, the only thought on James' mind is that he needs a stiff drink. He walks to the stockroom and gathers several empty boxes before returning to his office where he hastily packs his possessions. He hears a knock at his door, looks up and sees Alexander standing in the doorway. Neither speaks at first. James breaks the awkward silence. "Thanks for getting me home last night," he says, unable to make eye contact.

"No problem." Alexander pauses before continuing. "I hate seeing you like this. Anything I can do to help?"

"No. Just about packed up here. I'll go for a drive and maybe stop for a drink. Think things through."

"James, why don't you wait? It's almost lunch. I'll go with you."

James lays a hand upon his friend's shoulder. "Thanks, Alexander. You finish up here. I'll be fine."

Alexander looks beseechingly at his friend. "How about you skip the drink and head home?"

"If I stop, it would only be for one drink."

"I know. I know," Alexander says. "It's just... You know how it goes...."

James grows irritated. "No, Alexander, I don't. Perhaps you should enlighten me."

"Forget it. Just be careful. Okay?"

James gathers the boxes, his raincoat and briefcase. As he passes by his friend, he attempts a convincing smile. Then, without saying a word, he heads to his car.

James *loves* his car. It is a beautiful specimen of a vehicle that commands attention and makes heads turn. He relishes driving it and the power it makes him feel. He recalls the day he got it.

* * * * *

James bought the car himself—a present for his birthday, having had his sights on it for a long time. Actually, it had been Sally who had convinced him to treat himself, stating, "You've worked hard. Reward yourself."

That did it. They went to the Porsche dealership the next day—his birthday. Several hours later, like a kid with a new toy, James had driven off the lot with his brand new silver Boxster. A broad grin stretched from ear to ear.

* * * * *

Dazed, James stares at the road. He vaguely sees objects as they flash by—none registering. He feels as if he is contained in a glass dome. Nothing from the outside world can reach him. It is raining heavily. Through the moisture-induced haze, he sees the flashing red signal and the halo of light cast by the street lamps on the slick road. Occasionally, he spots the white dotted street lines weaving before the car and cannot understand why one minute his car is driving between them, while the next, one of the ominous lines creeps under the car, causing him to straddle it.

James pulls over to the side of the road to collect his thoughts and allow the car's defiant behavior to correct itself. He scratches his head and wonders at the darkness.

Why is it dark? Didn't I just leave the office?

He looks at the car's clock. It reads 8:15 PM.

That can't be right. Did I stop somewhere on the way home? Think. Think. Think.

His mind refuses to focus. He somewhat recalls sitting at a bar across town, munching on pretzels and peanuts, while having *one* drink.

James rouses with a start, realizing that he must have blacked out. Once again, he glances at the dash clock. A tremendous throbbing starts at the base of his neck, pounding without mercy against the left region of his head. Slowly, the digital numerals on the clock focus— 8:27 PM.

Twelve minutes have elapsed?

Forcing his body to obey his mind's commands, James pulls the car away from the shoulder and merges back into traffic. He is drunk and knows it. But he just wants to get home, where he can sleep it off.

His mind is a blur of thoughts and flashing information, none of which makes any sense. He stares at the windshield, trying to make out the road through the dripping haze.

Dripping haze?

He leans forward and looks more carefully at the windshield, realizing that the haze is vomit that had spewed from his mouth, covering the windshield and dash. His hands are covered with small chunks of undigested peanuts. Minuscule droplets of pretzels, encased in vomit, cling to the steering wheel. James tries to recall puking.

He wipes away the curtain of stomach contents and continues home, the two-lane highway appearing to fade into a single lane ahead. Staying in his lane is becoming more challenging. The bright streetlights cause his head to ache and feel as though it is in a vise—someone tightening the screw. The painted lines seem to jump off the highway one moment and completely disappear the next. Just trying to stay *on* the road proves daunting.

Should have accepted Alexander's offer.

Time passes by, ever so slowly. The road stretches on and on.

Want to get home. Make this nightmare end.

For a moment, time slips back through the years, delivering him to his favorite childhood amusement park. He feels like that small boy, trapped on the ride that had terrorized him—that ominous ride with its twisting curving track. He remembers its name—Colossus. It would forever haunt his memory. He would never forget how his friends convinced him to go on the ride and how he had puked, while the car raced at a terrifying speed down the severe drop. The track seemed to vanish from beneath the car as it sped down the track.

Remembering Colossus causes James's stomach to tighten and threaten to heave. He swallows hard and the sick feeling dissipates, along with the flashback of Six Flags Magic Mountain and *that* ride. James relaxes a bit.

Bright white lights come into view and blind him. Just as he notices that he has crossed the centerline, he hears a horn blare seconds before the steel-mangling collision. His car collides head-on with another vehicle and James has his last thought.

Not my car! Not my beautiful car!

CHAPTER 31

Sally's mother suggests that they go out for a bite of dinner. Sally is resistant, but eventually accedes.

The company would *be nice. Gotta get out of this house.*

They meet at a local Italian restaurant and sit in a back booth, sipping wine and enjoying a pleasant dinner. On her drive home, Sally appreciates the festive fall colors and pumpkins people have decorated their homes with, in anticipation of Thanksgiving.

Just as the trees have dropped their leaves and stand naked, looking dead, Sally, too, has taken on an appearance of near-death. Her cheeks hollow and her eyes sink in.

Sudden traffic causes Sally to crawl to a stop. By 9:15 PM, she has been at a dead stop for ten minutes.

What's up with the traffic?

The line of cars begins to inch along, and she with them. Up ahead, she sees an abundance of flashing lights. An inexplicable chill runs down her spine as she approaches them, causing her to shake involuntarily. A feeling of foreboding settles over her. As she rolls past the scene, she cannot help but turn her head to view the crumpled remains of the two vehicles. It had been a bad accident.

In horror, Sally recognizes one of the cars and screams, "Oh, my God! No!"

She pulls her car over, gets out, running. The jaws of life are peeling James' car open like a sardine can. Before she can get to the wreckage, her path is blocked by a police officer, who says, "I'm sorry, ma'am, but I can't let you pass."

"You don't understand. That's my husband's car. I need to get to him!"

"Just a moment, please." The officer walks over to an older gentleman, converses with him and points at Sally. The man nods and walks over to her.

Sally cries, "That's my husband in the Porsche. How is he? Can you take me to him?"

"I'm afraid I can't do that, ma'am."

"Why not?"

"It's too dangerous."

The blood in Sally's veins turns cold. She hears a ringing in her ears and, overwhelmed by a feeling of déjà vu, almost faints. She remembers that awful day at the beach when she had spotted Eric's still form lying at the water's edge, surrounded by the lifeguards and feels as though her legs might fail her.

From somewhere far away, she hears the officer. "Ma'am. Ma'am, are you all right? Come over here where you can sit down." He lifts the barrier tape and escorts her to the back of one of the fire trucks.

He motions to the nearest fireman. "This is the wife."

The man looks up. "Ah." To Sally, he asks, "Would you like a bottle of water?"

Sally, barely able to comprehend, nods her head. The fireman hurries off and returns a few moments later, hands her the water and then turns and leaves. She begins fumbling with the screw-off lid.

The police officer, noticing her difficulty, offers, "Here, let me." He takes the bottle, opens the lid and then returns it to Sally. "My name's Detective Reyes. You must be Mrs. Whitmore."

Sally nods and manages to put a few words together. "Wh…what happened. . .when?"

"We're not sure and are continuing with our investigation. Currently, your husband is trapped. They're working to get him out."

Sally listens as Detective Reyes tells her the facts. Her mind attempts to digest what she is told. Behind him, she notices they have peeled the Boxster open and are cutting away James' seatbelt to free him. She watches as they gingerly extricate him from of the remains of his car. She points behind the detective. "They're getting him out. That's good, right?"

Detective Reyes does not respond.

They lay James' limp body on a board, atop a stretcher. The EMTs circle, each busy with their lifesaving tasks. Sally watches, paralyzed with fear, as the paramedics talk to one another and then load James into the ambulance. They offer her a ride up front, which she accepts. With the lights flashing and sirens blaring, they make it to the hospital in less than ten minutes. James is immediately taken into surgery while Sally is handed a mountain of paperwork. She numbly sets about filling it out. She passes her remaining time pacing, fidgeting and crying.

After six hours, James' doctor comes out and tells her, "Your husband made it through surgery. He had a ruptured spleen, collapsed lung, shattered legs and ribs and he's lost a tremendous amount of blood. The next few hours will be crucial. We've done all we can. Now we must wait to see if his body will be strong enough to pull through. We've moved him out of recovery and into an ICU room. Would you like me to take you to him?"

Sally follows the doctor to James' room. It is quiet, with the exception of machines that beep, hum and breathe for him. She freezes in the doorway, barely recognizing James. His entire face is badly swollen and covered with myriad cuts and stitches along with a patchwork of green, yellow, black and purple bruises. There are tubes running in and out of him, each with its specific purpose. She watches the rhythmic rise and fall of his chest, which is synchronized with one of the machines, and marvels at how it sounds like Darth Vader. She remembers her son lying helpless, while machines breathed for him.

Sally crosses the room and walks to the side of the bed. A nurse, who is checking the monitors, startles her. She offers Sally a smile. "He's a strong man. Fighting hard to pull through. My name is Rose. You must be Mrs. Whitmore."

"Sally, please."

"I can only allow you to visit for five minutes. Can I get you something? Water? Coffee?"

"Coffee would be nice."

"Be right back."

Sally watches the young woman leave and then places one of her hands over James', sobbing quietly. "James, ah, baby. What have you done? Don't leave me. Damn it! Fight! For yourself. For me. For us. I can't bear the thought of losing you."

Rose returns with Sally's coffee. Offering it, she places a hand on Sally's shoulder. "It'll be okay."

Sally looks up at her, her eyes puffy from crying. "I hope so. I don't think—I've lost so much."

Rose gives Sally's shoulder a gentle squeeze in acknowledgement. "I'm sorry, but it's time for you to leave now."

"So soon?"

"Afraid so. You can return for another visit an hour from now."

Sally allows James' hand to slip from her own and turns to leave. To Rose, she says, "Thank you."

Rose smiles and resumes checking the monitors, logging their information.

An endless array of nurses and doctors come and go from James' room over the next twelve hours. Sally barely notices. She is focused on willing her husband to live. At 3:37 PM. the following day, she is startled out of a restless sleep by the sounding of alarms and buzzers. Nurses rush past her and into James' room. One calls, "Code blue! Code blue! We need a crash cart—stat!"

Sally, on her feet in an instant, stands in the doorway. "What's wrong?! What's happening?!"

One of the nurses tells her that a doctor will be out to talk to her. The blinds on the window are closed. Through a small crack, Sally watches the nurses and doctors feverishly work to revive James. At 4:08 PM. the movement in the room changes—it slows. The doctors step away from her husband. She sees one pick up a chart, look at the wall clock and then write something down. To her horror, the nurses begin turning off the monitors—one by one. She knows. Her husband, her rock, her savior is dead. She presses her face and hands to the glass, in an attempt to reach out to him. A guttural wail escapes her. "Noooooo!" She slumps to the ground, unable to stand.

A nurse rushes over to help. Knocking on the glass, she indicates Sally's condition. Rose emerges from the room. "Come on, Sally, let's have you sit down."

The two assist Sally into a chair. She looks up with her now dull green eyes. "This shouldn't have happened. I didn't have a dream this time. You...you said it would be all right. This isn't okay."

The other nurse leaves, and Rose watches Sally transform from a distraught widow into a lost little girl. Compassionately, she kneels in front of her and lays her hands on her knees. "I'm so sorry. We did everything we could. Is there someone I can call for you?"

Sally, engrossed in her own thoughts, does not hear Rose. She looks past her to the opened door through which she can see that the other nurses have finished turning off the monitors and are in the process of removing the now unneeded life-sustaining tubes from James' body. Rose tries again. "Sally. Is there someone I can call for you?"

Rose's words get through this time, and Sally responds, "Ma. I want my ma."

"Okay. What's her number?"

Sally rattles it off.

"Be right back, Rose says. "I'm going to place the call."

Sally nods, and her attention is drawn back to James. They have finished working on him. As the doctors and nurses leave the room, each walks over and offers their condolences, their words cutting through her like a knife.

Once they are gone, Sally goes to her husband. She takes his hand in her own, flinching.

It's cold...so very cold.

James' complexion is pale despite the bruising. She shivers as her mind flashes back to sitting in the emergency room beside Eric's body.

Rose returns and comes to stand beside her. "I was able to get a hold of your mother. She's on her way. Here, take this." She offers Sally another cup of coffee.

Mindlessly, Sally accepts it. She feels flat and empty inside and cannot fathom ever wanting to eat or drink again. For that matter, she cannot imagine doing *anything* ever again. She has lost everything. Her sons. And now her husband. The terrible reality begins to sink in. Something deep within her breaks, and she goes numb. In an attempt to block reality, her thoughts cease. Rose stays with her. When her mother arrives, she rushes to Sally and enfolds her in a tight embrace. "I'm so sorry, honey. Oh, God! I'm so sorry."

Sally offers no reaction or response. She too, appears dead and cold.

CHAPTER 32

Her mother takes Sally home and tucks her into bed. Sally utters no words—too consumed by grief. She awakes mid-morning the next day.

Where am I? What day is it? What time is it?

Slowly, the fog that clouds her mind dissipates. She is home, in her own bed, exhausted and has a horrible headache. Memories of the past few days worm their way into her consciousness, like an army making a stealthy attack. Remembering, she cries, "Oh, God! James . . . no." She sits up and closes her eyes in an attempt to block reality. Drawing her knees under her chin in a fetal position, she rhythmically rocks back and forth sobbing.

Don't want to get up. Or have this day begin. Or face life without James. Can't face it without him....

Grimacing, she thinks of the unpleasant funeral arrangements that she will need to begin today. She buries herself under the covers, in an attempt to delay the inevitable. After what seems like forever, knowing she cannot postpone things indefinitely, she gets up, sighs and dons her robe. She pads down to the kitchen, followed by Princess, where she finds her mother nursing a cup of coffee at the table.

Her mother gets up and goes to her with opened arms. "I'm so sorry, Sally. This is— Can I get you anything? Something to eat?"

Sally nods her head.

"Coffee?"

"No. Tea. James loved tea." Sally sits at the table, where she watches her mother busy herself. Her mother brings a mug of hot water and sets it before Sally, who adds a little sugar and milk. She rhythmically dunks a teabag in it, a lone tear escaping, as she recalls the many times James had performed the same act. When the liquid becomes stained from the contents of the teabag, she lifts the mug and cups it with both hands, comforted by the warmth it offers, before taking a sip.

Her attention turns to Princess, who is frantically walking the downstairs checking all the rooms. Every so often, she comes to her owner and looks at her expectantly. Sally reaches out her hand. As if on cue, Princess comes. Sally runs her fingers across her soft fur and says, "I know, girl. I miss him, too. He's not coming back."

Princess cocks her head, as if understanding, and lies down. Meanwhile, Sally's mother sets about preparing breakfast. "How do bacon, eggs and toast sound?"

"Great, Ma. Thanks."

Sally watches her mom turn on a burner, separate the bacon, placing each strip in the pan. The aroma of frying bacon quickly fills the room and takes Sally back to when she and James had made passionate love in this very kitchen as their bacon burned. Tears roll down her cheeks. Her mother looks over and says, "It'll get better."

"Just remembering…. James loved bacon."

"Hmm….sure did. He'd eat almost a pound of it in a single sitting. No one could put away bacon like that husband of yours."

Sally offers a pained smile.

When the bacon is done, Sally watches her mom remove it from the pan and place the pieces on a paper towel-lined plate before cracking a couple eggs and cooking them in the bacon's grease. As she pats the bacon dry, she asks, "Over easy?"

"Yeah."

Her mother drops two pieces of bread into the toaster and depresses the button. She flips the eggs before skillfully sliding them out of the pan onto two plates. The toast pops up, and she places one piece on each plate and then carries the plates over to the table. Sally watches all of this, marveling at its normalcy.

Nothing is normal anymore. Why are these simple tasks so fascinating? Seems like James is gonna walk through the door any minute. Wish he would. But he won't. Miss him—especially his quotes.

One of his favorites, by Luc de Clapiers de Vauvenargues, comes to mind and Sally mumbles it under her breath. "The things we know best are things we haven't been taught."

Her mother looks at her and asks, "What?"

A pained smile crosses Sally's face. "I was thinking of one of James's favorite quotes." Sally picks up her fork and begins mindlessly poking her food.

The two eat in silence. When done, her mother gathers their plates. "I've got these. Why don't you rest?" She rinses the dishes, loads them into the dishwasher and then goes about washing the iron skillet.

Sally stands at the ready with a towel to dry it. She says, "Keeping busy is good. Doesn't give me time to think."

They pour themselves another cup of hot water, add new tea bags and return to the table. Her mom says, "I've cleared my schedule so I can help you with the arrangements."

Sally sighs.

"Have you thought about where you want to lay James to rest?"

"We have plots on either side of our son." Sally slumps in her chair. "Never thought—"

Her mother reaches across the table and cups one of her hands over Sally's. "I'll call and make an appointment with their funeral director."

Sally looks at her mother. "Thanks, Ma. For being here."

Her mother gets up and places a hand on her shoulder. "That's what family does." She makes the call and sets an appointment for later that day.

When she is done, Sally calls Angel. On the other end, the phone rings twice before being picked up.

"Hello?"

"Hey, Angel. It's me, Sally."

"Sally girl? Been trying to get a hold of you. Where are you?"

"At home." She rushes through the next part in a monotone. "There...there's been a terrible accident. James is dead."

Angel gasps. "What?! Be right over."

Sally feels comforted knowing she will not be alone during this.

Those who love her most will surround her.

Angel arrives fifteen minutes later and lets herself in. "Sally? Sally, where are you?"

"We're in the kitchen," Gloria answers.

Angel rushes to her friend and embraces her. Sally's body shakes as she sobs quietly. Gloria watches them. Angel acknowledges Gloria with a tilt of her head. Silent words of understanding pass between them. Gloria asks, "Angel, can I get you a cup of tea? Sally and I were just discussing what needs to be done."

"Tea? Sure. Tea would be nice."

Gloria gets up and pours Angel a mug of hot water. She returns, hands it, along with a tea bag, to Angel and then adds more water to both her and Sally's mugs before sitting. "We have an appointment at the funeral home in a couple of hours. Would you like to come?"

Angel, dunking her teabag, looks towards Sally, who indicates, with a nod of her head, that her presence is wanted. "Sure. I'll do whatever you need."

Gloria glances at the clock on the wall and turns to Sally. "You should get ready, honey. Why don't you take a hot bath? We've got a long day ahead of us."

Sally says, "That sounds good. Will you two be okay?"

Her mother says, "We'll start calling people."

Sally looks at her mother and friend for several long moments. "Thank you both for being here. Couldn't get through this without you." She picks up her mug and turns to head upstairs.

Suddenly exhausted, Sally sits on the edge of the tub and turns on the faucets. She picks up the bubble bath and pours some into the stream of water. As if in a trance, she watches the mound of bubbles grow. Their iridescent shapes mesmerize her. When the tub is filled, Sally turns off the faucets and slips off her robe, letting it fall to the floor. She sinks into the warm steaming water, allowing it to wash over her, leans her head back and closes her eyes. A thousand thoughts assault her mind.

Why do all the men in my life leave me? My father. My brother. Eric Angel. James Charles, Jr. And now James. Why?

Sally remains in the tub for a long while with her eyes shut. When she reopens them, the water has grown cold. She turns on the hot water tap before washing herself. Climbing out of the tub, she reaches for an oversized bath towel and catches a glimpse of herself in the mirror. She barely recognizes the aged image reflected back at her. There are dark circles under her eyes. Her cheeks have deep hollows. Her eyes have a haunted expression—dull, flat, sunken. Appalled, Sally turns away and begins toweling herself dry.

Downstairs, Gloria fills Angel in on the details of James' tragic death. When she finishes, Angel sits in stunned silence before commenting, "I knew he was drinking more as a result of James Charles, Jr.'s death, but I never thought.... Sally doesn't deserve this."

She and Gloria take turns calling to notify people of James' death. Everyone is shocked, and offers their condolences and help. Just about the time the two are done placing their calls, Sally reappears in the kitchen dressed in a casual outfit. Gloria goes to her and gives her a hug. Pulling away, she sneaks a peek at the wall clock. "We should get going."

Angel looks at Sally. "Ready?"

"I guess. Both of you are going to be there with me the whole time, right?"

"Won't leave your side," Angel says.

CHAPTER 33

Angel, Sally and her mother drive to the funeral home in silence, none of them needing to talk, each lost in her own thoughts and memories. They are comforted by the others' presence. The people she sees along the way perplex Sally.

Why do they appear to be going about their business as if nothing is wrong? Don't they know? James is dead. My life has crumbled. Yet, they act as though today is the same as any other.

When they arrive, Sally's mother checks them in and returns to sit with her daughter and Angel. Catherine, a pleasant middle-aged woman greets them a few minutes later. Sally realizes she is the same woman who had helped her and James three months earlier with their son's arrangements. Recognition can be seen on Catherine's face as well. "I'm terribly sorry for your loss."

Sally nods in silent appreciation. They clasp hands for a moment, before Catherine escorts them down a hallway into a small room. She motions to several chairs, then walks around a large mahogany desk to take a seat. She allows everyone to get settled before addressing Sally. "I'm so sorry to have to see you again this soon."

Sally does not respond.

Catherine goes over the particulars regarding James' funeral: casket, flowers, number of attendees and viewing. They decide that a closed casket would be best, due to the extent of his facial injuries. Catherine confirms that James will be laid to rest beside James Charles, Jr. At the thought of father and son lying beside one another, Sally bursts into tears. Angel and her mother comfort her, and Sally regains her composure. They finalize the details and leave—each an emotional wreck. The car ride back to Sally's house is enshrouded in silence.

The following evening, at James' viewing, Sally functions on autopilot. She, exhausted from barely having slept since the accident, hardly recognizes the endless line of attendees who offer their condolences. The ordeal takes its toll on her body and mind. True to their word, Gloria and Angel never leave her side. They take her home, feed her a light dinner and put her to bed.

The next morning, Sally awakes as the morning light filters in through her window. Princess lays by her side of the bed. Roused by her mistress's stirring, she gets up and stands beside her, her face level with Sally's. Sally does not acknowledge her. Princess nudges her arm with her cold wet nose. This time, Sally rolls onto her side, smiles and scratches behind her lab's ears.

"Hey, girl. Up early too, huh? Gonna be a long day." She looks at the clock on the bedside table. "It's still early. Want to go for a walk?"

Princess circles, barking joyfully. She stops and prods Sally's arm in an attempt to get her up.

"Okay. Okay. Simmer down."

Sally rises and pads her way into the bathroom, where she uses the toilet, washes her face and brushes her teeth. Princess shadows her every move. Sally throws on old pair of James' sweats—still heavy with his scent—and heads downstairs. Halfway down, the aroma of fresh-cut flowers hits her. A grim reminder—one of many. A constant delivery of flowers from well-wishers had been arriving and overtook the downstairs. Her house was beginning to look like a florist shop. She ignores the flowers and continues into the kitchen.

Angel and her mother are still sleeping. She writes them a note, telling them that she will be back in an hour. She needs space and fresh air to help prepare for the arduously long day that lies ahead. She leaves the note by the coffee maker where she knows they will see it and heads towards the door. "Come on, girl. Let's go for that walk." Princess trots over and Sally leans down to click on her leash, before grabbing a scarf and heading out.

There is a chill to the air that causes Sally to wrap the scarf snug around her neck. She walks under the canopy of mature oak trees that line her street. She has no planned route, going wherever her feet take her. The birds begin to awaken and their chirped callings surround her. The streets are empty. Too early for anyone to be out, she has the streets all to herself.

As she walks the labyrinth of streets in her neighborhood, she allows her mind to recall the many good memories she shared with James. She turns corners and crosses streets, all of which go unnoticed. The memories she views in her mind torment her, and tears stream down her face. The beautiful trees, flowers and sweet melodies of the singing birds begin to rejuvenate her.

By the time she turns down her street and views her house, she feels strong enough to tackle this day. Squaring her shoulders, she walks up the porch steps and into her house, where she quietly calls, "Ma? Angel? Are you awake?"

"We're in the kitchen," she hears her mother reply.

Sally finds both sitting at the table, sipping hot coffee. Her mother fetches her a mug. "Your cheeks are flushed. Cold out?"

"A bit. Refreshing, though."

Angel scrutinizes her. "You okay?"

Sally sighs, "Think so."

Her mother returns to the table and places a warm mug in front of her. "Have a nice walk?"

"Yeah," Sally says, sipping her coffee. "It was good to get out and soak up some fresh air."

Angel puts a hand on her shoulder. "We'll be right beside you the whole time."

"I know. It's gonna be so hard to see James next to our son." Sally begins to cry.

Angel wraps her in a tight embrace. "It's gonna be okay."

Sally pulls back and looks at her. "That's what Rose, the nurse at the hospital, said before— It wasn't okay then, and it's not now. I can't imagine anything ever being all right again."

She allows herself to lean against Angel and freely cries. Eventually, she pulls away and they sit at the table, while her mom makes a light breakfast.

They eat in silence. Near the end of their meal, the doorbell rings as yet another delivery of flowers arrives. Her mom places them in the living room, amongst the others. Returning to the kitchen, she comments, "Such lovely flowers, and so many of them. James was well-liked."

The fragrance of flowers permeates every inch of the house. After they finish eating, the three clear the dishes and tidy the kitchen before going upstairs to get ready for the funeral.

On the drive there, her mother and Angel make small talk in an attempt to distract Sally. They fall silent as they round the corner and enter the cemetery. Tears leak from Sally's eyes as their car winds its way up the road and approaches the small chapel. Angel, noticing, squeezes Sally's hand. They park the car and enter the chapel where the presiding minister—the same one who officiated James Charles, Jr.'s funeral—greets them. Sally looks over his shoulder to the casket. Realizing that it contains her husband, her legs falter, and she takes a seat in the front pew. Her eyes never leave James's casket.

The guests begin to arrive, each making a point to address Sally and express their sorrow for her loss. The church fills to capacity, yet more mourners arrive, lining the walls and every available space. At the appropriate time, the minister begins the service. Alexander gets up to give James' eulogy. He stops beside Sally and places a hand on her shoulder. The bereaved widow cups his with her own in silent recognition.

At the podium, Alexander looks over the multitude of mourners and clears his throat. "As I look upon you, I see many aspects of James' life represented. Some of you knew him to be an amazing doctor, friend or colleague." He looks at Sally and smiles. "And some of you knew him to be a loving husband. I knew James most of my life. We met in high school, attended college and graduate school together and then wound up working at the same treatment facility. I guess you could say we matured together. I want to take this opportunity to share the man behind the mask—the man James rarely let others see."

Alexander pauses here to survey the audience. He can see by the looks on their faces that they are wondering what will be revealed. He takes his time before proceeding. "I doubt that there is one amongst you to whom James didn't recite his quotes. At times, they made him seem the pompous windbag and, as his best friend, I felt compelled to call him on it." There is a collective snickering in the crowd. "But there was a softer side to him. As a young boy, he was made an orphan when his parents were killed in a car accident that he somehow survived. He spent the remaining years of his youth in an orphanage. The summer of our sophomore year in college, we took a trip to Mexico to serve at a local orphanage. That's when I saw the real James. He had an uncanny way with children. As if he were the Pied Piper, they followed him everywhere and he seemed to thrive off of their energy and enthusiasm. He delighted in their insatiable appetite to become more knowledgeable. James was compassionate towards them and got to know each and every one as individuals. He had a unique way of making them feel special and through his attention they shone. He taught them about the great literary classics and fascinated them with his uncanny ability to find the right quote for any occasion."

Alexander stops here to look at Sally. "When he met Sally, his outlook on life changed—for the better. He told me that he wasn't complete until the day he met her—that he knew she was his soul mate. She gave his life purpose and direction. He was drawn to her intestinal fortitude. It fueled his tanks and gave him the conviction to be a better man and serve others more fully. In short, Sally completed his life."

He pauses and watches as tears stream down the widow's face. Angel and Gloria sit on either side of her, each with an arm around her, as she quietly sobs. Alexander gazes over the people present and sighs. "I have never known James to be as happy as the day he discovered he was going to be a father. Most of you probably don't know that in celebration of that momentous event, he and I ventured back to Mexico to the very orphanage we served at while in college. James felt an overwhelming urge to give back, to provide hope to those most in need—the children. And so he established the Sally McFee Foundation to provide scholarships to those children from the orphanage who demonstrated the ambition to continue with their education."

Alexander stops to clear his throat. "Each of us is left with our own cherished memories of the man James Whitmore was, and the impact he had on our lives. I choose to remember the lesser-known James, the one who would stand out in the rain and serenade his lovely bride, or the one who would give countless piggyback rides to the children of the orphanage until he could barely stand. And when the orphans squealed with delight and asked for more, he would smile and allow another to climb upon his back, galloping around the room. I choose to remember the man who couldn't stand to see another suffer and would go to great lengths to relieve their anguish. *This* is the man I choose to remember. My friend. My colleague. My confidant."

Sally experiences the service as if she is watching herself. She manages to make it through—barely. As each attendee files out, they stop and offer their condolences. "I'm so sorry." "Your husband was a wonderful man." "I can't believe James is gone." "He'll be missed." "The world was a richer place with James in it."

The faces of those who address her do not register, but instead blend together as one collective face born of immeasurable grief and suffering. Sally goes through the motions of accepting their comments. Once everyone has left, the funeral officials carry the casket to an awaiting hearse. It will drive the short distance to the private graveside service to be attended by only Angel, herself and her mother. The three watch as it is loaded into the vehicle before getting in their car to silently follow.

At the plot, Angel, Sally and her mother stand beside the open grave. The casket is taken out of the hearse and carried to the awaiting burial site, where it is placed upon straps that suspend it above the ominous pit. The three watch as it is lowered and swallowed by the awaiting hole. When the top of the casket falls lower than the surface of the ground, Sally catches sight of her dead son's grave beside that of her husband's. She remembers the day she and James met with Catherine, at Forest Lawn, to make the arrangements for their son's funeral.

My God! Was that only three months ago? Seems like a lifetime has passed.

* * * * *

Catherine had walked them to a showroom that displayed an array of high-end to affordable caskets. It all seemed morose, like some sick car dealership, only with coffins. Sally could almost hear the salesman's pitch. "Buy this one, and we'll throw in an extra year's warranty."

The minute her eyes fell upon the infinitesimal size of the boxes, she had frozen and James had needed to encourage her to move forward. She could still see the casket they had selected for their son. Its image was seared into her mind. It was powder blue and would later complement his father's grey one. It had a high sheen gloss finish that James had fallen in love with. He had commented on how it looked elegant. Later, his words burned in Sally's ears as she selected a grey one with a matching finish for him. Both were complete with plush beautiful white satin lining and pillows to cradle the occupants' heads.

* * * * *

In her mind, Sally views the image of them lowering her son's coffin into the ground just as they are lowering that of her husband's. Something deep inside her shatters, and she cries, "Stop! Don't lower it! I want my son and husband back." She rushes to the ground between the two graves and falls to her knees. Reaching out to both, she begins wailing—utterly broken.

Angel and her mother rush to her and try to pick her up. She pushes them away and collapses on the ground again. They attempt to raise her once again only to be met by an unexpected surge of strength. Sally fights them off, as if her very life depends on her staying where she is. Her mother tries to reason with her. "Come on, Sally. You've got to let them finish their job. They've got to lay James to rest. He won't be alone. He's got James Charles, Jr. by his side."

Hearing these words, Sally wails louder, inconsolable. Her mom takes a step back and looks at Angel, who kneels down next to her grief-stricken friend and places a loving hand on her back. "Sally girl, you've got to let him go. You can't stop what's happening. I know your heart's breaking. Mine too. Come on, let them finish here." Angel offers her hand to Sally, who looks up with tragic eyes made lifeless by the emotional storm she has endured.

Sally takes Angel's offered hand, rises and follows her lead, walking as if her entire body is anesthetized. Angel steers her away from the grave to the awaiting car. They get in, never glancing back. Gloria drives away. Angel sits in the rear seat, with Sally leaned up against her—a loving arm encircling her broken friend. As they wind away from the graveside, the three never see the men lowering James' casket into its final resting place. Father and son are reunited.

CHAPTER 34

Following James' funeral, Sally shuts down completely. Her mother and Angel take her home and put her to bed. Then, alone in the kitchen, the two make hot tea to soothe their shattered nerves. Angel toys with her teabag, raising and dunking it. She looks up at Gloria and comments, "This is way worse than I've ever seen Sally. It's too much—losing both sons, and now James. I...I can't imagine what she's going through."

Gloria grows reflective and takes a sip of her tea. "I agree she's overwhelmed. Who wouldn't be? Let's give her some time."

Sally's condition worsens. She doesn't eat, hasn't spoken since leaving the gravesite, remains in bed and is too numb to be comforted by Princess. Gloria and Angel take turns watching her—afraid to leave her alone in her diminished state of mind. After a week of watching Sally slip further and further away from reality, into her own world, the two are faced with the difficult decision to check her into a facility where she can receive the psychological attention she needs.

They research locations through the help of James' colleagues and decide on Whispering Pines, which employs some of the best mental health professionals. It is a beautiful center located on sprawling acreage, with rolling hills, mature trees, streams to forge and trails to explore.

Gloria meets with the doctor who will be handling Sally's case. His name is Dr. Anthony Friedman. Standing barely five and a half feet tall, he is hunched over and closely resembles a troll. His salt and pepper hair splays wildly in every direction and his eyes appear inordinately large behind his bottle-glass thick glasses.

The doctor takes Gloria on a tour of the facility and its grounds, during which she discusses Sally's current condition, the losses she has suffered. Once back in the building, Gloria asks, "Can you help Sally?"

"Your daughter's suffered a string of terrible losses, Mrs. McFee."

"Gloria, please."

"All right, Gloria. I am confident, however, that we'll be able to work through them. Please have her here tomorrow at 10:00 AM." He struggles to stand, crosses the room and, placing his gnarled fingers bent with age on the door handle, opens the door, signaling the end of their meeting.

Gloria gets up and walks to him, offering her hand. "Thank you, Dr. Friedman. You and Whispering Pines come highly recommended. Having met and spoken with you, I can see why."

Driving back to Sally's house, Gloria is confident that she has made the right decision. She and Angel discuss how her meeting with Dr. Friedman went and her confidence in his ability to help. They discuss with Sally how they think it would be best for her to check into Whispering Pines, so she can get some rest and treatment. She acquiesces.

The following morning, Gloria and Angel pack a suitcase for Sally and the three head to Whispering Pines, arriving a little before 10:00 AM and are greeted by her new doctor. "Hello, Sally. My name is Dr. Friedman. We're going to be working with one another."

Sally looks at him but doesn't respond. He continues in a gentle tone. "At this point, you'll need to say good-bye to your mother and friend so we can get you settled."

Her mother and Angel take turns hugging Sally. They tell her that they love her and that she is going to be fine. In the meantime, a nurse has appeared by Dr. Friedman's side. "Sally, this is Lilly. She's going to take you to your room and help get you moved in. You and I will meet again in an hour. Does that sound agreeable?"

Sally, void of emotion, nods her head.

"All right then." He turns and walks down the hallway.

Lilly picks up Sally's bags. "Your room is this way."

They walk down the hall to her room, where Lilly helps her

unpack before taking her on a tour of the facility. She points out the cafeteria, recreation room, health office and medication dispensary. When the tour is complete, she delivers Sally to Dr. Friedman's office to begin their meeting.

Sally listens to what the doctor has to say. He explains how they will be meeting twice a day for an hour at each session. He also informs her of what the remainder of her daily routine will entail. When asked if she understands, she acknowledges with a slight nod of her head.

Sally is non-communicative her first week at the facility. When her mom and Angel come to visit, she does not speak to them. Gloria grows worried and discusses her anxieties with Dr. Friedman. "Should we be concerned that Sally isn't talking? She's usually so chatty—never been at a loss for words."

"We have to be patient. Sally's been through a tremendous series of shocks, and her mind is trying to process them all. One tool the brain uses to protect itself when overwhelmed is to shut down. I'm confident that in time she'll come around."

Encouraged by his words, Gloria relaxes.

After a week of treatment, Sally begins talking again while in session with Dr. Friedman. Her thoughts are fragmented—almost in code. "Ever feel like you're on a carousel going round and round—never really getting anywhere?"

"Yes, Sally. Everyone feels that way at some point."

"I've seen things I recognize because I've seen them before."

Dr. Friedman waits for her to continue. After a moment of reflection, she does. "Going clockwise, I come across the lies, reality, truth and finally end up at the fantasy side of the ride. I have enough time to barely experience each of these—but only for a short time." Sally stops, uncertain how to proceed. "I see things that are in code. But are they really?"

Dr. Friedman interrupts, "Your dreams?"

"Yeah. How long have they shown me things I didn't understand? A month? A year? A lifetime? I try to figure them out, but can't. Wish I could understand what they're trying to tell me—sooner."

Dr. Friedman's voice is soothing. "Some things are meant for our understanding, while others are not. Events happen in their own time. We cannot force our will on them."

Sally looks into his eyes for the first time. "The meaning of my dreams horrifies me. I guess I'm beginning to understand. Life is a shit-hole. I know it. I don't object. Used to fight it. Why bother?"

"You're absolutely right, Sally. We all have to experience and feel what life throws at us. Sometimes it's unpleasant. But if it weren't for the bad times, we wouldn't be able to appreciate just how wonderful the good times are."

Sally stares out the window, lost in thought. "Good times," she mocks. "I guess."

Dr. Friedman looks at her and smiles. "I think we've made excellent progress. I'm proud of you, Sally. You've experienced a tremendous amount of pain and grief. It takes courage to face it and allow yourself to feel it."

Almost in a whisper, Sally states, "A man who is 'of sound mind' is one who keeps the inner madman under lock and key."

Dr. Friedman looks intrigued. "That's interesting. Did you just think that up?"

"No, it's a quote from Paul Valery. My husband used to say it. I find it comforting."

Dr. Friedman ponders before responding, "Hmm, it's a good quote. I'm glad you find comfort in it. I think this is a good place for us to stop."

Over the next few weeks, Sally opens up to Dr. Friedman. They explore her premonition dreams in greater depth, how she cannot control them and how they haunt her. They discuss how all the men in her life have left her: first her father, then brother, then Eric Angel, followed by James Charles, Jr. and finally her husband. They examine how these losses have left her feeling abandoned, seeking the approval of men in any form.

After four weeks at the facility, Sally has a major breakthrough while in a marathon session. The anger she has held onto through the years and the frustration she has swallowed begins to seep out like a steady line of ants—first a few tentative scouts, followed by a deluge of an insatiable army. It comes in the form of a tirade.

"Why is it that men are so hard on women?" Sally asks. "Why do they feel compelled to assault them with verbal attacks? 'You've put on a few pounds?' 'Take better care of yourself.' 'Wear more makeup.' 'Wear less makeup.' 'Are you really going to wear that?' 'You look like shit.'"

Dr. Friedman considers for a moment before responding. "Well, Sally, some men are very insecure with themselves. The way they make themselves feel better is to put down others."

Neither speaks, allowing what has been said to be digested. After several minutes, Sally continues, "Men have it so easy—they enter and leave this world with basically the same body. They're not forced to undergo a monthly battle of mood swings, bloating and craving of foods. They don't have to surrender their bodies, to bring new life into this world. Once they dip their dicks, their job is done. The women's forms, however, are forever altered." Tears spill from her eyes. She does not notice. Staring ahead unseeing, she looks tired and defeated as she continues. "Their boobs sag from feeding their young. They're ripped apart by men screwing them and by delivering babies. Their vaginas are *never* the same. They're torn and surrounded by scar tissue that has no sensation. The men's penises remain the same, while their women are frustrated by less sexual awareness. The men are self-centered and cruel. They're able to reach orgasm the same as always. *Nothing* has changed for them."

Sally pauses to stare out the window, reflecting on the two sons she had brought into the world—the ones she will never be able to watch grow up. Dr. Friedman waits patiently. Her next comments seem to almost be a personal assault on him. "Why is it that women are called sluts when they spread their legs for sex? Doesn't seem to matter whether it's one or a thousand men we take on, we're still labeled. However, the men we're with are elevated to a position of being on a pedestal. Why is that?"

She shifts positions in her chair. Her anger boils. Her icy stare penetrates Dr. Friedman, causing him to flinch. He responds, "Sally, that's one of the oldest questions. There is no answer."

"Fuck that!" Sally spits the words out, laced with venom. "You men, you're all part of the problem . . .no, you *are* the problem!

You're all selfish, self-absorbed little boys who think nothing of anyone else unless it serves you or your dicks. You don't give a damn who you steamroll to serve your own needs. You ask for forgiveness after screwing us over, claiming, 'I didn't mean to hurt you.'" Her face contorts with a mixture of sadness and anger. More tears stream down her face, and she gruffly brushes them away. "Fuck that! It *is* your intent. You'd sell out your best friend in a heartbeat if a piece of ass comes along. Go ahead, try to deny it."

Her intense glare dares him to disagree. Dr. Friedman remains silent. Sally takes this as affirmation to the accuracy of her comments and is disgusted by his inability to refute her charges. "Yeah, that's what I thought. You sex-driven bastards are worse than us women. You align yourself to any female you think you can conquer— knowing that you'll walk away from the experience raised to a godly status by your peers. We, on the other hand, are also human and have our needs, yet society punishes us by attaching negative labels to us when we attempt to fulfill them."

Sally's speech becomes rapid as her impassioned words spill from her lips. "Many men portray a bad-boy, tough-guy image, thinking it will win over the ladies. It does…for a while. Down deep, every woman wants a bad boy she can play with, but it's just that—play. Don't men understand? Women don't want to keep bad boys." She lets out a sardonic laugh. "They'll satisfy their desires and toss their bad boys aside once they're done toying with them. Women only want to keep men who show honesty, integrity and those who treat them with respect. James was one of those. That's why I married him."

Dr. Friedman does not interrupt her diatribe.

Sally leans back in her chair, closes her eyes and rubs her temples for several long minutes. She sits upright and looks at the doctor. "In my experience both as a hooker and a stripper, I've seen the same pattern over and over—middle-aged men who fuck girls half their age. Their male friends view these conquests as validation to their maleness, showering them with praise, 'Way to go, dude.' 'You're the man.' 'You've still got it.' The young, naive women get used and tossed aside. Both feel empty, by the end of the experience. Why do you suppose men prey upon these younger women?"

Dr. Friedman, who suddenly looks worn out, leans back in his chair. "I'm not sure, why don't you tell me why *you* think they do."

Sally grins. "Aren't these the same men who are the first to grab their shotguns when an older male threatens to take advantage of their own daughters? What a bunch of hypocrites. Don't they realize that *they* are the lowly older males whom they claim to protect their little girls from? Perhaps they're perverts who, excited by their own daughters, go out and tap someone else's." Sally shakes her head, saddened by her revelation.

Dr. Friedman attempts to interject some male wisdom. "Sally, perhaps they are attempting to reclaim a part of their youth—the thrill they experienced when they were young."

Sally refuses to be calmed, growing more belligerent. "No, they're looking to control and dominate. That's all they do—it's what they live for. These men know that within the first few minutes of a conversation with women their own age, they will be discovered for the manipulative, male chauvinistic bastards they are, so they seek to conquer younger, more naive girls, in an attempt to feel better about themselves and put themselves in a position of control. In the eyes of these younger females, they are viewed as something worthwhile instead of the worthless, womanizing, useless pieces of shit they are. They hold no respect for women or themselves."

Sally laughs. "Don't they realize that they're not in control? Like Peter Pan, they refuse to grow up and, as Lost Boys, are left feeling empty." She pauses. New understanding dawns on her. She stops pacing and faces Dr. Friedman. "I find it amusing. You set out to screw us, when in the end it is you who are most screwed. We are smarter and more in control. We know what we're doing and make the conscious decision to proceed. We've learned the ways of men well. We know what drives you and have learned that either way we'll be labeled, so we might as well get something out of the experience that we do control. You men have taught us well. We've learned to manipulate you, as you set out to take our reputations, in an attempt to boost your own. Fuck all of you!" Sally, feeling empowered and alive, has a knowing grin on her face. She recites, half to herself, a quote by Oscar Wilde. "The aim of life is self-development. To realize one's nature perfectly—that is what each of us is here for."

Dr. Friedman leans forward. "What?"

Sally chuckles. "That was one of my husband's favorite quotes. I never understood it before. But now I get it. I really get it!" For the first time ever Sally sees things clearly. Her face illuminates with the dawning of absolute understanding. "I've always thought that if I looked too closely at my past or at life, it would make me crazy—I've just discovered the opposite. I get it, now!" She looks up. A smile creeps across her face. As if awakening from a long dream, the joy and illumination she feels radiates from within her. "I've learned from my journey how to accept and like me. And now I understand what my purpose in life is. It's to share that acceptance with other broken women—to help them become whole."

Dr. Friedman smiles at her. "How are you going to do that?"

Her eyes twinkle, and Sally responds, "I have absolutely no idea. And that's okay. I'll figure it out as I go."

CHAPTER 35

Sally's breakthrough is huge! A few days later, she leaves Whispering Pines and returns home with a clearer understanding of what path her life is meant to take. She celebrates with her mother and Angel that evening. After eating, they sit in her living room and enjoy a fire whose flames crackle and pop. Sally, seated on the sofa with Princess curled at her feet, looks up and states, "You know, I've been thinking."

"About what, honey?" her mother asks.

Sally feels serene. "It doesn't matter that my life doesn't have a house with a little white picket fence and flowers surrounding it, complete with a husband and children, playing in the yard." She gazes into the fire. "*This* is my life, and I'm comfortable with who I am and where I'm at. Doesn't matter what others think of me. Only what I think of myself. I've outgrown my childhood rebellion, have overcome my addiction to crack and have survived the death of my two sons and husband." She turns away from the fire and looks at the two most important women in her life, noting each of their smiles, before continuing. "I have a best friend, an amazing relationship with my mother and am whole and happy. I couldn't have gotten through all of this without your support."

Angel looks at her lifelong friend with compassion. "Looks like you've found yourself."

Sally studies the glowing embers in the fire while a smile plays at the corners of her mouth. "James used to say that we should strive to replace our old victories with new standards of excellence." She turns to her mother and friend. "I want my life to *mean* something. I wanna set goals and dreams." She tilts her head slightly and grows reflective. "Hmm…."

Angel asks, "What?"

"I was just thinking of one of James's favorite quotes, by Edgar Allan Poe."

"Which one?"

"Those who dream by day are cognizant of many things, which escape those who dream only by night."

Her mom shakes her head in amusement. "James and his quotes."

Sally continues. "I want to dare to dream and then fight like hell to make them happen."

Later, alone in bed, Sally rubs behind Princess' ears. "Tomorrow, girl...tomorrow."

The ringing of the phone wakes Sally the next morning. Fumbling for the handset, she knocks it on the floor. "Damn!" She leans over the side of the bed and feels around for it. Locating it, she answers, "Hello?"

"Sally? You okay?"

She flops back in bed and pulls the covers over her.

"Oh, hey, Angel. Yeah. Just knocked the phone off the nightstand."

"Sorry. Did I wake you?"

"Don't worry about it. Had to get up anyway."

As if on cue, her alarm clock begins buzzing. She reaches over and smashes the off button, sending the clock skittering across the nightstand in the process.

She can hear Angel's laughter on the other end. "You always did hate alarm clocks. How many have you broken?"

Sally joins in her laughter. "Too many."

"How did you sleep last night?"

"Good. Feel great this morning."

"Any plans today?"

Sally swings her legs over the edge of the bed, rubbing the sleep from her eyes. Princess lets out a grunt, gets up, stretches and then lays her head in Sally's lap. Sally pets her and replies, "Thought I'd hike Chantry Flats with Princess."

"Want some company?"

"No. This time I have to go alone."

The concern can be heard in Angel's voice. "You sure?"

Sally grows reflective. A smile of contentment shapes her face and she responds, "Yeah."

"Give me a call when you get back?"

"I will."

Sally hangs up then goes to the bathroom. While reaching for her robe on the back of the door, she catches a glimpse of her naked image in the full-length mirror. She does not turn away this time. Instead, she studies her reflection, seeing, for the first time, what James had—a beautiful woman.

She combs her fingers through her thick auburn hair, which drapes over her shoulders, conceals one of her voluptuous breasts and cascades halfway down her back. Sally smiles at how the sunlight, streaming through the window, makes her natural highlights shimmer. She runs a hand along the side of her face and marvels at the china doll visage captured by the mirror. She slowly turns her head from side to side, noticing the contours of her chiseled features, and gently traces the faint mask of freckles that spill off the ridge of her nose on either side. She notes her emerald green eyes—the same as those of her brother and Eric Angel. They twinkle when the light catches them. Tiny crow's feet, like those of her mother's, form at the corners of her eyes. She allows her eyes to travel the length of her body, noting her long slender neck, her petite shoulders and hourglass figure. She reaches up and traces one of her breasts, remembering Eric Angel suckling as an infant. She winces slightly when she recalls how James Charles, Jr. never had the opportunity. She witnesses her near-flawless skin tone, which displays slight traces of stretch marks. She allows her eyes to linger on her legs. They are shapely and sculpted, as if Michelangelo himself had carved them from stone—the muscles clearly defined. She smiles at the woman reflected back at her and cocks her head to one side.

Is this what James saw?

She turns to Princess. "What do you think, girl?"

Her eyes crinkle at the edges, and she smiles at the mirror. "*I like what I see. For the first time in my life, I like *who* I see."

A little while later, Sally and Princess descend the steep dirt pathway that leads into Chantry Flats' lush vegetation. Princess, unleashed, eagerly runs ahead, in search of anything she can chase. They wind their way over a quaint wooden bridge and past dwellings, arriving a short time later at the waterfall where she had sat with Angel, nearly four years earlier, mourning the loss of her first son. She sits on the same rock she had then, and throws a stick into the pond. Sally watches Princess rush after it and then closes her eyes, allowing thoughts of Eric Angel to freely flow through her mind.

Hey, baby! Momma did it. Fixed myself. I'm not lost anymore.

The nudge of Princess' soft muzzle against her thigh makes Sally open her eyes. She takes the stick and throws it again then returns to her thoughts.

Hope you're enjoying your little brother, Eric Angel. I wish I could have buried him beside you, but.... Are you looking down on me? Do you see Momma smiling up at you? I think about you all the time, little man. It's okay. I'm not sad anymore. I cherish the good times we had. Laugh often and teach your little brother how to silly dance. Have fun and look out for each other.

Sally's startled out of her thoughts by a spray of cold water. She smiles at Princess who has finished shaking herself. "I'm done here. Let's go home."

That night, Sally pulls out her spiral-bound journal, just like the one James originally gave her, and begins writing:

I managed to drive part way up to Chantry Flats, before it hit me—the overwhelming feeling of utter joy. I smiled and began crying from happiness. Thought it would stop. It didn't. Tears came from deep within me. The more I cried, the more joy

I felt. I must have looked frightening, as I pulled into the parking lot-a crazy woman sobbing uncontrollably. Didn't care. Too busy riding waves of happiness.

When I got out of the truck with Princess and headed down the steep dirt trail, everything came into clear focus. I wondered at every new leaf. Wild mustard dotted the hillside along with violet and mauve lupines. It was breathtaking and made me cry from its beauty. Princess kept running back to check on me, and I assured her that I was fine.

The sound of a stream caught my attention. I leaned over a bridge to get a better look at the flowing water beneath. Lizards scurried across my path. I couldn't help but laugh as Princess chased first one and then another.

At some point I stopped crying and began smiling from the inside out. I get it now. I really get it! Until now, I haven't fully understood my purpose. I know that I should seize the day. Now I see these moments for what they are-steppingstones. How could I have missed this before? If I'm brave enough to believe in and then blindly follow them, they'll lead me to a joy *beyond my wildest dreams.*

Sally closes her journal, her eyes twinkling, filled with a sense of peace. She replaces the cap on her pen and looks down at Princess who is peacefully lying beside her. "I want to live in the moment. Wonder what's gonna be revealed next in this journey called life? Can hardly wait. Bring it on!"